WITHDRAWN

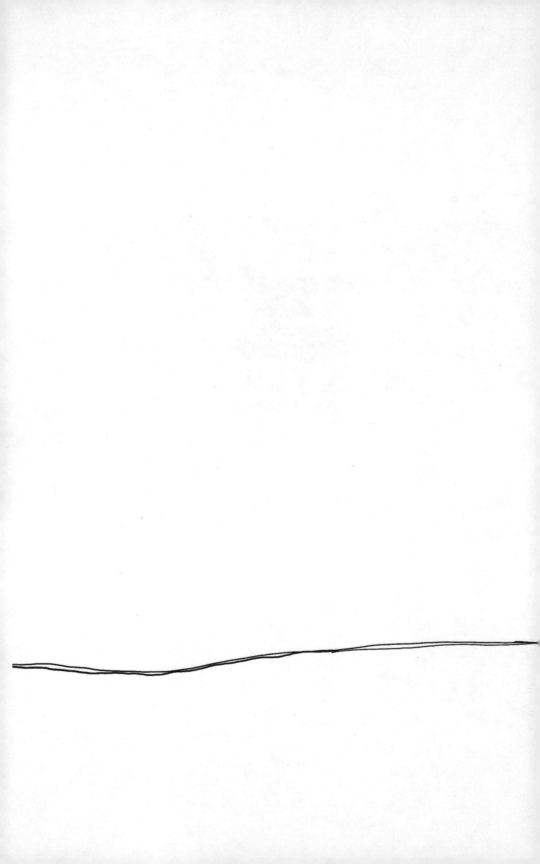

RANI PATEL IN FULL EFFECT

BY
SONIA PATEL

Cinco
Puntos
Press

• EL PASO, TEJAS •

FIRST EDITION
10 9 8 7 6 5 4 3 2 1

Library of Congress Cataloging-in-Publication Data

Names: Patel, Sonia.
Title: Rani Patel in full effect / by Sonia Patel.
Description: First edition. | El Paso, TX : Cinco Puntos Press, [2016]. |
    Summary: Rani Patel, almost seventeen and living on remote Moloka'i island, is oppressed by the cultural norms of her Gujarati immigrant parents but when Mark, an older man, draws her into new experiences, red flags abound.
Identifiers: LCCN 2016013016 | ISBN 9781941026502 (paperback) | ISBN
    9781941026496 (cloth) | ISBN 9781941026519 (e-book)
Subjects: | CYAC: Self-esteem—Fiction. | East Indian Americans—Fiction. |
Immigrants—Fiction. | Sexual abuse—Fiction. | Hip-hop—Fiction. | Family life—
Hawaii—Fiction. | Molokai (Hawaii)—Fiction. | BISAC: JUVENILE FICTION / Social Issues
/ Self-Esteem & Self-Reliance. | JUVENILE FICTION / Social Issues / Sexual Abuse. |
JUVENILE FICTION / Family / Marriage & Divorce. | JUVENILE FICTION / People & Places
/ United States / General. Classification: LCC PZ7.7.P275 Ran 2016 | DDC [Fic]—dc23
LC record available at https://lccn.loc.gov/2016013016

Cover Illustration by Zeke Peña
Design & Layout by Rogelio Lozano / Loco Workshop

Hats off to AMBER AVILA, JILL BELL, STEPHANIE FRESCAS & SANTIAGO MONTOYA.
We pushed you around, but you learned quick.
Go interns!

For Hansa, my mother, my foundation.
For James, my husband, my inspiration.

WIDOW

Moloka'i, 1991

I caught him. Red handed. In the alley behind Kanemitsu's.

My father and the barely out-of-adolescence homewrecker, making out.

I can't stop bawling.

I grab the scissors and electric razor from the closet. I rush to the deck of our pole house, almost tripping over the leg of the piano bench. The ocean air stuffs itself in my nose. The sticky breeze doesn't do anything to cool me. I flip on the light, toss my black Clark Kent glasses onto the table and start cutting. Clumps of hair and sloppy tears cover my face. I can't see. I can't breathe. I just cut. That's me, a cutting slashing machine.

When I'm done, I throw the scissors onto the table and take hold of the razor. I switch it on and shave my scalp clean.

I'm friggin' bald now. I catch my breath and blow and push the little hairs from my face with my breath and my shaking hands. I turn off the light, stand under the starry sky and imagine that the electric razor in my hand is a *Star Trek* communicator. And I'm the alluring Lieutenant Ilia. Cocoa skin, oval eyes, and high cheek bones now accentuated by my bare head, made all the more resplendent by the daggers coming out of my eyes.

I put on my glasses, searching for the outline of Lanai across the wide Moloka'i channel. I find it. My index finger and eyeballs trace it. I relax and listen to the Pacific's gentle grazing of the naupaka on the miniscule patch of south shore beach below. My troubles and my hair are gone, at least for this minute.

Sniffling interrupts the tranquility.

It's my mom. She's behind me. She says, "I heard the buzzing, Rani."

The wooden deck planks creak as she takes a step closer. Then I feel her rough fingers running down the back of my head. I don't turn around. Or move.

"Betta, why?" she asks in a heavy Gujju accent. The concern in her voice is unsettling. I haven't heard that before.

Really? I had to shave my head for you to notice me?

She walks around me, inspects me as if I'm a statue. "Widows are forced to shave their heads in India," she mumbles. She crosses her arms and pauses, ruminating. Then she laments, "Vidhwa ne kussee kimut na hoi. Thuu vidhwa nathee."

Yeah, Mom, I feel just like a worthless widow. A kimut-less vidhwa.

I picture myself in a thin, white cotton sari. It's draped over my bald head. I'm standing close to a scorching funeral pyre. Like countless other widows in India, I'm ready to fling myself into the conflagration. For a second, the sati Is almost real. I feel my skin burning. I flinch and my hand immediately checks.

Skin cool and intact. No burn.

Just a mental scorch.

Mom asks again, "Betta, why?"

Finally I whisper, "It was this or banging my head."

She collapses on the teak-slatted chair. Her face is frozen in suffering: Picasso's *Weeping Woman*.

Then she pulls herself together. "Betta, I didn't know what else to do," she says. She gets up from the chair and approaches me. "Sunil dada taught me that husband is God, so husband's word is law."

I look the other way. Is she talking about the same Sunil dada, my grandfather, who lives in Nairobi, the one who encouraged me to pursue a career and *not* get married?

"I didn't know what else to do."

"Mom," I say after a while, "Dad's so busted. It's Wendy Nagaoki. I saw them together at Kanemitsu's." I move to the edge of the deck and lean against the railing. Looking up at the moon, it hits me again. Dad's gone and I don't have anyone. I turn to face Mom. "Look, I didn't know what else to do either. But I figured shaving my head was a good start."

Mom breaks down and falls into the chair again. Her head's in her hands as she rocks back and forth. She sobs, "I wish I was dead, I wish I was dead."

I'm not saving you this time. It's your turn to save me. Only I know you won't.

PACIFIC EYES

"Rani, whoa!"

I don't hear Mark's voice or the sound of his heavy work boots striking the rickety, wooden steps.

It's a slow Sunday morning at Maunaloa General Store. No customers means I get time to sit on the front porch. It's in bad shape, like the entire store building. Hardly matters, the porch is many things to many people. A town hall for some. A living room for many. A studio for others, allowing for spur-of-the-moment ukulele and percussion jam sessions. For me, it's my clandestine lyrical lab. The place where I write my best rap.

Today I'm writing something different, something to write away my sadness and my worries. Hunched over my notebook, I'm lost in the words.

Mark taps my shoulder. I push my glasses further along my nose and look up. My eyes refocus. I see his baby blues fixated on my head. *Uhh*. Immediately I'm under the spell of his hotness.

He raises one eyebrow and gives me a closed mouth smile. Then he nods and says, "You look fierce, girl."

Only I don't take in what he's saying because I've been cast into some kind of dreamlike state. And I can't hear. All I can do is stare at his heavenly face.

Ahhh, Mark. Mark Thoren.

I've known him for a couple of years from the store. He's by far my favorite customer. Even when he comes in dirty, sweaty, and shirtless. Especially when he comes in dirty, sweaty, and shirtless. He's a groundskeeper for Moloka'i Ranch. His last name says it all. He's strikingly handsome and built. Exactly how the god of thunder should be. His surname, blond hair, ocean eyes, square jaw, and height—about 6'2"—make me think he's Swedish. His body is cut, like Tupac, only white. He looks like he's in his late twenties. When I'm working the register, he's always friendly, asking me about school and stuff. I get butterflies every time I see him, which is practically every afternoon. But all of this is strictly on the down low.

"Rani?"

"Huh?"

"Girl, you're fierce." He whistles in approval.

Embarrassed, I remember that I'm bald. I touch my scalp. "Oh. This. Thanks. It's kind of crazy, right?"

"No way. You look fine." He squints his eyes and bites the side of his lower lip. It's like he's gawking at a table of chafing dishes overflowing with kalua pig, lau lau, lomi lomi salmon, poi, and chicken long rice. And he wants to gobble it up ASAP.

I feel myself shrinking at the hungry look on his face and the generous words he spoke. Fine is not an adjective anyone has ever used to describe me. I'm not even that good-looking with a normal head of hair. He probably thinks it's a rebellious teen angst thing. And pity compelled him to give me some feel-good comments.

"I wouldn't say that," I mumble.

My favorite customer sits down on the bench opposite me. *Hmm.* To what do I owe this privilege? I have nothing to offer Mr. Thunder God. And he's never sat on the porch with me before. Usually he buys his packs—Salem Lights and Bud Light—and chit-chats a bit while I'm ringing him up. Then he leaves, with my eyes searing through his jeans as he exits. Little does he know he's the sole reason I look forward to work. I've even fantasized about delivering groceries to his light blue plantation house near Maunaloa Elementary School.

I knock on his door. He opens it, shirtless of course, but this time smelling of Drakkar Noir. Leaning against the door frame, he asks me in. I set the grocery bag on the kitchen counter. An orange rolls out then falls to the floor. I bend down to pick it up...

"What're you working on?" he asks, his incredible eyes perfectly matching the Pacific behind his head in the distance.

I hesitate. No one knows that I write.

Actually, no one knows much about me. Anonymity suits me just fine. I realize that's about to change because Mark's sexy smile drags the words out. "A poem, a slam poem," I say, uncrossing my legs and pulling my jean shorts down a little. I close my notebook and lay it flat on my lap. I'm sweating. I don't want to let go of any more secrets.

"Sorry, Mark, but I have to go finish stocking..."

Mark cuts me off before I can say "the beer," which seemed way cooler than what I really do have to finish stocking—cans of Spam.

"A slam poem? Really?"

His curiousity is disconcerting. No one has ever been particularly interested in anything I do. Except Pono. But he doesn't count because he only cares about the class council stuff we work on together.

"Yeah...but poems aren't usually my thing." I get up, hugging my notebook tight, and seal my lips so that the spontaneous freestyle flowing in my mind stays safely locked away.

Clutching my notebook close to my chest,

as if it's a question-proof vest.

Boy, you got me stressed

and mentally undressed

with your direct requests.

I'm about to put myself under house arrest

lest you guess I'm

messed up and depressed.

"So, what's your usual thing?" His attention holds me hostage. I settle back down on the bench.

"Oh, that. It's kind of classified," I say, relieved that my dark brown skin hides the blushing.

Mark leans forward. "Come on, Rani, you can tell me."

Tell him about playing piano, not about the rap! I mean, that's fully legit. Even if it's really for Dad.

Mark's like a male siren. I can't resist his song. The truth leaks from my lips. I slide my palms under my thighs and study my bright pink toenails. "Rap is kinda my thing," I confess, avoiding his eyes.

"Rap? Really? Who would've thunk?"

I half smile, shifting my eyes back to his glorious face. Then to his robust biceps. Then to the outline of his tight abs through his sweaty, white t-shirt.

"That's cool. So do you call yourself Lil Rani or something?"

"Something a little more original than that. MC Sutra."

Seriously, Rani? Shut the hell up!

"You know nothing much surprises me. But this, I never would've guessed this about you, Rani. I mean MC Sutra." He pauses then asks, "You seventeen, yeah?"

"Yeah, just about." I'm straining to keep my cool. I'm freaked out that he'll leak my secret about MC Sutra. I end up clasping my hands and begging. "Please Mark, don't tell anyone about the rap or about MC Sutra. Please, please!"

"I won't if..." he says real slow, "...if you read me the poem."

He stretches his arms onto each side of the railing. For a second they appear more sinewy than usual. But then I see something I've never noticed before—a dreamcatcher tattoo wrapping around his right upper arm. But before I can ask him about it, he says, "I'm ready."

I take a deep breath. "It's called 'Widow,'" I mumble. I open my notebook and flip to the right page. As I start reading, the anxiety slowly melts away like a half-eaten shave ice in the summer sun. I change up the speed, the volume, and the tone to match the words, pausing strategically along the way. Full on Patricia Smith.

I shaved my head.

Waist length, thick, good Indian hair

gone in five minutes.

Hair shed,

saying the unsaid.

To my mom whose arranged marriage

my dad disparaged,

so daughter became child bride.

He divides

me and her.

He kept me close, his little princess,

his little missus

and witness

to Mom's "accidents" from

years of banging her head on hard cold walls, numb.

Brandishing knives in desperate suicidal threats.

Rani betta, my little darling, just forget.

Let me comfort you

with teenage back rubs, taboo.

But they help him pull through.

A dark web of emotional and sexual merging,

and I am emerging

as his mirror.

He tries to make things clearer.

He says,

I escaped India,

my mother's frustrations,

my father's perversions,

my own victimization

by immigration to America.

A better life was my intention.

But he had no foundation.

So he made me his reincarnation.

Attempts at normal friendships

elicit Dad's guilt trips

and snubs.

His revenge: psychological break-up.

By him I am now ignored.

His insatiable thirst for being adored

quenched by another, half his age.

At first, rage.

New lover?

New daughter?

Winds of fury

intensify waves of sorrow,

steadily, one after another,

they smother...me.

I'm worthless.

Nothing.

Dead.

Mom's suicidal frustrations in my head.

I punish myself and shed

hair, self-worth, dignity.

It, not she.

I realize I'm standing up. And crying. I sit back down on the bench and look quick at Mark. His expression is somber and his eyes wet. I had no idea my words could move a grown man.

"Is this about what happened at Kanemitsu's last night?"

"Yup," I whisper.

Mark speaks softly. "That line about your Mom near the end, I can totally relate."

He's frowning and seems more sad. We sit in silence, reliving our own painful memories. And despite the solemn mood, I'm astonished at all the firsts. First time a hot guy paid attention to me. First time I told anyone about my passion for writing rap. First time I told anyone about some of my family problems. Somehow I don't feel so alone.

Instead I feel connected and grateful. Also butterflies. But not the usual few. A thousand of them.

SMOKING ROSE

At 9:15 p.m. on Saturday, September 7—two hours *before* Kanemitsu's—Mom and I were closing up the restaurant. And I still sorta had my act together. Sorta because I'd been on the verge of losing my marbles for months. See, I'd been ninety-nine percent sure that my dad was having an affair. I figured the definitive proof of his goings-on would present itself soon enough since Moloka'i is small. With only about six thousand people on this thirty-eight mile long, ten-mile wide island, how could it not? Besides, everyone knows everyone. What I didn't know was that before this night was done the truth would be fully in my face. And it would all go down at Kanemitsu's.

On that day, I was exactly one year and three months shy of eighteen. Adulthood was approaching. But my dad's attention had slipped away awhile back. And with it so had my sense of well-being, my sense of how things were supposed to be. Of who I was. Of my value. I couldn't figure out how I'd been managing to keep myself together.

I was thinking about this as I carried the last of the dirty dishes from the dining area to the sinks in the back. Whenever I think about something deeply, my mind just naturally gets a rhyme going.

My self is sliding away.

Self-worth, astray.

Self-confidence, flying like an angry jay.

Self-esteem, on the way to faraway.

Self-respect, not sticking around for these rainy days.

Two hours before Kanemitsu's, I still had a full head of hair. And all the customers had gone home.

I'd let my hair out of the bun that had been sitting on top of my head, so tight it felt like I'd been balancing a donut up there. I tilted my head back and shook out my thick black locks.

Aah.

My waist-length Indian hair flowed down my back like the river Styx. Some of my Gujju aunties on the mainland called it sahrus var—good hair. My mom called it vagrun var—wild woman hair. I didn't call it anything. Mostly I tried to tame it by making it into a bun or a French braid or a ponytail.

Except when I was alone. Then I let my hair down. Loose and free.

I was thinking about where to start cleaning first—the floors, the table tops, the bar counter—when I heard a garbled male voice.

"Hey there little lady pretty Hawaiian."

My mom was supposed to be the only other person in the restaurant. And she was in the back. Startled, I whipped around to see who it was, grabbing my hair to push it back up.

"No, leave it down. It's gorgeous," mumbled a balding, forty-something-year-old pasty white man. He looked like a happy clown with his sunburned nose and big smile.

Probably a tourist. He must be drunk, ignorant, or both. I bet both. Because first of all, everyone on Moloka'i knows I'm not Hawaiian. I'm the only Gujarati girl on the island. Second, guys never notice me. Pretty lady? Gorgeous hair? What was he talking about? Moloka'i boys won't even look at me. To the fine local studs my age, I'm a sixteen-year-old dorky four-eyed flat-chested curry-eating non-Hawaiian nobody.

"Let's you and me take a drive," he suggested, winking. He propped his elbows on the bar. He tracked me with his beady eyes.

That'll take chloroform.

"Tempting," I said, pulling up my glasses by the hinges. Then I crossed my arms and shifted my eyes and chin slightly up and to the right. As if I was actually contemplating his offer.

Not.

I looked back at him. With a bogus pout I said, "Sadly I have to stay and clean up." And with that, I continued the closing process, ignoring him and his stalker eyes. I shut off the stereo. Silence replaced Leahi's *Island Girls*. I switched off half the lights—a nice contrast to the bright, loud, busy evening I'd spent waitressing. Fortunately, the rowdy mainland visitors were gone. Unfortunately, they left behind their boozed-up compatriot.

I looked at him out of the corner of my eye. He hadn't moved from his spot at the bar. I grabbed the broom from the tiny closet in the hallway and started sweeping vigorously, hoping he'd get the hint and leave.

In case you haven't noticed, Mr. Drunk-Ass-Creep, West End Cafe is closed now.

He hadn't noticed.

He pushed himself off the bar and stood up. For a couple of seconds he swayed like a coconut tree in the trades. Must've been all those Primos he ordered. He recovered his balance, then staggered towards me. His red golf shirt with *Kaluakoi Resort, Moloka'i* embroidered on the left chest was untucked and lifted up on one side. *Ugh*, I could see his hairy beer belly. Smirking, he slurred, "At least gimme one hug. C'mon, make this old man happy."

I didn't expect that he'd have the chutzpah to actually do it. But as soon as he was close enough, he threw his arms around me. Locked in. And squeezed. One of his thick, calloused hands tumbled down my back and crash landed on my okole. Luckily I was still holding the broom, which I used to shove him away. He stumbled back and wobbled, like he was balancing on a tightrope.

Please don't fall. I don't want to deal with this. Get out!

He found his footing, gave me major stink eye and yelled, "What the hell! You're too skinny anyway, you crazy bitch."

He lurched out, slamming the screen doors behind him.

Drive safe, s'kebei.

Thank God. I shut and locked the front entrance, turned around and leaned my back against the door. The humidity hit me like a ton of bricks. My uniform—a black t-shirt with the restaurant's name printed in large white cursive letters on the front—clung to my skin. Not fast enough, I hoisted it up and off. I chucked it onto the bar and pulled up my hot pink tube top. AA cups require frequent tube top manipulation to prevent slippage. But I refuse to be denied the right to rock my style. And, just because I'm flat as an anthurium, why shouldn't I enjoy the natural ventilation a tube top offers? Luckily my baggy jeans were already cool—as in temperature and excellence—by virtue of their billowing roominess and the strategically located holes.

The chill out moment ended all too soon. Mom called from the kitchen, "Rani, do the pouthu, I'll do the vasun."

"Ok," I called back. I took out the mop and bucket.

She had no idea what had just happened on the other side of the saloon doors. But that was nothing new. She's always been oblivious to most things that involve me. Except the piano. That's the only thing she's ever really talked to me about—besides what I have to do at the store and restaurant. It's always been one of two short edicts:

Practice piano.

Play piano.

Anyway, I think she's been out to lunch with regards to me because she's been living in Naraka ever since her arranged marriage to my dad seventeen years ago. Living in hell is probably the opposite of the blissful adult life she imagined as a girl growing up in Kenya and Gujarat. Her chance at a happy life was ripped away by my dad and the vaitru he demanded. And here she is still doing his work today.

Though she's been blind to things happening in my life, I've been a gecko clinging to the wall of her life, listening and watching. Arguments with Dad. Phone calls to relatives. Interactions with customers. And without ever having any heart-to-hearts, I've picked up many tidbits about her life. I know she wanted to be a doctor. I know about a handsome man she met at her Gujarat college who wanted to marry her. And she him. I know she never wanted to marry my dad. But as this observant gecko has gleaned, her desires didn't matter. She had to conform to the expectations set forth by her parents and backed by an entire Gujarati culture. They controlled her life. She submitted. It was all chalked up to naseeb. And boy oh boy, was fate cruel to her. Sometimes I wonder if she thinks it's a fate worse than death.

I rolled the bucket to the back room to fill it up. Mom was immersed in washing a mountainous stack of dishes in two of the gigantic industrial-sized sinks. I added a couple of capfuls of mopping solution to the bucket and tugged at the pull-down faucet. Water gushed out and the sudsy mixture rose.

I gripped the mop handle. I hated to clean. I shoved the bucket like it was a gigantic boulder and I was Sisyphus. When I got to the dining area I surveyed the mess. I blew the loose strands of hair from my face. Napkins, beer bottles, remnants of rice, hamburger steak, and Portuguese bean soup were scattered across the tables and hardwood floor. The soles of my precious hot pink, baby blue, and creamy white Adidas high tops clung to the boards. A strange groan and shudder emanated from my body. It was so bizarre that I decided it should have its own word. A grudder. Or a shroan.

I hate my life.

I freakin' hate my life.

Then I felt guilty for hating my life because I realized it would never be as bad as my mom's. Still, I was resentful. I mopped away the tourists' dinner evidence and their sticky dregs. The monotony of mopping allowed my thoughts to wander. But like always, they returned to my dad. Things had been out of whack. Worse since the roses.

In early August, Pono Kamakou and I, both reps for our senior class of 1992, were at Moana's Florist. Now I'm definitely not one to front like I know much about Hawaiian culture because I most certainly don't. But I know that it's customary in local culture nowadays to present honored guests with lei. So Pono and I were selecting lei for the University of Hawaii at Manoa college admissions officers flying over for an assembly early the next morning.

Incidentally, Pono's got to be the hottest vice president on the face of the earth. Since I'm president I get to hang with my towering, hunky VP outside of school for official class business like this. In my humble opinion, it's the biggest perk of being president—a position I was elected to only because no one else ran for it. I've been crushing on him since the beginning of junior year. Too bad he's had a girlfriend pretty much since then. The perfect Emily Angara. Not that it would matter even if he was single because like all Moloka'i boys, he wouldn't be interested in me even if I was the only girl in school.

Pretending like I was carefully inspecting ti leaf and pikake lei, I was secretly ogling Pono's amazing brown eyes, silky black hair, and dark, smooth skin. He's three-quarter Hawaiian, one-eighth Filipino, one-sixteenth Spanish, and one-sixteenth Chinese with the lean, muscular body of a die-hard surfer. Which he is.

The front door creaked open. That's when I spotted the back of my dad's head. I knew it was him. He's the only man on Moloka'i with that jet black coarse wavy Indian hair. Pared down like a round, sculpted Chia Pet. I call it his Indro. He didn't see me.

Pono dropped the maile lei he'd been looking at and touched my shoulder. He inched closer so that he was standing directly behind me. Then leaning down, his breath warm and sweet, he whispered into my ear, "Isn't that your dad, Rani?"

Pono's hands are on my body!

My euphoria burst out like when you drop Mentos into a two-liter bottle of Diet Coke. I took a deep breath and nodded. I whispered back, "Wonder why's he in this place."

Dad picked out a bouquet of a dozen red roses. My heart began beating like war drums and my thoughts raced like the dude Pheidippides from that Robert Blacking poem.

I knew.

He *never* bought flowers for my mom. Ever. Plus they'd been fighting more than usual.

Dad sashayed over to the line at the cash register. He looked as happy as that day last April, the first time he came home at 4 a.m. The night before he told me he'd be out late at a water activist meeting. I saw him creep back into the house early in the morning. He was like a teenager trying to sneak in without waking his parents. Not that I'd ever done that because the only reason I'd be up at that hour is for homework. Which I happened to be doing since 3 a.m. that morning. As he tiptoed past my room, I saw the spark in his eye. That spark was the first time I noticed something had changed. I knew fighting to preserve Moloka'i's water from the careless clutches of the Ranch and Kaluakoi Resort made him feel like he had a purpose. But elated? That seemed sketchy. He was like a different person. Not the stoic Gujarati man I knew.

And Dad's been pretty much MIA since then. At home less and less. Working less and less, and recently not at all. All the while, Mom's continued to work at the store and restaurant twelve to eighteen hours a day, seven days a week. I've maintained my after school and weekends work hours.

Last year he'd gotten into water activism as a way to "stick it

to the Man." That's how he described it to me. "The Man" was the
Moloka'i Ranch. The Ranch owns about one-third of the island and
most of the west end, including the land, houses, and business
buildings in the tiny town of Maunaloa. Back in the day, when the
Ranch leased a large portion of their land to Libby McNeill & Libby
and Del Monte, Maunaloa mainly housed pineapple workers. Today
the Ranch rents the houses to their own employees, Kaluakoi
employees, and former pineapple workers or their families. And they
rent the store and restaurant buildings to my parents.

Dad's pissed because the Ranch didn't renew our lease on the
store or restaurant, leaving us only two more years to run the
businesses. Well, only one more year now. Dad's been fixated on
revenge ever since. He knew that the Ranch and Kaluakoi had been
wanting full access to Moloka'i's only source of fresh water to irrigate
and expand the tourist potential of the dry west end. He also knew
that many people on Moloka'i didn't want the island's limited water
supply to be wasted on tourist development projects. Especially when
many Hawaiian homesteaders didn't yet have access to the water for
their agriculture. I'm no local but I've always agreed that the water
should be for the Native Hawaiians first and foremost. You don't have
to be Einstein to see the logic in that. Dad eagerly jumped on the "no
way in hell is the Moloka'i Ranch or Kaluakoi getting our fresh water"
activist train. He even became one of the conductors. For him, it's
been the perfect "fuck you" to the Ranch for "fucking with him."

Anyway, Dad's in line at Moana's. He turned his head and dug
around in his front left pocket for his wallet before realizing it was in
his back pocket all along. That's when I spotted his new beard. So
George Michael. Short boxed, closely trimmed. I inhaled sharply. In

the two weeks that I hadn't seen him, he let his five o'clock shadow grow. He never allowed himself to keep any kind of facial hair before. Come on now, the guy used to ridicule guys with hair.

Rani, what do you call a man with a beard?

I don't know, Dad. What?

Unemployed.

Oh the irony.

I snuck up behind him and tapped him lightly on his shoulder. "Hey, Dad!"

He spun around. The gigantic bouquet brushed my face. "Oh, hi Rani. What're you doing here?" he asked, pretending to be unphased.

"Pono and I are ordering some lei for school. Who are the roses for?" I asked, my fingertips touching the red velvet band that held the stems together. I tried to sound calm though my heart was pounding.

Dad didn't skip a beat. "Your mom, of course," he said, then gave me a self-righteous smile.

Yeah right.

How could he straight up lie to me—with absolutely no hesitation? After he left, I paraded back and forth in front of Moana's, debating. I decided a call to Mom was in order. I rushed to a nearby pay phone and dialed. Like a sportscaster, I laid out a play-by-play and wrapped it up with my hunch about Dad's two-timing.

Mom refused to believe my girl's intuition.

The roses were on the kitchen counter when we got home from work later that evening. *Duh*. Obviously he had to drop them off. He'd even scribbled a fake ass card.

To: Meera. *From*: Pradip.

Pathetic. No "Love, Pradip," of course. Mom didn't say a word. Her face remained impassive as she filled a tall, crystal vase with water and added an aspirin.

I pushed the mop faster. The scowl on my face grew as I thought about the smug look on Dad's face as he held the bouquet that day. For me the roses were the penultimate piece of the puzzle. B.R. (Before Roses), I was skeptical. Seriously, since when do activist meetings run all night? A.R. (After Roses), I was completely done falling for it. But I had no clue that the final piece of the puzzle would be revealed in less than two hours.

Mopping done. Moping, not so much. I rinsed out the mop and bucket and propped them against each other on the floor to air dry. Mom was wiping down the sinks. She wrung out the towel and hung it, then sat on the rusty metal chair in the corner.

"I'm starving, Mom. Time for Kanemitsu's. You want anything?" I asked, smiling, trying to be cheerful.

"No, I'm tired." Her face was sour like amchoor. I watched her massage her swollen left ankle.

She had twisted her ankle here three weeks ago running around as both cook and waitress. Time to rest and heal her ankle? Ha! That's a luxury Mom hasn't had since we moved to Moloka'i five years ago.

Mom yawned. "I'm going home. I'll eat the leftover shaak and bhatt." Her eyes were vacant, as if she were peering through the paneled wall.

By then it was 10:30 p.m. It was the earliest we'd ever been pau on a Saturday. We locked the back door and headed down the ramshackle stairs to the unpaved parking lot shared with the Big Wind Kite Factory and the Maunaloa Post Office. Besides those two businesses, a gas station down the road, a Moloka'i Ranch office, and our store and restaurant, there aren't any other shops or offices in Maunaloa. My eyes adjusted to the night. I saw a thick, eight-inch centipede zip past my mom's feet and make its way under the raised restaurant building.

She didn't notice. I walked more cautiously, deliberately lifting my kicks a few inches higher than normal. Didn't want any centipede guts on my Adidas beauties. I climbed into our green 4runner. My waterworks started when I saw Mom lift her ankle into our dusty Cressida so carefully. I cried in the darkness. My mind went straight to that summer day in '87 when we still lived in Connecticut, the day Dad came home from work and dropped a bomb.

"I'm moving to Moloka'i. Come if you want."

He left the next day. That's exactly how it happened. Without telling Mom or 12-year-old me, Dad had purchased Maunaloa General Store and West End Café, leasing the buildings they were in from the Ranch. And, despite every fiber of her being rejecting the idea of leaving the East Coast and her Gujju social network, the strong Indian subservience flowing through my mom's veins took over. On her own, she packed everything, sold the house, and said her tearful goodbyes. Dutifully she and I boarded one of the first of several planes, setting out on our journey to the remote Hawaiian island we still couldn't properly pronounce.

Ever since then, the three of us have been living in cultural isolation on Moloka'i. No other Indians here, let alone Gujaratis. I've had five years to stew about all this. It's clear to me that the wheels of our severe family dysfunction had already been in motion on the East Coast, but they went into cruise control on our time capsule-island-of-turmoil—Dad's ego stroked and inflated by his increased ability to do whatever he wanted without the meddling and gossip of our Gujju friends and relatives, Mom cut off from her protective Gujju connections. And me, fully dependent on Dad's attention for any semblance of worthiness. A self-sustaining state of disarray. Our family roles became carved in volcanic stone. Dad—raja, the king. Mom—kam vaari, his servant. Me—rani, his queen.

But, slowly and steadily, the trade winds of seclusion have been eroding our rocky foundation. And Dad's deceit started a landslide.

I rubbed my eyes. *Must. Not. Cry.* After all, I'd been looking forward to Kanemitsu's all week. Couldn't show up puffy-eyed. I cranked the stereo cassette player. Queen Latifah was rapping about the *Evil That Men Do*, a track I'd had on rewind for a couple of weeks. As I listened, I pretended she was the big sis I never had. Her supreme vocal presence soothed me.

Womaned up, I pulled out of the gravel parking lot.

KANEMITSU'S

The single lane "highway" between Maunaloa and Kaunakakai was pitch black—nothing new because there aren't any street lamps. No stop signs or traffic lights either. Nothing to break the tedium of the twenty-five minute drive. Most nights I don't pass any cars.

A while back, Pono told me something that still kinda freaks me out every time I'm driving back from Maunaloa. He said that at sunset or sunrise I should be wary of huaka'i po, particularly near the sacred Kapuaiwa Coconut Grove that's one mile before Kaunakakai. Makai of the highway. When I'm driving alone in the dark, even if it's way past sunset, I get scared I'll hear the drums of the 'oi'o. And they'll be chanting and marching near me. If you look the ghosts of the departed warriors in the eye, you'll die. *No thanks!*

But thankfully my rumbling tummy directed my attention to images that weren't frightening: Kanemitsu's famous hot bread slathered with melting, gooey cream cheese and sweet and tart liliko'i jelly. Wiping the drool from my lips, I swerved a bit. Driving was a challenge when all you could see was fresh bread.

Finally I saw the Chevron. I slowed down and turned left onto Ala Malama Avenue, the main street in Kaunakakai. Everyone on Moloka'i calls Kaunakakai "town." Most people on the island live in town, in small, single-wall construction homes spreading out in a three-to-four mile radius of the main street.

Technically that makes the short strip of one- or two-story business buildings on Ala Malama Avenue "downtown." Downtown's got the two best-stocked grocery stores on the island: Friendly Market and Misaki's. It's got the only pharmacy. It's got a couple of restaurants and banks. A library. A post office. The police station. A fire station. A few other retail stores. Some state and county offices. And of course, Kanemitsu's Bakery & Coffee Shop.

Kanemitsu's was jumping. I counted ten trucks and cars already out in front. Instead of hanging out with friends, my weekly Saturday night social reality has been standing in line with a bunch of people I only sort of know. Together we wait for a delicious late night treat.

It's an adventure that only locals know about. The bakery's storefront is actually closed this late at night. To get the prized loaves, you have to walk to the back door that's tucked away from the main street. Every time I make my way down the shadowy alley to get there, I hear Duran Duran's *A View to a Kill* play in my mind's boombox. I'm always alone on the stealth walk so I pretend it's dangerous. Like I'm heading to some big drug deal. Not that I've ever used drugs. Or alcohol. Or even cigarettes. Although I am kind of an underage dealer since I sell booze and smokes on the daily at the store.

I parked next to a Moloka'i Ranch flatbed.

Is that who I think it is?

If Mark was in line, that would take the night to a whole new level. I pulled my hair into a high ponytail and did an appearance check in the rearview mirror.

Ok, somewhat passable.

I quickly sniffed my pits.

Uh-oh, barely passable.

I shrugged and hopped out of the truck. Girl's gotta eat.

The prospect of seeing Mark in line distracted me from making my usual 007 jaunt down the alley. Before I knew it, I was queued up behind twelve other hungry souls. The lady at the front of the line knocked on the dilapidated wooden door. Then she stepped back to wait for the mysterious bearer of bread—a curiously odd, delicate man with a raspy voice—to take her order.

Marky Mark—sans the Funky Bunch—was the last in line. *Oh yeah*. I welcomed the *Good Vibrations*.

He was standing with Stan Lee, a newbie at the Ranch. Stan recently moved here from Honolulu, so I don't know much about him. Except what I could see. That he's full Korean and about twenty-four. A couple of weeks ago, Mark and Stan Lee came into the store after work, engrossed in a conversation. I overheard Stan Lee saying something about his mom's batu-smoking boyfriend beating her up again. Stan Lee said he felt guilty because he'd been out when it happened. I wonder if he moved to Moloka'i to protect his mom.

So there I was, standing behind them in the bread line. I heard Stan Lee speaking all hush-hush to Mark. For a second I considered staying quiet, thinking I should let them go on with their convo. But I changed my mind. I decided a loud clearing of my throat was the most logical way to interrupt. Mark whisked around at the sound.

"Hey Rani, howzit?" His speech and smile told me that he was well into the cold pack he bought earlier.

I lifted up my glasses by their corners. "Oh hey, Mark. I didn't expect you here." Hoping my speech and smile didn't tell him that I was well into thinking about the six pack I knew he had under that shirt. "Just finished work. I'm starving," I added, as lukewarm as possible to douse the heat rising in me.

"Yeah, us too. We're going down to the wharf to eat. Come hang out," Mark suggested.

Butterflies.

Stan turned his back to me at that point. I swear I heard him let out a small grunt, a mixture of an annoyed sigh and a half-whispered *fuck*. I was about to say yes to Mark when I heard my dad's laugh behind me. My head swiveled around at the sound. Even though it was dark, I could make out his tall thin build and Indro. He was walking with some woman down the alley. Dad skyscraped over her. They sauntered arm-in-arm. When they got near the only faint light fixture, I saw him chatting away and gazing down at her. She was looking up at him, all bright-eyed, like a fascinated student. The way I used to look at him. They stopped for a second and he leaned in for a kiss.

My thoughts sprinted.

Fight or flight? Fight, then flight.

What happened next was a blur of tears, confusion, jealousy, and contention.

I charged towards them. My arms moved purposefully, strictly in sync with my steps. As if someone ordered me to do a military quick march.

Dad's never walked arm-in-arm with Mom.

I stopped.

Dad's never talked with Mom like this. And he hasn't confided in me since the end of last school year.

I took a second to knuckle up, then bolted forward again.

Dad's never kissed Mom in public. Come to think of it, I've NEVER seen him kiss her. But he's kissed...

My body was paralyzed at that point. It was as if I was standing on a track and a train was charging at me. I could see the conductor and he sounded the whistle. But I couldn't move. I was about to be bulldozed when in an instant the train took a detour. I was face-to-face with my dad.

Dad folded his arms and gave me a look. *The* look. The one where he rolls his eyes and sighs in exasperation. Like I did something to let him down, to frustrate him.

The hussy smiled. Yep. She stood there and smiled at me.

"What the heck, Dad?" I asked. Half yelling. Half crying.

"Shhhh. Keep it down, Rani," my dad whispered firmly, pressing his straightened index finger on his lips. Then he put his arm around the slut and said, "You know Wendy. Wendy Nagaoki."

That's right. I remembered where I'd seen her. Misaki Market. Wendy the checkout girl who never smiles at customers. Word on the street is that Wendy was addicted to batu the year after she graduated from Moloka'i High & Intermediate School. I think she got her MHIS diploma in '87.

That makes her about 21. Yuck!

But then her mom gave her some straight up tough love and threatened to kick her out of the house. I guess Wendy got herself together. Somehow she must've managed to get off the stuff. I'm betting there's more to the story than that. I don't care because she's obviously stolen my dad.

I'm thinking Dad met her at Misaki's. I could see it. Deadpan Wendy. Ringing up customers. Dad next in line. He makes some witty remark and her lips curve up. Then she laughs. And that was that.

I think about how young she is.

Ugh.

And she's not all that good-looking. Short. Short black bob. Lackluster eyes. Baggy grandma shorts and flowery blouse. No flava. Still she was the one smiling. Not me. I exhaled loudly, agitated. I envisioned getting up in her face and screaming something venomous. Instead, I kept my eyes and head lowered and muttered, "Skeeze."

"Rani, let's talk about..." she started to say.

But I wasn't about to stay and jabber with this plain-Jane-Dad-thief. I ran past them back to the truck. My gut was tight, my chest empty and aching. I fumbled with my keys and finally got the truck door open. I grabbed the steering wheel and hauled my sorry ass onto the seat. I put the pedal to the metal and gassed it all the way home, doing sixty in a thirty-five. Windows down. Warm air blowing through my vagrun var for the last time. Because I knew full well what I was going to do as soon as I got home.

That was last night.

This morning I'm sweeping up the tangled spread of my hair on the deck. I use a small brush to coax it into a trash bag. Then I walk to the railing and prop my elbows on the wide top cap. The Pacific is pacific. So is my mood. My eyes turn to the east. I run my palm over my scalp.

And me and my bald head marvel at the spectacular Sunday—September 8th—sunrise.

GUILT

"Hey, Patel," La'akea calls out as she cruises to the back of the store. Her eyes are fixed on the beer chilling in the fridge. She grabs a six-pack of Bud Light and strides to the checkout counter. I don't realize that I'm gawking at her with a ridiculous grin on my face. Not until she says, "Patel! Why you all da kine l'dat?"

"Huh? Oh. La'akea. Howzit?" I ask, blinking my eyes several times to shake myself out of my lovesick thoughts. Mark left an hour ago. I was in the middle of going over a blow-by-blow of our convo. I was just getting to the part I hadn't quite figured out, the part after I read him my slam poem.

"I like one pack Marlboro Lights," La'akea says.

I give her a fake smile as I reach for the cigarettes. I'm kinda annoyed that she interrupted my daydreams. I study her a minute. She looks like a raisin. The dark brown skin on her face is wrinkled and full of sores. She appears years older even though I know she's only twenty-two. Her teeth resemble short, rusty nails.

She reaches into her pocket and pulls out a shoddy plastic baggy full of pennies, nickels, and dimes. She drops it onto the counter.

La'akea's an occasional customer at our store. All I know about her is that she lives in Maunaloa with her uncle and aunt. That she's more than seventy-five percent Native Hawaiian. That she's unemployed. And that she never buys anything here besides her toxins of choice. I've heard whispers about her and batu, but that's hearsay.

Is this what batu does?

So now I'm staring at her. I cover my mouth with my hand to keep in the *ewww* sound that wants to escape. La'akea is staring back at my bald head. Neither of us says anything. I'm remembering the first time I saw her a couple of years ago. It was the way she held herself that was unforgettable. She had perfect posture, carrying her strong body the way I imagined an ali'i would've back in the day. But it was more than that. Her aura was sublime. It felt like I was in the presence of someone almost divine. But today she looks like she stepped out of a casket that's been buried for fifty years.

I dump the coins onto the counter and start counting. Sadness whizzes about in my head. Guilt too. It's not like I'm Captain Cook or Lorrin Thurston. And I haven't directly stolen La'akea's land. Or killed her family. Or given her a deadly disease. But here I am maxin at the store, thinking about Mark or when I can write my next rap, and all the while she's been scrounging for coins to buy substances that'll probably kill her from the looks of it. She destroys herself by buying things from our store while we make money.

But I didn't ask to move here. I didn't ask to work here. Thanks a bunch, Dad.

I'm about halfway through counting the pennies and my mind wanders. I think about what Pono and I were talking about on Friday after Hawaiian history class. About how most people on Moloka'i have an understanding of Native Hawaiian issues that goes beyond the textbooks and classrooms. Pono was born and raised on Moloka'i and his parents are active in the Native Hawaiian sovereignty movement. And since I've been to many activist meetings with my dad, I've heard the perspectives of Native Hawaiians on the island with regards to land, water, culture, and history. It isn't all hula girls, tikis, grass shacks, and mai tais. It's about a people that prior to foreign contact were a highly structured and refined society. It's about how the Native Hawaiian culture was all but wiped out by the negative impacts of colonialism. The depopulating. The heisting of land and health. The educational, economic, and political powerlessness.

I finish counting the loose change. As usual, La'akea has the exact amount. "Exact to the penny. Thanks," I say under my breath.

I force myself to look at her. To try to really see her. I peer into her raven eyes. I'm surprised by the hope spilling from her dark brown irises. It seems at odds with the devastation of her body. It demands acknowledgement and drags a half smile from my lips. A little louder I say, "Take care, La'akea."

She gives me a crooked smile back and says, "Later, Patel." Then she throws me a raised shaka and heads out of the store.

My brain is about to self-combust with guilt when Omar Ellis steps into the store. He and La'akea give each other a strong chin-up as they pass near the entrance. Omar's strutting. I'm talking Aerosmith and Run DMC *Walk This Way* strutting. And like that rock and rap collaboration, Omar is a cultural collaboration. He's half African American, a quarter Hawaiian, and a quarter Samoan. His hair towers in the most incredibly tight hi-top fade. It's almost as high as Kid from Kid 'n Play. Today he's sporting some baggy jeans slung low. A black t-shirt under a black and white flannel shirt. Both oversized. And a pair of white-on-white Air Force 1's. His head-to-toe hip hop style is undeniable. Impressed as always, I give him a subtle chin-up.

Like me, Omar's sixteen. We're both young seniors. Our birthdays are actually only one day apart. He lives in Maunaloa with his mom and comes to the store all the time. But I didn't meet him here. I met him at school in '87. He's the first person who talked to me. For some reason he took me under his wing. Maybe he felt sorry for me, watching me struggle to understand pidgin initially. He called me "IH," Indian haole, for weeks. He's been teasing me ever since.

Omar usually greets me by throwing his arm around my shoulder and asking "Howzit my sistah from anotha mistah?" Omar hasn't seen his mistah since he was five years old. His dad's been in prison on the mainland for murder. From what Omar's told me it was someone else's drug deal gone bad. And his dad got framed. Rotten naseeb, I guess. Although I think that qualifies as a particularly tragic fate. Totally cruel. I mean his dad never touched drugs or alcohol. Omar likes to talk about how his dad treated his mom. I swear he puffs out his chest whenever he brings it up because he's super proud of his honorable role model. Omar says that even from prison his dad shows how much he respects his mom. Whether it's over the phone or in letters, his dad treats his mom like royalty. And his mom is committed to being supportive to his dad throughout the imprisonment.

I'm in awe of his parents. The way they act towards each other is the exact opposite of my parents.

Anyway, I know Omar's only joking when he says the whole "sistah from anotha mistah" thing. And even though most of our other verbal exchanges also involve him teasing me and me trying to keep up with the repartee, I know he cares. He's the closest thing to a friend I have.

Omar's preoccupied today, presumably by my homage to Sinead O'Connor. He's standing in front of me at the counter, gouging out a hole on my bare head with his keen pupils. "For the first time in my life, I'm speechless," he murmurs. Then he snaps out of his daze and chuckles. "Nah nah, Rani girl. You look fly."

I don't say a word. Instead I form a biting smile and use my middle finger to slowly, very slowly, push the bridge of my glasses up my nose. My sarcastic gratitude. Omar raises an eyebrow. Then our eyes meet in confrontation. Neither of us can hold out for very long and we end up cracking up after less than a minute. We cool out and then Omar glimpses around the store to confirm it's empty. He says, "Hey Rani, I wanna hear all about your voyage into baldness, but I'm here on urgent business. And it ain't because my mom and I are out of milk. Let's go talk on the porch."

For Omar and me, the porch is our sober watering hole. Pretty often we hang out there and chitchat about this and that. But never about *urgent business*. Needless to say, I'm curious.

"Shoots," I say, stepping out from behind the counter. Then I add, "Hold up." I run to the chill and grab two cans of guava nectar.

"Tanks eh." He shakes the can but then puts it down on the bench next to him without opening it. His head drops and he starts some accelerated foot tapping. Like he's digging some ultra quick beat.

He's stalling.

Omar's usually not one to stall. Now I'm really curious. I take a sip of the sugary, syrupy juice. "What's up, Omar?" I tilt my head sideways to try and meet his downturned eyes.

He jerks his head up, stomps both his feet, and slaps his hands on his thighs, as if my words are a drill sergeant's command to sit at attention. Then he blurts out something that doesn't quite register the first time.

"It's your parents."

"What?"

"Your parents. They were having a huge fight at the restaurant."

I scrunch my face and wait for his account.

"I was on my way to check our P.O. box for a letter from my dad. I got near the restaurant and heard shouting. I went to check it out. Your mom was crying and yelling at your dad. She was screaming in Indian so I couldn't understand. Your dad was standing there. He looked pissed. Then your mom sunk to her knees and grabbed onto his pant legs. It seemed like she was begging or something. Next thing I see, she's pounding her head with her fists."

The look on Omar's face wavers between apprehension and indignation. Punching his right fist into his left palm, he grits his teeth and asks, "Why wasn't your dad doing anything? Why would he let her do that? What did he do to make her so sad?"

Now my eyes dip. Then my head. And my face lands in my hands. I proceed to blubber.

"Oh no, Rani. Sorry. You ok?" Omar slides forward on the bench.

I take my glasses off, wiping the tears from my face and snorting in some major hanabata. "Yeah, I'm ok."

My answer must not have convinced Omar because he says, "Come on, Rani. Talk to me. You my sistah. We got each other's back."

Of everyone I know on Moloka'i, Omar is the one I should trust the most. After all, he's trusted me with all his family stuff. I contemplate hedging. But I can't keep in the words or the tears. "My parents," I manage to utter between sobs, "that's why I'm bald." I take deep breaths to prevent a complete emotional breakdown. I slip on my glasses and regain my composure. Then I proceed to recount everything. My suspicions this past year. The mounting evidence. And finally last night at Kanemitsu's.

But why was my mom yelling at my dad? Was she calling him out? Was she telling him off? Was she asking him to come back to her? I think about my slam poem. About Indian families. About Gujarati families. About Patel families. About my family.

Why is this happening to my family?

This isn't supposed to happen in Gujarati families. Especially Patel families. I mean Patels are supposed to be family-oriented. Extremely patriarchal, yes. But family first. I think there are more Patels in the United States than any other Indians. And we're not all related! Not by a long shot.

Patels came to the U.S. to better their lives, to get better jobs and more financial security, to get more educational opportunities— just like every other immigrant. Patel parents are willing to work hard to make all this happen. All those 7-11's. All the motels. Patel parents work their fingers to the bone to ensure a brighter future for their offspring. Patel parents do that. And from what I've seen in the Patel families we knew on the mainland, the husbands were the boss. But they talked considerately to their wives. Sure, I've heard of a couple of Patel divorces. But never the blatant carrying on of affairs. I cross my arms tight across my belly and stare at the ocean.

Patel Dads aren't supposed to have affairs.

Patel Dads aren't supposed to neglect their wives.

I'm digging my long, sharply filed nails into the soft, fleshy part of my inner arms. Deep. I don't even know I'm doing it.

Patel Dads aren't supposed to be indecent with their daughters.

I wrench my mind out of its gutter. But not before my nails get what they want.

Why is my Patel family like this?

I suppose there are exceptions in every culture. In every last name. I feel something wet on my fingertips. I scan my arms and hands. It's then I spot the blood.

BUTTER PECAN

The tiny, self-inflicted lacerations ground me. The pain makes me feel calm. I don't know exactly why. Maybe because I know how to deal with pain I can see. I can wash it with soap and water in the shower, then put a little antibacterial ointment on it. Which is what I did. But pain I can't see, the pain in my mind, I don't know how to deal with it. I usually don't deal with it. I usually try to forget it.

And now I want to forget what Omar told me about my parents' fight. Forget the intruding thoughts and agony that followed.

I pull *Catcher in the Rye* from my backpack. I'm two books ahead for our A.P. Lit curriculum and I intend on making it three. Sprawling on the carpet in my room, I flip open to my bookmark. Holden's at Mr. Antolini's house. A few pages in, my eyes droop. I'm too pooped to get extra ahead. Salinger gets tossed onto my desk. And I toss myself onto my bed ready for sleep.

But as soon as I switch off the lamp and hit the pillow, sleep escapes me. My mind tracks the emotional rollercoaster ride of the day.

COASTING: waking up with a bald head

ASCENSION: writing *Widow*

BARREL ROLL AND VERTICAL LOOP: hanging out with Mark

FIRST DROP: La'akea guilt

ASCENSION: hanging out with Omar

SECOND DROP: what Omar told me about my parents

The slamming of the front door ends the ride. I check the clock: 11:45 p.m. I got home about two hours ago because Mom never lets me work past 9:00 p.m. on Sundays. Or any other school night. I double check the clock. Yup. 11:45 p.m. Mom's home later than usual. The restaurant must've been busy. I wonder if Shawn stayed for the full shift. He's the cook, but he's notorious for leaving work early. Or missing work completely. Too much pakalolo will do that. The thought of Mom cooking and serving alone drops guilt on me, again, like a ton of bricks. I push back the comforter and jump out of bed. I open my bedroom door and hear Mom rummaging in the freezer. I slink to the kitchen, hoping that she'll be in the mood to talk. I still don't know if she finally believes me about Dad and the homewrecker. How much more proof does she need than me seeing them together at Kanemitsu's? And they had an intense fight today. I should ask her if she believes me. Point blank.

But I should start by saying sorry for how cold I acted last night. Then we could talk about her day. Then I could ask her about the fight. If there was a resolution. If she believes me about Wendy. And I really want to ask her how she feels about everything.

But more than anything I wish wish wish she would ask me how I feel. And hug me. And tell me everything will be all right.

46

"Hi, Mom," I say.

"Mmm," she mumbles, not taking her head out of the freezer.

I stand there and try to muster the courage to apologize. She grabs the new half-gallon of butter pecan ice cream and slams the freezer shut. Incidentally, the only flavors of ice cream she really likes are butter pecan and pistachio because they taste "almost Indian," like the kulfi flavors from her childhood.

Then she jerks open the silverware drawer for a spoon. I get a load of her expression. Her brow is in its permanent V-shaped crease. It makes her look constantly angry. I think of the V as her tiny scarlet letter. Well-defined from years of silently "putting up with Dad's bullsheet," as she often mutters under her breath. The skin on her face Is otherwise relatively wrinkle free and soft. Her thick, shoulder-length mostly gray hair is parted in the middle. She always wears it pulled back in a low ponytail with two brown-metal Goody hair clips, one on each side holding the shorter hairs in place. She's worn this hairstyle for ten years. At least. But the almost complete change from black to gray hair was unexpected since she's only forty. Probably stress. That's how she explained it to Preeti masi over the phone a few months ago, adding, "Pradip nu salu aahkuu mathu kaaru che hagi."

Yeah Mom, I hear ya. Dad's full head of black hair is like him saying, "In yo' face, Meera. This pimp ain't gonna work at all. How ya like me now?"

Umm, not at all, Dad.

Ice cream and spoon in hand, she plods to the den. I follow her. I stand in the doorway and watch as she inserts a VHS of a Bollywood film with Amitabh Bachchan. *Agneepath*. She settles onto the sofa and digs into the carton. Within seconds, she's by herself in another world of intense Indian drama and dessert. And I don't exist. But I'm still standing there. Still trying to gather the courage to say sorry, then begin the rest of my planned conversation.

I decide it's too hard to start with an apology. So I ask, "Mom, how was your day?"

"Fine," she mumbles, her mouth full of creamy goodness and her eyes cemented to the screen.

"Must've been busy. I hope Shawn stayed the whole time."

No response.

So I keep going. "You're home so late. I wish I'd been there to help you."

Not a peep. She keeps watching and eating, hypnotized by her ritual of screen and ice cream. I cross my arms and keep watching her. Waiting.

Come on, Mom, look at me, please. What do I have to do now to get you to talk to me? You don't even have to talk about what I want to talk about. You can tell me to practice piano! Anything!

I'm not sure what else to say. The fleeting emotional connection she exhibited last night is gone. What's weird is that when I shaved my head she knew something was up. And she reached out. It was like she really saw me. I think she could feel my pain. I think she was trying to help me. She talked to me the way I've imagined moms should talk to their daughters. Getting a taste of it last night left me wanting more. Because for the first time I knew she could do it.

She reached out and I retreated. *Did I mess it up by not responding?*

Now that I'm back to playing my usual talkative role and reaching out, she's retreated. And I'm chasing her again, like she's a patang on Uttarayan, Gujarat's Kite Festival. We're in Vaso and someone cut her string. I'm darting through the narrow streets filled with dung and trash. I'm weaving around decaying concrete buildings. All in hopes of trying to get her back before she's stolen.

But she's always just out of reach.

I wait a bit longer.

Zilch.

I drop my arms and walk back to my room. *Ugh*. Frustrated with myself that I expected anything more. Why should I?

The roller coaster plunges down, down, down.

STILL A LOSER

Monday morning at school. The stares are piercing, the whispers deafening. Bald head down, I trudge, wishing for another Trekker somewhere in the partially enclosed hallways of Moloka'i High & Intermediate School. With all the rubbernecking, I might as well be Lieutenant Ilia, the Deltan alien. Starfleet wouldn't even have to make this Deltan declare the Oath of Celibacy. Because the last time a human teen showed carnal interest in me was, *hmm,* let's see. Oh yes. That's right. Never.

"Hey, Baldy!" someone shouts from a picnic table on the grassy area near the cafeteria. I turn to see who it is. Jacob, Paka, and Roger—all seniors—are sitting at the table. They're laughing. Not a simple "ha ha." Nah, that wouldn't cut it. They're pointing at me and straight up belly-cramp laughing. Paka almost falls off the bench.

Baldy.

I've heard worse. Back in Connecticut, the white, black, Latino, and non-Indian Asian kids bonded over their relentless tormenting of me.

Hey brownie, I saw you eating a brownie. EWWWW. Gross, you cannibal.

Feather or curry? Must be curry because you stink.

Go back to India, you cow lover.

Hey Rani, I saw you eating monkey brains for lunch. And I hear your dad rips out people's hearts.

Thanks *Indiana Jones and the Temple of Doom* for that last one. Although right now it's pretty accurate. Dad has ripped out two people's hearts. Even though Mom won't admit that one is hers.

"Eh, bolo head. Try come!" one of them calls out again.

"Shut up!"

I look back again and there's Omar standing in front of them. His feet are wide apart and he's leaning slightly, his head tilted back a little. Then he crosses his arms. His B-boy stance reminds me of Joseph "Run" Simmons in one of those classic black and white photos of Run DMC in Hollis Queens, NYC. Circa 1984.

"What, Omar? We was jus makin' anykine." Jacob approaches Omar, toe-to-toe.

"I said shut up."

They stare at each for a couple of seconds. Then Jacob grins mockingly and sits down.

Omar comes over to me. "Wuzzup, sistah?"

"Not much. Thanks for that."

"Ain't no thang. How you doing?"

"Hangin' in there, I guess."

"You gonna be ok, Rani. You'll see. Anyway, I gots to get to the library. Research that's due next period awaits. Talk to you later." He gives me a chin-up and heads off.

I watch him until he turns the corner to the library, thankful for my one true homie. I walk towards the cafeteria.

Unfortunately, bolo head rings in my ears. It feels like a pinch of salt in a gaping, raw wound. The pinch soon becomes an entire twenty-six ounce canister of Morton Salt as Kapena's *Masese* fills the air. Someone once told me that this song is a bunch of Fijian words that sound good together when sung and the actual meaning isn't clear. Something about being bummed and lighting up cigarettes and drinking kava to feel better. I could use some kava right about now because there in front of me is Emily leaning back against Pono.

Emily. Pono's Filipina girlfriend. With silky, cascading waist-length hair. I follow her every move. She sits up on the picnic table bench and fiddles with the volume knob on Pono's boombox. Then she drops her head back and shakes out her luscious locks. She turns the knob more to the right. Then she smiles, presumably satisfied with the loudness. And I sneer. Full on Billy Idol. Not wanting to draw attention to myself by fist pumping and rebel yelling, I shift my gaze to Pono. He looks like a T&C model in his black tank top and tapa print board shorts. Only when he wraps his arms around Emily and kisses her shoulder do my eyes become unglued from his broad, chiseled shoulders.

Nothing new about this scene. But with my hairless head and everything going on, I'm feeling like more of a reject than ever.

Didn't think that was possible.

It is.

I go back to Connecticut again. The harsh feather or curry mocking was only part of the story. Back in Constitution State, I was perpetually ostracized. The social scene was like in *Grease*.

The popular white kids were The Pink Ladies and the T-Birds. I was Eugene Felsnic. P.E. wasn't about physical education training. It was about being picked last for teams. And not picked at all for parties. The girls, in their fancy Benetton, Esprit, and Gap outfits, CCD, and country club weekends, pointed at me, giggled, and walked away. The coups de grâce: the boys avoided me like the plague. A bespectacled loser, I watched the cool kids live their cool lives from the sidelines.

And here I am at MHIS six years later, still watching the cool kids. Today the view's perfect from behind a bushy purple bougainvillea. All I need now is some popcorn and a large Coke. Emily turns her head and kisses Pono back. On the lips.

Shoot me now.

Pono asked Emily out at the beginning of junior year. To my dismay, they can't keep their hands and lips off each other in public. I wonder what they do when they're alone. An image of their naked, intertwined bodies flashes in my mind. I shudder and refocus on the scene in front of me.

Pono stands up, stretches, and grabs his ukulele. He nods at Emily. She skips the CD forward to *Reggae Train.* He starts strumming along with the song, totally in sync. Pono's a ukulele virtuoso. The whole scene is pretty much like a free Jawaiian concert. And who on Moloka'i doesn't love a good Jawaiian jam? A crowd of kids surrounds them, blocking my view. I drag myself away from the life film I'll never be a part of. Not even as an extra.

The aroma from the cafeteria draws me in. Nothing like a hot sloppy joe and tater tots to make everything better. Lunch is the surefire highlight of my school day. The lunch ladies are like the aunties I wish I had: funny, thoughtful, sweet. One of them, Auntie Mary, always gives me a little extra of the sides. Winking, she'll whisper some version of, "I gotta fatten you up, Rani." Is it really that or can she tell I'm having a bad day? Every day?

I search for an empty table. That's when I hear my name.

"Rani! Over here, Rani!"

I know that sound—the clinking of multiple gold Hawaiian bracelets. I scan the cafeteria.

It's Crystal. From a distance, her arm looks like it's gold-plated. She's waving at me. "Rani, there's room here."

Oh no.

I head over in what feels like slow motion. *The Empire Strikes Back* theme song blasts in my head.

Crystal Polani's also a senior *and* the most popular girl in school. A beautiful Hawaiian girl, with long, straight black hair. When she dances hula, everyone, including me, is spellbound. She's always May Day Queen. She's even a cheerleader. She's sitting with Rayna and Richelle, also cheerleaders. They all have boyfriends. And hickies.

Seeing the Pink Ladies of MHIS, my brain offers me a concise, bulleted list of my loser qualifications. How thoughtful.

Rani! Listen up.

—You're not popular.

—You're an IH.

—You wear big ass glasses.

—You can't dance hula.

—You're not a cheerleader.

—You don't have any girlfriends.

—Boys will never like you like that.

—You've never even been kissed by someone not related to you.

—You haven't even stepped up to bat with a boy.

—And now you're BALD!

Dang.

I feel like I'm about to get a root canal. I sit down next to Crystal. Their shocked eyes lock in on my head. The normal insecurity I feel around them triples. I take a bite of my sloppy joe. Juice runs down my chin. I forgot to get a napkin. Of course.

Sloppy Rani.

"Oh here," Crystal says, handing me an extra napkin.

"Thanks." I wipe my chin.

They watch me devour the rest of my lunch.

"Everything ok, Rani?" Crystal eventually asks.

"Yeah, everything's ok." I keep my eyes on my lunch tray.

"Do you have cancer?" Richelle blurts out. Crystal kicks her under the table.

"No. No cancer. No chemo. I did this to myself." I rub my smooth head.

"Oh." Richelle tucks strands of her long black hair behind her ears.

"Why?" asks Rayna, leaning forward.

"It's a statement," I say, adjusting my glasses and hoping the interrogation will stop. I tell myself they're genuinely worried. I mean it's startling that I shaved my head. No girl has ever done this at our school. And it's not like my bald headed "statement" makes me some badass fashion icon. Nope. I ain't Grace Jones.

Then I panic. *What if they ask what statement I'm trying to make?* I don't want to let anything about my parents slip.

"Thanks for letting me sit here." I stand up like someone lit a fire under my ass. "But I gotta go. Got some homework I need to finish up before next class." That's a big lie. I always get my homework done before school starts.

I hear them whispering as I walk away. Must be how rumors start.

Maybe a tattoo, like Mark's dreamcatcher, would've been better than shaving my head. So far people have mocked me. Now they think I have cancer. No one understands my pain. Well, especially since I haven't told them anything.

Boo hoo.

I walk to the gigantic banyan tree at the front of the school and sink down with my back against the semi-smooth trunk. The long branches and densely packed leaves block out the bright sun. I close my eyes and get a major kanak attack.

Next thing I know, someone's tapping my shoulder. It's Pono. He's sitting beside me under the tree saying, "Rani, Rani. Earth to Rani."

"Sorry, Pono. Miles away in dreamland, I guess." I slide my hands under my glasses and rub the sleep out of my eyes.

"You lookin' fierce, girl." His voice is low and torrid, like he's telling me a smouldering secret.

Fierce? Funny, that's the same thing Mark said.

Then he grasps the corners of my glasses as if they were made out of a single dry spaghetti that would snap if handled without care. He realigns them on my face.

Our faces are so close...

"Thanks." I don't say anything else because I have to focus on willing myself to not grab his face and kiss him. I'm taken aback by his sweetness. If he's this charming to me, a mere classmate, what's he like with Emily? I'm holding my breath.

"No worries. Anything you wanna talk about?" His amiable eyes reassure me and suddenly I envision we're in a confession booth. He's Father Damien and I'm a churchgoer ready to admit everything. Tell him all about what's going on with my family. Pour my heart out about how much I've liked him since last year. That I wish he wasn't going out with Emily.

But all that stays locked up in my mind's confessional. I'd never tell him the stuff about liking him because I ain't one to stir the pot. And I'm no homewrecker. Mos def. Unlike that skeeze named Wendy.

"No."

"Ok, but you know you can talk to me anytime, right?"

"Yeah, I know. Thanks."

"Oh, and here are some receipts for the assembly." He hands me a brown clasp envelope.

"Thanks V.P." I slide the envelope between my books.

He smiles, then checks his ultra manly G-Shock. "Time for A.P. Calc." He jumps up, then holds out his hand for me.

Bald nobody and class hottie. Walking to class. Like *Beauty and the Beast*. Only in reverse.

THREE STRIKES

The large, copper svastika, the Hindu symbol of auspiciousness, hangs on the front door of our house. Trouble is, it reminds me of a Nazi swastika. The Nazi party turned the traditionally positive symbol forty-five degrees to the right to make it their own. The symbol creeps me out, at any angle. And with the recent inauspicious happenings in my life, I can't help but think I'm walking into a Nazi lair.

Not exactly my idea of home sweet home.

I push the door open. The smell of Indian food drives away the thoughts of Aryan supremacy. I'm comforted by the scent of cinnamon, cumin, and coriander, redolent of the states of Punjab and Gujarat. Definitely matar paneer. Bubbling dal and bhatt too. In an instant, I'm ravenous.

I pull my Adidas high tops off, almost knocking over the Ganesh statue on the shoe cabinet. Maaf kaaro, Ganesh. Forgive me.

I've been at a student council meeting that lasted until 6:30 p.m. It went well. We got everything squared away for the school dance on September 20th. It's a fundraiser for our senior class luau in May.

That's why I didn't help Mom at the store today. My frequent unwanted visitor—guilt—comes knocking. *Forgive me, Mom*.

She's kneading wheat flour in a large stainless steel thali. She's bearing down on the dough with all her might, like she's pushing down on a bike pump that's stuck only she doesn't know it's stuck. I look around to see if there's anything I can help her with.

That's when I spot two Island Air plane ticket receipts next to the plate of the bakhri she's already made. I wonder who's going on a trip. Like a robber, I swipe one of the golden brown bakhri and take a bite. I close my eyes and savor the bite. It's still warm and crisp on the outside. It tastes delicious. It puts loaf bread to shame. I open my eyes and worm my way closer to the receipts. I take another bite and lean forward on the counter. I sneak a peek at the printed names.

Pradip Patel.

Wendy Nagaoki.

And I check out the destination.

Moloka'i to Hawai'i.

So they went to the Big Island! I drop the bakhri on the counter and my arms fall to my side. I take a step back, feeling nauseous. I clench my fists under the countertop.

I guess Mom believes me now. That's three strikes:

1. Roses—Tuesday, August 6, 1991.

2. Run-in with Dad and Wendy at Kanemitsu's—Saturday, September 7, 1991.

3. Plane ticket receipts found—Monday, September 9, 1991.

Three strikes and you're out, Dad.

Too bad Mom hasn't said one word about any of it. So it's back to me being Nancy Drew.

Rani Drew.

I need to solve the mystery that is my mom. I should just ask her about the receipts. Seems pretty basic. But communication has never been our strong point. Not like Nancy Drew and Hannah Gruen. I mean poor Nancy never knew her mom. I think she died when Nancy was a youngster. And I feel bad for anyone who loses their mom. I can't imagine. But at least Nancy had Hannah—her loving Mom figure and counselor. Mom's not Hannah Gruen.

There's no Meera Gruen.

Not even close. Mom doesn't discuss difficult situations with me. Saturday night was an anomaly. I mean, I was out of my mind with emotions. I didn't have my usual wits about me to talk myself out of telling her anything. And she acted like a real live human being.

But now it's back to our standard operating procedure. And the (Enormous. Elaborately adorned. Indian.) elephant in the room of our lives sits pretty. Eating juguu with its long trunk.

I keep my face calm. "You ok, Mom?"

"I'm ok." She doesn't look up from her kneading.

"I'm worried about you."

"I'm ok." She kneads furiously.

Dang, she's strong.

I stand there still as a mannequin watching her wallop the dough. I wonder how long it took her to become such a master bakhri maker.

"Need some help?"

"No."

I rest my elbows on the counter and cup my face in my hands. My eyes follow her hands as they divide the dough into small balls, then flatten each dough ball into individual discs. With a velan, she rolls each disc into a circular flat, like a tortilla. Perfect six-and-a-half inch diameter circles. Each exactly the same size and thickness. Without using a mold. Last time I tried to make bakhri each one turned out to be a different shape, thickness, and size. Kind of like the Hawaiian islands.

I linger and psych myself up to ask her about the receipts.

Come on, Rani, you can do this. You got this.

I'm sweating. I have to pull at my shirt to keep it from sticking. Moist pits and all, I picture myself as Rocky Balboa. Donning my gloves. Hopping about in my gold and maroon colored robe to stay warmed up. Then I step into the ring.

"Hey Mom, what about these receipts?"

Silence.

After five more minutes of nada, I devise a different strategy.

Try playing piano. Maybe that'll relax her and she'll open up.

I walk to the living room and play *Für Elise*. It's my mom's favorite, I think, because I've noticed she usually gets a half-smile when I play it. My fingers press the keys and I peek at her. I'm hoping the beauty of the piece will draw her out of her shell.

Nope.

She doesn't seem to hear it, still completely absorbed in making the bakhri. So I stop playing halfway through. I drop my hands into my lap and stare out the sliding glass doors at the channel. It's calm, like I wish I was. I get up and head to the entryway for my backpack. I wrap my fingers around one of its straps and lug it to my room.

I'm about to shut the door to my room when I hear my mom's voice. Groaning. I drop my backpack and slink into the hallway. All the sweat gets sucked back in and I'm dry as a bone. My eyes become binoculars and my ears a highly sensitive wire tap. I match my breathing to my heart beat and maintain complete stealth.

By now I'm lying on the hallway carpet. I commando crawl to the beginning of the hallway and peer around the wall at my mom.

She's shaking her head and grumbling. She's done this before—complain out loud to herself when she thinks no one's listening. But generally she cries while she gripes. Today's different. More anger and no tears. I didn't think it was possible, but the V-shaped crease on her forehead is deeper than usual. I mentally record her solo tirade, translating it from Gujarati to English.

"Salo Pradip. He's never taken me on vacation anywhere. Maybe I'm the stupid one because I don't ask for anything. I just do all his work. My girlfriends on the mainland get fancy clothes and houses. They go on trips. I know they speak up. I've seen it."

I'm stunned. I'm holding my breath.

She continues her rant. "Their husbands treat them like wives and their kids like kids. Not their wives like servants and their kids like princesses."

Oh snap!

"And now he's got a new princess. Wendy. That kutri. She gets to have it all. His attention, no work, vacations. And what about poor Rani? And she thinks he's such a good dad."

She thinks about me! Maybe she doesn't hate me!

My eyes dart around on a crazy search for nothing in particular. All I can hear is my heart beating and pushing the blood through my arteries. I let out a long, slow breath. The corners of my lips venture towards my eyes, which send tiny wet emissaries to greet them.

WATER OVER FAMILY

I creep my way through the bodies and plop down in the chair Pono saved for me. He gives me an inviting chin-up. His "it's so on" smile kindles my activist flame. And ignites my Pono fire.

He goes back to scribbling on his notepad while I consider how much I need a cold shower. I look around the large hall of the Kaunakakai Community Recreational Center. Locals are spilling out of the open entryways on either side. I can tell the meeting's gonna be intense. My heart is throbbing at lightspeed. I'm not quite sure if it's because the gorgeous brown skin of Pono's arm is touching mine or if it's the meeting. I order my brain to focus on the meeting.

Fortunately my brain obeys. But then I realize this is my first activist meeting without my dad. I scan the room to make sure he's not here. No sign of him. Today it's just me. Skittishness tries to oust my courage.

You can do this without him. You know your stuff.

Courage triumphs and I'm ready to fight for the environment.

As are most of the locals here. Public Enemy's *Fight the Power* runs through my mind. And so does my own spontaneous rhyme.

Everyone wants a piece of it—

Moloka'i's water. Admit it

all ya'll plotters wantin' a judicial writ

to give you free reign to buss out yo' tool kit

and construct for profit.

But we won't submit.

We ain't soft.

So you best back off

cuz you bout to be iced out—Jack Frost.

I envision going up to the standing mic at the center of the room and spittin' my rhyme as my testimony.

The lights dim. I swag walk to the standing mic.

A spotlight comes on. A DJ drops my beat. I spit...

Pono elbows me back into reality. "Hey, Rani. You gonna give a testimony?"

"Uh-huh."

"Cool. Me too."

"Yours is the one I'm looking forward to hearing," I say, smiling.

He smiles back. It almost makes him look shy.

Did he just blush?

But before I can read into his face anymore, the EPA Chair calls the meeting to order.

After today's hearing, the EPA will decide if the Moloka'i aquifer is truly its principal source of drinking water for the island and if contamination of it would be a health hazard for the inhabitants of the island. If they determine it is, then Moloka'i would get federal Sole Source Aquifer Designation. So any federally funded development would have to get EPA approval to make sure it doesn't pollute the aquifer. This would be huge for keeping Moloka'i Moloka'i.

The Chair calls for the first testifier. Auntie Hannah. She and Auntie Lani are the main activists fighting to protect the island's water. I think of them as Moloka'i's dynamic duo. The Salt-N-Pepa of water activism because first, Auntie Hannah is white and Auntie Lani is a brown Native Hawaiian and second, because they've got mad verbal skills. Watching them testify at public forums is the most inspiring thing I've ever seen.

There's buzzing in the audience as Auntie Hannah walks to the mic. The Chair calls for silence and Auntie Hannah introduces herself. Pono and I exchange ecstatic glances. He puts his left arm around the back of my chair. His fingers barely graze my arm. I do my best to listen to Auntie Hannah's testimony and ignore my urge to leap out of my chair and jump on Pono's lap.

Then I hear a familiar voice.

Oh no.

No. No. No.

I pivot a bit to the left and see my dad weaving through the chairs to a couple of empty ones near the front. Freakin' Wendy's behind him. Dad and I make eye contact, but he looks away before I can make out his expression.

So this is what it's come to. My dad is willing to fight for the water of Moloka'i. Willing to fight for Wendy. But he won't fight for our family. For Mom. For me.

My eyes don't release my panic yet. First I feel my heart shaking. Literally. Then my entire body. My eyes eventually release salty fluid almost as an afterthought. The secondary tears drip onto my lips and into my mouth.

I feel Pono's hand on my back. "What's wrong, Rani?" I turn to face him. His eyebrows are lifted and his eyes wide.

"I don't feel so good," I say, my eyes shifting to my dad and Wendy. Pono's eyes follow mine, then return to me. Suddenly, it's like someone shoved plugs into my ear canals. I see Pono's lips moving but I can't hear what he's saying. And I can't see him clearly because it's as if someone put an opaque plastic bag over my head and tied it at the neck.

Air. I need air. Help!

Next thing I know I'm near my truck. Trying to catch my breath.

MOM'S EMANCIPATION

Dad's home for the first time in I don't even know how long. It's strange having all three of us in the house at the same time. It's like Dad's a guest, a visiting raja from a faraway kingdom—with a new foreign rani—who stops by unannounced. In the spirit of hospitality, we all sit down for the gourmet meal his old kam vaari prepared. It makes me miss the days of our previous family dysfunction when our roles were well defined.

Mom serves us the food. A million questions spring up in my mind, slow at first, then faster and faster. Like microwave popcorn.

Why is he here tonight?

How can he leave us?

If I'm not his rani anymore, what am I?

If Mom's still working her butt off, but Dad's not around, is she still his kam vaari?

I watch Dad tear off a piece of bakhri, wrap it around some vegetable korma, and put the unsealed dumpling in his mouth.

It's freakin' delicious, right? Bet Wendy the slut can't cook up anything half as delectable.

I have this powerful urge to slap the food out of his hand and grab the plate away from him.

Selfish bastard. You don't deserve Mom's cooking. Go back to Wendy and let her try to cook something this good.

He takes another bite. His eyes are focused on my head. Midchew he says, "I always wanted a boy." His words and amused expression stun me, but my lips are wired shut and my vocal cords are paralyzed. He snickers and finishes chewing. I used to think he said the funniest things. Not right now. Right now, I'm irritated. I run my left hand over my head. I'm surprised by the bit of stubble I feel.

We finish our meal in silence, heads down. The quiet is unbearable, making my motoring thoughts louder. I swear I'm about to burst like a huge Hubba Bubba bubble some little kid blew. I keep my eyes on my plate and focus on each bite to keep myself in one piece.

After dinner, Mom and I clean up. I dry the last of the dishes. The tension is thick, like Mom's homemade paneer. I wade through it and head back to my room. Before I make it halfway down the hall, I hear Dad's booming voice.

"Rani. Meera. I want to talk to you. Come sit at the table."

Finally. He's realized what a terrible mistake he's made. That he loves us so much. That he's going to leave Wendy and things will go back to our normal with me and Dad. Dad and me. Raja and rani.

Hopeful, I sit down at the dining room table, my back straight. I press my quivering hands under my thighs. I glance at Mom. As usual, I can't read her expression. I look at Dad and smile.

Dad clears his throat and adjusts himself in his chair, like he's getting ready for a long flight. "Wendy's going to move in with us. It's best for everyone," he announces.

My mouth is too shocked to curve down. I sit there like a ventriloquist puppet with a painted-on permanent smile.

"I've asked her to move in this weekend," he continues.

The reality of what he's saying strikes me. Like a mallet. That's when my mouth drops. I contort my face in disbelief.

"Wh-what?"

I flash a pleading look at Mom, but she doesn't notice. She's sitting with her hands folded, staring at the table.

"Mom, say something! Come on." She doesn't utter one word.

Panic. Dad's talking nonsense and Mom's not doing anything. It's the opposite of their usual fight. What the heck do I do?

"It's the most logical solution for all of us," Dad continues.

"How!?"

I shove my chair back and vault up. I pace. My breath becomes rapid. Instead of a peacemaker, I become a prosecutor. I question the defendant. "Protecting the water of Moloka'i from the Ranch is pointless if you break apart your family. They're using up the water and destroying the land, but you're using us and destroying our family. How are you any different from the Ranch?"

"Don't question me, Rani. Sit down."

He's never talked to me like this before. Is this how Mom feels when he bosses her around? Does she feel hopeless and worthless when she does whatever he demands, even if she doesn't agree? I shake my head and the tears start. "You made Mom move to Moloka'i. All she does is work," I wail. "You broke her, and now you've left her."

Dad's eyes are on the table. He lifts his stainless steel pyalo and swirls around the remaining water. He takes a sip then says, "Mom needs me, Rani. I can't leave her. And I won't leave Wendy. I love her." He's looking directly at me now.

He's talking to me like Mom isn't even here. I take off my glasses and massage my temples with my fingers. Then I bury my head in my hands.

"What about me, Dad?"

"You don't need me anymore."

What?

A whirlwind of images, chronicling my life as Dad's rani, zoom through my mind. Quarter Pounders at McDonald's, despite Mom's pleas to him to raise me vegetarian. Hiking in the Appalachians without Mom. The trip to Oahu the year before he declared he was moving to Moloka'i while Mom stayed behind and worked.

Even after moving to Moloka'i, it was still him and me. At the store and restaurant. The activist meetings. Hiking and fishing. I think he genuinely wanted the best for me. A better life than he had growing up in Gujarat.

But Mom paid the price because she was never on his radar.

Over the years, he gave me all of his many forms of attention— the I love you's, the countless hours spent, the private conversations with no filters. And like a sponge, I soaked it all up.

Rani, you're all I need.

Rani, it's just you and me.

Rani, tell me what to buy Mom so she calms down.

Rani, Mom's gooso. It's because she had a rough childhood. Just stay out of her way.

70

Then there were the other private things. An all too familiar shiver creeps down my spine and my body trembles. I think about my slam poem.

So daughter became child bride...

I can't let myself go there. Mom's here and she doesn't know about all that. Quickly, I lock those memories away and toss the key.

Instead, I dredge up other memories—the ones of him praising me. All he had to do was shower me with his affection and attention and I'd let him do anything to me. And I'd do anything for him—anything to ensure I'd keep getting my fix.

So child bride became Dad's attention junkie...

I'd ask him about his day. Make him feel better if he had a bad one. I'd listen. Obey. Never talk back. Straight A's—always. Chores and work at the store and restaurant—above and beyond. On-call expert couples' counselor. And I didn't need a degree. I had lots of experience.

Sometimes I'd even forget I had opinions of my own. In my mind, he could do no wrong. He knew everything. If I stayed close to him, I'd feel good and everything would work out. If I listened to him, I'd succeed in life.

And I didn't mind the isolation. It meant he wanted to be with me the most. If my friendships went beyond casual, Dad interfered. This one time, after we first moved to Moloka'i and still lived in Maunaloa, he accused two of my new friends of letting all the Ranch cows into our yard. There was cow shit everywhere and Dad was furious. Thinking about it now, there's no way two kids could have done that. How could he not know that? Guess it was a good excuse to cut me off from them. At the time I didn't think anything of it. A life outside of him seemed unnecessary.

It was all about him. I got good at all about him. An authority on the subject, in fact.

And the ultimate reward was when he said, "I love you, Rani. What would I do without you?" His approval became my life-sustaining force.

I've looked up to him for so long, I don't know where else to look.

And now he's saying I don't need him.

"It's not fair, Dad! I'm the one you really love. Not Wendy! What about me? Don't you love me?"

"I do, but I'm committed to Wendy now."

I'm speechless. My head hurts. I rest my forehead on the table. No one speaks. Minutes pass. Dad tries a new tactic. Running his fingers over his stubbly beard, he whispers, "Rani betta, you have to help me."

I lift my head up. "How could you even ask Mom and me to live with Wendy?"

"Don't you want us all to stay together?"

"Of course I want *us* to stay together." I draw an imaginary circle with my finger encompassing the three of us. "But not with Wendy."

"I'm not leaving Wendy, Rani. You've always helped Mom and me fix things. You have to help us all stay together."

I almost fall for it. Then I take a look at Mom. Even though she hasn't moved, tears streak her cheeks. There are no words of self-harm. Only silent sorrow.

"I'm not going to fix things this time!"

Dad opens his mouth to retort.

"Bhus. Chuup. Both of you. That's enough," Mom says.

Flabbergasted, I press my lips together. My tears stop.

"Pradip, you need to leave," she says, wiping her cheeks with the back of her hands. "You and Wendy aren't welcome here."

This is the first time I've ever heard Mom stand up to Dad. I let the significance of it wrap itself around me like a pashmina shawl.

No headbanging. No knives. No "I want to die."

"Meera, I won't leave you. You need me."

"I don't want you in my life anymore. I'll hire an attorney to handle our divorce and divide everything. Don't come back here or to the store or restaurant."

Dad's eyes and mouth are stuck wide open. He looks like one of those busts of dead old guys you see in museums.

"If you try anything funny, I'll call the police. I'm not following you anymore."

She grips the armrests of the chair and labors to push herself up. She limps over to Dad. I can tell her ankle is still bothering her. My eyes well up again.

"Get out now, Pradip."

RAP SAVED MY LIFE YO!

"Get out now, Pradip."

Mom's words echo in my ears. Dad's won all the battles, but she just won the war. I'm shell shocked. And restless. I walk in circles around my room like I'm a dog chasing its tail. The three-foot tower of CDs in the corner beckons me, urging me to find some lyrical healing. I run my finger on the CD spines, making my way down the stack. My eyes fix on LL Cool J's *Mama Said Knock You Out*.

I pull it out quick so none of the other CDs shift. I drop the disc into my boombox and skip to its namesake track. I want to blast it, but it's late and Mom's probably sleeping. So I settle on volume five. I hurl myself onto the bed and glue my eyes to the ceiling. I imagine a sold-out arena. I'm announcing on stage. Then Mom appears amidst the bright flashing lights and starts full on rapping. She delivers each of LL's lines with precision. Her thick Gujju accent adds to the performance. She's working the crowd in her stylish hip hop outfit. Baggy jeans. Oversized black hoodie with a huge Indian flag on the back. A long 24K gold chain with a four-inch diameter, diamond-studded, Om pendant. Black and gold Adidas high tops.

I smile, feeling less sad and worried. Every time I listen to this hard-hitting LL track, it's like I've won a boxing match without throwing a punch. It's the ultimate stress relief. There's something timeless about it. I can picture myself listening to it even when I'm forty, when I've had a bad day at work, when I want to kick my boss where the sun don't shine, but I can't because I don't want to lose my job or get charged with assault in the third degree, even though it's only a misdemeanor. So I blare *Mama Said Knock You Out* instead. Miraculously, everything's all G.

I'm sure LL knows he's influenced people from all walks of life. But does he know that his dynamic rap has provided much-needed solace to a first generation Indian teen girl? If I ever met him, I'd probably give him a chin-up and say, "S'up LL." *Naw*. Let's be real. I'd give him a big bear hug and say, "Thank you. Thank you for *Mama Said Knock You Out*. It's cheaper than therapy, man."

My thoughts drift back to Mom and what else she said to Dad.

I'm not following you anymore.

Mighty words for a woman who followed him for seventeen years. From Kenya to Gujarat, where they met for the first time after being matched by their parents. Then around a Hindu marriage fire in Gujarat, where Mom did the Saat Phere and followed Dad around the holy fire witness Agni. I've seen the photos. With each round, they recited vows to each other. After the seventh vow and circle, they became man and wife. I've been to a few Hindu weddings. The vows enthralled me—so simple, practical, and beautiful, spelling out married life between two loving partners. Through the years, though,

Dad hasn't been a loving partner and he sure hasn't kept any of the vows. Trust Mom with her decisions about the household? No. Consult with her about their source of income? Nope. Seek her and only her to experience all the seasons of their life? Heck no!

I take off my glasses and flip over on the bed. I bury my face in the pillow. It becomes a soft sponge for my wet eyes.

Mom kept following him. To New York. To Connecticut. Finally to Moloka'i. How could she possibly know that Dad would say the words but do the opposite?

My grandparents followed the traditional Gujarati Patel's Chha Gaam—Six Village—marriage arrangement system. In this system, you can only marry someone from one of the six villages (actually sizable towns) that isn't your home village. I'm no geneticist, but talk about limiting the gene pool.

Yuck.

I think about my grandparents. Bet they got together one day and said to each other, "Hey! Let's get Pradip and Meera married even though they don't know anything about each other!" Easy peasy. No discussion like, "Well, maybe they should get to know each other first," or "Maybe because Pradip is self-centered and Meera can't speak up for herself, we should think about this more carefully." A cruel joke. A game of dice for bored parents.

I jerk up on the bed and shake my head. I roll off my bed. I want to to write some rhymes. Time to use the adrenaline pumping in my body and the strange mix of sadness and relief to create a rap masterpiece. I plop down on the thick cushion of my desk chair, open my frayed notebook and slip on my glasses. Then I see the large envelope Pono gave me the other day. It's laying flat on my desk. I look back at my notebook, but it's like the envelope uses a tractor beam on my eyes. I grab the envelope and tear it open. Pono said it was receipts, but inside there's only one sheet of paper.

MC SUTRA

BE PREPARED TO PERFORM ONE ORIGINAL RAP

AT AN AUDITION THIS SATURDAY.

IF THE CONTENT, FLOW, AND DELIVERY

OF YOUR RAP IS DEEMED WORTHY,

YOU WILL BE INVITED TO BECOME A PERFORMING MEMBER

OF 4EVA FLOWIN', AN UNDERGROUND CREW ON MOLOKA'I DEDICATED

TO THE INNOVATION AND PERPETUATION OF HIP HOP.

MEET THE PROFESSOR

7:15 P.M. SATURDAY

HO'OLEHUA POST OFFICE

BURN AFTER READING!

Underground crew dedicated to hip hop?

I take off my glasses, wipe the lenses with my shirt, and slide them back on. I read it again. Yep, underground crew dedicated to hip hop. On Moloka'i? Is Pono messing with me? He doesn't even know I rap. Only Mark knows about MC Sutra. Is Mark pranking me? Do Mark and Pono know each other? This has got to be a joke.

Not funny.

Rap's no joke to me.

It's most definitely helped me cope with my family conflicts. I fold the invitation in half lengthwise then crease the top right corner to the center pleat. Tonight, LL's rap got me through my family's final rupture. But it goes back further. I think about how way way back it goes for me as I fold the invitation into a paper plane.

It started when I was little. The fights were happening all the time. With warning. Without warning. Terrible intense fights. So intense there was usually a threat of Mom getting hurt.

The memories are flying around my brain like a hundred paper planes, one in particular.

I'm seven years old, standing at the top of the stairs. There's light in the kitchen and a terrifying thumping. My mom is banging her head full force against the hard wall, screaming, "I want to die" over and over again. My dad is slumped on a nearby chair, staring at the floor, doing nothing, saying nothing. I run and squeeze my way in between Mom and the wall. "No, Mommy, no! Stop! I love you! Do something, Dad, come on!" My mom wails, then dives forward with her arms and torso stretched out in front of her. Like she's in child's pose.

My dad doesn't move. I grab his hands and pull him out of the chair with all my might and push him over toward Mom. He stands staring at her, arms limp at his side, head turned away. I tug at Dad's hand and try to pull him down toward Mom, try to force him to hold her hand. "Say sorry to her, Dad, come on."

Dad drops Mom's hand and grabs both of mine. He fixes his eyes on me and says, "Rani betta, thu mari chokri chu, mari princess."

I flick away a tear right before it reaches my jawline. The paper plane invitation in my hand seems to clamor for takeoff. I launch it across my room and watch as it glides a couple of feet before diving onto the carpet.

My brain is fast-forwarding to every fight that ever happened so it can get to the most recent one. Ten years of saving Mom from hurting herself. Ten years of her ignoring me. Ten years of being the focus of Dad's attentions. Ten years of being their peacemaker. For what? In the end I couldn't save their marriage or our family. He's with another woman now. They might as well have gotten a divorce back in the beginning.

Then my brain rewinds to a particularly rough fight my parents had in our Connecticut house when I was eleven. That's when rap claimed its position as my savior. It went down like this. Mom held the tip of an eight-inch chef's knife to her chest, screaming, "Mhare mari jawuu chhe." Torment covered her face and tears flowed like the Ganges during monsoon. As expected Dad sat at the kitchen table doing nothing. I pulled the knife away from Mom. Settled her down. Told Dad what to say to her. And brokered a peace treaty between them. Then I locked myself in my room, emotionally exhausted. I cranked up the radio so they wouldn't hear me sobbing.

Run DMC's *It's Like That* was playing. I'd never heard it before. I couldn't stop my head from moving to the beat. And Run DMC's flow somehow blocked the flow of my tears.

That was it. I'd found something that made me feel better when Dad wasn't giving me his undivided attention. Feel better after saving Mom's life. Feel better when I was lonely.

Rap saved my life yo.

And it's been saving me ever since. A year ago I put my own pen to the pad. Writing rhymes to lift myself up. To give myself a road map to life. To swagger and display courage, in hopes that one day I'll truly feel that level of confidence in myself.

I retrieve the paper plane and flatten it. I scan the invitation's words again and scowl. No one talks about rap on Moloka'i. It doesn't add up. On this island it's all about reggae and Jawaiian. That's what's everywhere. Oozing out of trucks, cars, and houses. Kids on the beach playing ukulele and singing it. It blends into the culture and adds a bit of defiance to traditional Hawaiian music. A subtle non-Western rhythmic form of resistance woven into daily life.

I don't know what to make of this 4eva Flowin'. But I know what I have to do.

Invitation in hand, I walk to the kitchen. The lights are all out. The only sound, the steady low hum of the fridge. I flip on the light switch and rummage through the drawers looking for the disposable lighter. I cram it into my pocket. I open the sliding door to the deck and step out, treading down the stairs to the beach. The Pacific laps at the south shore. I sit on a random tree stump, which the ocean sometimes delivers from some other shore. Alone in the darkness, my eyes adjust. I feel calm and secure. Because I know that rap's there for me. That it'll save me whenever I need it. And that no one's going to mess with that.

Belie dat.

I slip the invitation under my thigh so the trades won't carry it off. With my thumb, I turn the spark wheel and press down on the fork of the lighter. It catches on the first roll. The flame's a bright orange in the black night. A momentary lull in the winds protects the flame so my free hand doesn't have to. For a second, I watch the flame toss itself around. I pull out the invitation and touch the flickering light to the paper. Quickly the white disappears, swallowed by a glowing yellow mouth with dark brown and sizzling orange lips. Pieces of char fall to the sand. I stand up and take a few steps to the water's edge. As the flames reach the corner of the paper, I drop the burning remnant into the water.

BUTTERFLIES HIGH ON COKE

Either the Gujarati men I know have trouble understanding English or they're complete narcissists.

There's no other way to explain why Gautam uncle, a successful banker in Alabama and my dad's former best friend, is on the phone asking me to reconsider letting Dad and Wendy move into our house.

I'm fairly certain this is how it went down. It started with Dad.

I told him, "I'm not going to fix things this time!"

Dad heard that as, "I'll come around. Keep asking me until you get your way, Dad."

Then Mom told Dad, "Get out now, Pradip."

Dad heard that as, "I'm mad, but I'll cool off. Just in case, Pradip, why don't you ask Gautam to help convince Rani? That way, you'll be sure to be back in the house in no time."

Funny thing is Dad's been estranged from Gautam uncle for years. Dad said something about being disgusted by Gautam uncle's banking success. "Gautam's become so greedy, bigoted, and egotistical," my dad told me.

That's all out the window now that Dad needs help.

And I'm sure Gautam uncle thinks he's the big man who'll swoop in and save the day. With his words of "reason," he'll rescue Mom and me from the depths and restore us to sanity, self-respect, and common sense. *How gracious of you, uncle dearest.*

I listen to Gautam uncle rattle on in Gujarati about how my dad misses us. That he really wants us all, including Wendy, to be one joint happy family.

Yawn.

He pauses for a breath and I jump in. In my somewhat broken Gujarati, I say, "But, Gautam uncle, Mom doesn't want to live in the house with Dad and his lover." Seems pretty straightforward.

He rebuts. "Your Mom doesn't mean that. Doesn't matter because your Dad has a right to live in the house. Your Mom isn't allowed to keep him out."

Wow. In three dismissive sentences, the level of woman-hate by these Gujju men is loud and clear. Showy even. Like the kaju barfi my mom neatly arranged on the stainless steel thali in July. She'd made it for my dad's birthday because it's his favorite Indian sweet. With artistic meticulousness, she'd even decorated the diamond-shaped delicacies with edible gold and silver foil. We never got to sing him happy birthday because he didn't come home until after Mom and I had gone to sleep. Dad didn't mention a word about the barfi to Mom the next day, even though we'd left it on the kitchen counter with a card.

"Besides, Rani betta, raja had more than one wife."

I realize two things about Dad and Gautam uncle. And perhaps about the entire male-dominated Gujju culture that raised them. More like brainwashed them.

1. They don't take a woman's words seriously.

2. They can do anything they want, but a woman can't.

And I thought the creepy, old, okole-grabbing tourist guy was a misogynist. As it turns out, maybe he was more of a straight-up jerk under the influence. My dad and Gautam uncle are sober and scheming. And a bunch of other *S* words. Sly. Sneaky. Slick. Selfish.

Right about now, I'm thinking that's worse.

To my chagrin, Gautam uncle keeps talking. "And betta, don't worry so much about studying. Forget being a doctor. Your Dad and I are looking for a nice Chha Gaam boy for you. Better to get married when you are young. Not like these American women."

Over my cold, dead body.

There's no way you're arranging my marriage to some hairy Indian boy who only wants a nokrani. And for the record, I'm never getting married. You think I want to end up like my mom? No way! I'm heading straight to the state of Independence. Maybe if a guy actually likes me, someday I'll have a boyfriend. And move from Singleville to I-Got-A-Man-ville. But, marriage. Nope. Not ever. Also, I most definitely will be a physician, thank you very much.

Rolling my eyes, I say, "Gautam uncle, I have to go. Customers just walked into the store. I'm the only one here." Slight exaggeration. Really only one customer: Mark. But any excuse to end this call.

Not listening to me, he continues with his spirit-crushing lecture. "Money's not a problem. I'll pay you $10,000 for each baby you have. Even more if it's a boy. You need to have lots of babies. We need more Hindus in this world, right? Too many blacks and Muslims."

I feel sick to my stomach. The casualness of his enmity towards anyone who's not a Gujarati male makes me want to vomit. I can't believe he thinks I completely agree with him. I picture him in a white robe with a blood-red Hindu svastika on the left chest, a tall, pointy white hat, and a face-covering white cloth mask with eyeholes. That freaks me out big time.

"Bye, Gautam uncle," I say. I drop the phone onto the receiver like it's covered with a horrible virus. A couple of seconds later, the phone rings again. I know it's him, so I ignore it.

"You look like you just saw a ghost," Marks says, hoisting a 12-pack of Bud Light onto the counter. I can tell he stepped out of the shower a few minutes ago because he smells like a warm spring day. He smiles at me. His eyes sparkle like the dime-size sapphire earrings I once saw Lalita ba wearing. His black t-shirt hugs his strapping torso like I wish I could. My mind flashes to the slide show of the French sculptor we learned about today in art class: Auguste Rodin. Before I know it, I'm picturing Mark and me strolling through the streets of Paris. Suddenly he's a walking sculpture in the Musée Rodin.

He sits down and I envision myself on his lap. My left arm is around his neck and his right hand is on my hip. Hold up! We're naked! He leans in. We give Rodin's The Kiss a run for the money.

I smile and forget about Gautam uncle's asinine comments.

Don't stare.

"I wish it was a ghost," I say, aligning my glasses with both hands. "No, it was my dad's crazy friend on the phone trying to turn me into a woman-hating racist."

"Ooh. Sounds like my dad." He laughs. "May I have a pack of Salem Lights, please." I'm In a daze, my eyes following his hand as he runs it through his sunny hair.

Down, butterflies, down!

I grab his cigarettes from the display case, wishing there was a neon sign over my head that read, "How about some Rani with those Salem lights?" Might as well throw in a bunch of flashing arrows pointing at me. That would make things easier. Maybe then he'd stay a little longer and talk to me. I ask myself if there's anything I can do to make that happen. What would Beverley Joliet do?

"Flirt, Rani," the gorgeous 28-year-old Beverly whispers into my ear.

At least that's what I imagine she'd advise. Besides, that's how Beverly got Juan in that steamy romance novel *South of the Border Passion.* Yes, one can learn a tremendous amount about love and courtship by reading romance novels. My mom has a stash of at least a hundred. I mean a woman's got needs and I'm pretty sure Dad wasn't attending to hers. So Mom got her action through books. Some nights she stays up into the wee hours of the morning reading.

I sneak her books into my room and feast on every delicious word, each sentence like a bite of warm, syrupy, rose-essence gulab jamun. Especially the descriptions of making out. Those sections are worth rereading. And making out is usually preceded by flirting.

I better flirt like crazy with Mark! I lift up the left corner of my glasses and take a deep breath.

Here goes.

"You know smoking and drinking will kill you," I say coyly, half smiling. I lean forward with my elbows on the counter and balance my chin on my interlaced fingers.

"I guess you're partially to blame since you're my dealer." He flashes me a devilish grin.

He's flirting back!

"Yeah, I guess I'm your dealer. Must be my bad girl side." I raise an eyebrow and give him a subtle smile. Full on Beastie Boys *She's Crafty* style.

He grins and looks at me in this sexy ass way. Oh boy. Chicken skin to da max. Then he says, "Why don't you come hang out on the porch for awhile. Keep this customer happy so I'll keep buying."

It's working! High five, Beverly! I owe you!

The butterflies in my stomach fly around like they're high on coke. Well, what I've heard a coke high is like. Amped up. Euphoric beyond measure. I follow him onto the porch and we both sit on the same bench. The sunset adds to the amorous vibe.

The setting sun over the ocean paints the sky a deep orange. And they lived happily ever after.

If only.

Mark cracks open one of the ice cold beers and offers it to me. That's when I get a load of a nickel-size, dark reddish-brown spot on his hand. It looks like a burn. And I'm surprised by the thinness of his outstretched arm. I can even see some veins popping out. His arms are usually filled out by all his muscles and taut, smooth skin. I don't say anything about that because I'm kinda in a tizzy. Instead I say, "Can't drink on the job," hoping I sound nonchalant. Can he tell I've never had a beer?

"Right." He takes a big swig. "Ahh. Glad it's Friday. And payday."

"You do realize that this is the extent of my Friday soiree, hanging out on the front porch of the store with a customer." I let out a loud, dramatic sigh.

"A customer?! Ouch! That hurts," Mark teases, holding his closed fist to his heart. "I thought I was more than a customer. More like a friend."

Friend?

I'm giddy. "Yeah, I guess so," I say.

"By the way, Rani, how are things with your dad?"

"Lousy." I shake my head. The sheer joy of having Mark's attention motivates me to talk. Things I would never tell anyone start coming out of my mouth. I can't shut myself up.

"It's like a soap opera. *Days of Pradip's Life*. He wants Wendy to move in with us. Can you believe that? He actually thought we'd be ok with that."

"I'm guessing your mom's not down with it."

"Thankfully she's not into polygamy." I kick off my slippers and lift my feet onto the bench, hugging my bare knees. "She kicked him out. She straight-up told him he's not welcome near us."

"Go, Meera." He finishes off his beer and lets out a silent burp. Then he opens another can. "How are you doing?"

"I don't know. I keep trying to figure out how to fix everything." I hug my knees tighter. "Dad's gone and Mom still won't talk to me." I exhale loudly. "I feel kinda lonely." A wave of sadness pulls me under. "I know what you're thinking, '*Boo hoo, Rani. Stop feeling sorry for yourself. You have it easy compared to most on the planet.*'"

I try to hold back the tears but I can't. Like a faucet left slightly open, a few trickle down my cheek. "That's what you're thinking, right?"

He puts his beer down and slides closer to me. With an almost tender tone, he says, "Hey, look at me."

That's what Dad used to say.

I turn my head to him and look into his eyes expectantly, biting my lower lip and holding my breath.

"I get why this hurts."

The floodgates open and I sob. My head drifts down and ends up on his shoulder.

"It's ok," he says, softly patting my bald head.

After a minute I stop crying, but keep my head on his shoulder. "Thanks, Mark. For listening and not judging me."

"I'd never judge you. You my homie." With his free hand, he grabs his beer and takes a big gulp.

Really?

The fog of depression lifts and infatuation takes over. I pat my eyes dry under my glasses, then push them up. Wish I had some tissue to blow my nose into. I end up snorting the snot back in. Loudly. Embarrassed, I try to get a grip. I sit up straight and face him, laying my hands flat on my thighs. I change the subject to lighten the mood. "So, you got a girlfriend?" I ask, with a bit more enthusiasm than I'd intended.

He almost chokes and practically spews out the sip of beer in his mouth. "Wasn't expecting that one." Smiling, he says, "No girlfriend. Haven't had one in over a year."

Hee hee!

Tingling all over. Just like what Beverly felt. Casually I say, "That's surprising. A hard-working looker like you. I wouldn't think you'd be single for long."

"Well," he pauses like he's mulling it over. He fixes his eyes on me. "I'm talking to this one girl. She's smart, beautiful, and funny. I'm definitely interested in her, but I don't think she'll go for an old guy like me."

Dropping that Molotov cocktail, he picks up his open beer and the rest of the 12-pack. "I gotta get some sleep. Haven't slept good in a couple of nights." And with that he walks down the porch steps. Unexpectedly he turns around. I jerk my eyes off his derriere and fiddle with my glasses, feigning spectacle malfunction.

Grinning, he says, "See ya around, Rani."

"See ya, Mark."

Who's he talking about? Could he be talking about me? No way, Rani! Shut up! You have no chance with a guy like that.

The phone rings. I run inside and answer it. It's Mom.

"Rani, I need that big box of wine bottles. The restaurant's really busy. Close up the store and come here," she says, out of breath.

I check the clock. It's already 7:30 p.m. I shut down the store as fast as I can. Struggling with the heavy box of wine, I cross the street to the restaurant. Rambunctious customers are spilling out of the restaurant's front door. I guess I didn't notice them when I was caught up in mackin' on Mark.

Only Mom's in the kitchen. Pots and pans boil and sizzle on all four burners of the gas stove. Partially plated entrees sit on the counters, their beds of cabbage patiently awaiting the Korean ribs. The thirty-cup rice cooker is open, half empty. Don't need any more clues. Mom's been cooking and serving.

"Where's Shawn?"

"He didn't show up," Mom says.

No Shawn. No Dad. I watch Mom load the rectangular stainless steel tray with three steaming dishes. This is like a microcosm of Mom's entire life. She does all the work while Dad's off doing whatever he wants.

"Just do the cooking, Mom," I say, grabbing the tray out of her hands, "I'll wait on tables."

Nothing like three hours of serving drunk tourists non-stop to make time fly. Hungry customers occupy the five booths and eight bar stools all night. As soon as a booth or bar stool clears, it gets filled from the line of boisterous tourists outside on the porch. Most of them are already drinking because they've ordered liquor while they're waiting. They sit before I have a chance to wipe down the tables. I try to smile and engage in their small talk about Moloka'i as I take their orders and serve their food and drinks. *What's the best beach on the island? The most beautiful hike? Is Kalaupapa worth it?*

Finally the last customer leaves. By the time Mom and I finish washing the dishes and cleaning the kitchen and dining area, we're ready to collapse. Mom winces as she balances the last pot on the dish rack.

"Your ankle?"

"It still hurts." She leans her weight against the sink.

She looks drained. I want to give her a hug, but I can't get myself to do it. I get her a glass of water instead.

"I'm going to ask Auntie Maile's niece and nephew if they can work at the store and over here. This is too much for us."

"Sounds good."

I swear I hear violins playing as I watch Mom limp down the stairs. She grips the hand railing as she takes one slow step down at a time. It's like I'm watching a Leela Chitnis Bollywood film of the archetypal suffering, selfless Indian mother.

I hate you, Dad.

We make our way to the truck. I help her into the passenger side. I sneak a peek at her every few minutes, trying to think of something to say. She's staring out the windshield into the dark night. She doesn't move her head. I'm not even sure if she's blinking her eyes. I sigh and grip the steering wheel as tight as I can, like I want to crush the life out of it. A hurricane of emotions builds—anger, sadness, confusion, irritation—and quiet tears storm down my cheeks. I want to tell her how much I care about her. Love her. Know she's miserable. Try to comfort her with my words.

But I don't have the strength for a monologue. I want some words from her. I want her to say something to me. Heck I'll take anything.

Throw me a bone here, Mom.

I want to scream.

I end up keeping my mouth shut and waiting out the swirling category-4 emotions.

I accept that it's going to be twenty-one miles of shared silence.

I force my eyes to stop seeking connection with her and focus solely on the road ahead. But as soon as we pass Chevron, I can't stop myself from looking in her direction. The heavy glow from the streetlamps spotlights her. That's when I feel this ache in my gut. Because I see her pull her hand away—*was she trying to touch me?*—and turn back to stare out of the windshield. There are tears on her cheek. The ache in my gut turns to a searing panic in my chest.

ATHEIST NIGHTMARES

I'm flailing to escape. My grandfather's arms encircle my child waist. He hauls me from the mobile stairway onto the Kenya Airways jet. I scream and reach for Mom. On the tarmac, Dad pulls Mom away. She screams and reaches for me. In an instant I'm a teenager, sleeping peacefully in my twin bed. Out of the blue a tall, older man, his face out of focus, appears in my room. There's something familiar about him. He takes off one shoe, one sock at a time, arranging them carefully near the foot of the bed. He takes off his pants, neatly folds and lays them on top of his shoes. He takes off his boxers and drops them on the floor. He lifts the white comforter and slides into my bed. I wake up startled by his movement. He grabs my hands and holds them over my head. He climbs on top of me. I struggle trying to extricate myself. He grips my hands tighter with his right hand and moves his left hand under the comforter, pulling off my panties. That's when I get a clear view of his face. It's my dad.

Crowing roosters. I jolt up, trembling. The beads of sweat on my forehead trickle into my eyes and down my cheeks. I blink several times, then rub my eyes. It's dark. I realize my pj's are drenched and sticking to my skin. I'm chilled. I curl into a compact ball for warmth and squeeze tight. I grope the desk for my glasses. My fingers find the frames and I slide them on.

The dream. No, the nightmare. I reassure myself that I'm safe. He's with Wendy now. He hasn't "tucked me in" recently. My mind waffles.

Your nightmare used to be reality.

Get over it, Rani. You're not crippled. You're not starving. You're not homeless. You're not poor.

I try to make the nightmare go away. I glimpse out the window. The glow of the big Moloka'i moon offers solace and reminds me of *Moonlight Sonata*. I played it last night after Mom and I got home. It helped quiet my painful churning emotions. Mom went straight to bed, but I played my heart out. I haven't wanted to play recently. Last night was different. The moonlight was streaming through the sliding glass doors, illuminating my fingers. I felt connected to Dad as I played.

But it's too early to play right now. So I listen to *Moonlight Sonata* in my mind and close my eyes, trying to find good Dad-memories. He introduced me to the piano when I was six years old. He drove me to lessons every Thursday without fail. Why he picked the piano is a mystery. I mean he doesn't play any instrument. But he encouraged me to practice hard, that it would all be worth it someday. He'd hold my hand and smile at me. I believed him and felt secure. I practiced everyday. I wanted to make sure my piano teacher would have nothing but rave reviews to give my dad after each lesson. I try to hold onto these memories as I wipe the remaining sticky sweat from my forehead. But it's no use. Thoughts of the nightmare charge back in. I realize it's the same nightmare I've had over and over since Dad starting being distant last spring. I feel myself sinking.

'Nuff already.

I kick at the damp comforter—and the loitering hurt—then jump out of bed.

I shower and dress. Then it's to the kitchen for breakfast. Finding tasty leftovers for the most important meal of the day is never a problem when your mom's Gujarati. There's a note on the counter. Mom's handwriting.

"Rani, eat the prasad. You have the day off. Lani and Colt are covering the store and restaurant with Auntie Maile and me. Mom."

Yes!

It's the first Saturday I'll be free in months. Too bad I have no friends to go holoholo with me.

I dig into the prasad: strawberries and sweet cream. Delicious. Since kicking husband-God out, Mom's restarted her daily sewa of her true Lord of the House, Thakorji. Service to Thakorji includes the offering of food and drink. I scrape up the last bits, relishing every bite. Yummy *and* holy, what could be better?

I wash and dry the prasad bowl and spoon and carefully place them in the kitchen drawer reserved for Mom's Thakorji stuff. This drawer is a treasure chest of Thakorji paraphernalia. Miniature silver toys. Multi-colored cloth frame coverings with silver and gold trim. Matching clothes. Tiny sparkly jewelry. Deep burgundy and yellow velvet pillows. Silk blankets. All the makings of a luxurious hang out for her beloved Thakorji. Today I find a buried prize amidst the spoils. Partially hidden under a gadi, the bent, glossy edges of old photos jut out. Like a pirate, I claim my pictographical loot.

The first photo is of Mom and me. She's wearing a gorgeous green silk sari with gold paisley print. Holding me. Gazing deep into my eyes. Smiling. I must be around two years old. I'm sitting on her lap, my arms wrapped tight around her slender neck, smiling back at her. We're seated in front of Thakorji. Maybe she was in the middle of teaching me a prayer. I bring the photo closer and examine her eyes. There's tenderness and love. I try to match my smile in the photo. My eyes get moist, thinking about life before Dad hijacked my childhood.

The next photo is of Mom, Lalita ba, and Sunil dada. Mom's draped in a red sari, weighed down from all the intricate gold embroidery. It's her wedding sari. She's beautiful, with her neatly braided hair, layers of ornate gold and diamond jewelry, kohled eyes, and cryptic smile. I can't take my eyes away from her loveliness. Her mangalsutra hangs around her neck.

The mangalsutra noose.

Lalita ba and Sunil dada are expressionless.

Hereditary poker face, huh, Mom?

Their faces were anything but blank the year I lived with them in Nairobi, Kenya. Dad sent me there when I turned six because he didn't want to do the extra parenting while Mom took a year-long intensive computer technician prep course for General Electric. I frown, remembering that day on the JFK tarmac which I often relive in my dreams. Like this morning.

It was Lalita ba who first introduced me to strawberries and cream prasad and the intricacies of Thakorji worship in their small

Nairobi apartment. She told me that she'd learned the rituals from her mom, Agneya ba. She also told me what happened to Agneya ba. Even though I was only six years old I remember every detail of her description.

Mom spent her childhood in those cramped quarters with Lalita ba, Sunil dada, and her two younger brothers. Beatifically, I reflect on how Mom and I both experienced the hot, lazy afternoons there as children watching Lalita ba lead a gaggle of other bas in satsangs.

Sunil dada worked hard as a travel agent, but he really knew how to play. And when he played with me he practically turned into a kid himself. We laughed. We sang. We chased each other in a sprawling Nairobi city park. We went on adventures. My mind drifts to the day he and I danced with the Maasai in a random river on the outskirts of the city.

Then there was the feminism. On the car rides home from our exploits, he'd convert back into a grown up. Then he'd say some version of, "Rani, don't get married. Get your education instead." Thinking about his words, it's pretty clear that Sunil dada was quite the champion of women's rights for an old school Gujarati male. And that must've been radical in the culture back then. Come to think of it, seems like it still is.

That's why it doesn't make sense that he told Mom that "husband is God." Especially since I'm sure he knew what happened to Agneya ba. I wonder if Lalita ba thought of Sunil dada as her God, along with Thakorji. My brows furrow and I shake my head.

The last photo is of Mom and Dad in front of our large, modern Connecticut house. I recall the view of the house from the bottom of the long, steep driveway. The same view I had each school day after stepping off the bus. With its sharp, angular design and frosty gray color, that house resembled big icicles at the start of winter. Growing more cold and rigid with time. I took this photo of them on the day we moved in. They bought it right after I got back from Kenya. Standing shoulder to shoulder with big grins, they look like a happy couple. But things got worse after we moved in. Much worse.

Mom worked longer hours than Dad. Sometimes she was gone overnight, fixing computers in other states. Many days I didn't see her. She still did all the cooking and housework. She'd have meals prepared for Dad and me ahead of time. Dad didn't lift a finger at home. By the time I turned eight, the shift in Mom's life from full-time mom and housewife to full-time computer technician and housewife made her bitter and distant not only from Dad, but also from me. The closeness she and I once shared evaporated like the waters of Lake Nakuru in the Kenyan sun.

The nightmare from this morning surfaces in my head again. I drop my face into my palms, breathing deeply. I need to get out of my head, out of the past, and out of this house.

Hopping into the 4runner, the thrill of my free day builds. A full belly and a full tank of gas. Perfect combination for a drive east. Only thing missing—a girlfriend partner in crime. I wish and sigh. Driving alone, I'm left with my thoughts. Then again that's nothing new.

Rani, my princess, I need you. Why do you need friends?

You're gone, Dad. Stop commandeering my thoughts and dreams.

I pop in my *The Devil Made Me Do It* tape and fast forward to *Break the Grip of Shame*. Oscar Jackson, Jr, aka Paris, raps. I nod my head to the dope beat. I lip sync his socially conscious lyrics and try to zone out. I apply the words to my situation with my dad.

And eureka!

Ok, I'm not Archimedes, but I think I get it. I haven't let go of him. He's already let go of me and let Wendy in. I'm still clinging to him in my mind, so of course he'll enter my thoughts and dreams.

With each mile east, I imagine cutting the cord connecting us. But by the time I get to Murphy's beach at the 20-mile marker, I realize I can't do it. I can't sever the cord. Especially the strands of hope that maybe he'll come back. How is it that he can so easily excommunicate me, but I can't stop having faith in him? Even after everything he's done?

I drive further east. The road becomes more narrow and winding. No signs of human civilization anywhere. The foliage grows lusher and more vibrant. I pretend I'm exploring some faraway land. Reaching the lookout, I pull over to the side of the road. From this vantage point, Halawa valley is picture perfect. The falls, deep in the mountains to the left, gush. To the right, the bright blue ocean purls the small curvy beach below. Everywhere else is intensely green.

I drive down into the valley and come to the end of the road. I park on the side, near the sandy path that leads to the beach. On the opposite side of the road, the stony skeleton of an old church overgrown with jungle, catches my eye. Every time I'm in Halawa valley I notice it. Like most people, I forget about the archaic remnants of the building as soon as I look away. But today I'm drawn. I cross the road and stand in front of the church, like I'm Dr. Henrietta Watson "India" Jones, the brilliant archaeologist sister Indiana Jones should have had. And I've stumbled upon a mysterious place of worship. A career-making find.

The ancient atmosphere fills me with awe. On each of the three steps leading in, I pause, and soak it all in. Inside there are only four partial walls with sky as the roof. Who prayed here long ago? If it was the original Native Hawaiian inhabitants of the valley, what did they think of western religion?

Sitting in the far right corner, I ease my head back against the wall and stare at the sky. The peacefulness makes me drowsy. Hoping for a nap I close my eyes.

Instead of sleep, I fall into distressing Dad-thoughts. Dad berating Mom to her face and behind her back to me. His continuous mocking of her dedication to daily prayer. How she relinquished her daily worship because of his derision. His scorn of Hinduism and all religion in general.

Rani, there is no God. If there is a God, why are there wars and starving people? Anyone smart is atheist.

Of course I wanted to be smart. So I didn't believe in God. I believed in Dad.

Mom was raised to think husband is God. That's why she followed and obeyed Dad. All along, through Dad's words and actions and Mom's lack thereof, haven't they also raised me to believe that Dad is God?

How do you stop believing in God when He's stopped believing in you?

I try to stop all the thoughts. I force myself to follow a gecko as it makes its way across the cracked cement foundation. I take my glasses off, fold them, and lay them on the ground. I thump my forehead with my lower palm. But I can't shut off my brain. I'm breathing fast and shallow. I drag my legs up and wrap my arms around them. With my head on my knees, I sob.

I shut my eyes tight to try to contain the surge. At some point the tears stop. The first thing I see is blue. That's when I realize I'm on my knees. My head lifted to the sky. My hands in prayer.

THE PROFESSOR AND ME

A small gray-brown mongoose took five in front of the Ho'olehua Post Office sign. It cocked its head in my direction. From its smug expression, I swear it was thinking, "You fell for it, sucka." I leaped up from the sidewalk and shook my fist at it. "Beat it!" I shouted. Then I flipped it off. That's right. I gave the finger to a mongoose. It deserved it.

Talking to a furry critter in a deserted parking lot—a new social low, even for me.

As it scurried away, I yelled, "Me and my decked out MC self got some place to be!" It turned its head back and smirked right before it disappeared into a bush. No joke.

Decked out? Fo' sure. Baggy dark blue jeans sitting low on my hips. Now I ain't in the Lo-Life gang, but I made sure the Polo name logo on the waistband of my black and white Ralph Lauren plaid boxers is clearly visible. XS cropped white male basher. My answer to the wife beater. Tummy showing, of course. XL gold hoop earrings. A couple of thick gold chains. A wide black belt with a gold buckle. Black Adidas high tops with gold stripes and insignia. And tonight my black nerd glasses add a special touch of mysterious intelligence. I hope. Salt-N-Pepa would approve. It's all about *Expression* after all.

So you see, you four-legged hater, I'm MC Sutra in effect.

Darkness is descending so I check my Egyptian hieroglyphic design Swatch. Almost 7:00 p.m. No Professor in sight. I'm starting to feel ridiculous.

After I got home from Halawa valley, I spent the rest of the afternoon locked in my room listening to hip hop CDs. The goal was to lyrically overcome the emotional smorgasbord from the morning. I emerged a couple of hours later all Bobby McFerrin. By the time 5 o'clock rolled around, I was trying to figure out what to do until hot bread time. That's when the 4eva Flowin' audition resurfaced in my mind. Guess all the hours I'd spent immersed in beats and rhymes left me wanting to believe that something so good could be true. Besides, things couldn't get any worse could they? I went back and forth for the next half hour.

In the end I couldn't resist. I had to see for myself whether or not 4eva Flowin' was real. Maybe it was the mystifying moments in Halawa. Or maybe it was something else. But I decided to take a chance.

I check my Swatch again. 7 p.m. I crumple my face. Five more minutes. That's it. Then I'm leaving. Defeated.

I haven't seen a single car or truck pass by since I got to Ho'olehua. This town is almost in the middle of the island. There's lots of land here but very little development. It's where MHIS, the airport, and most of the Hawaiian homestead lands are. I take in the view. From where I'm sitting at the post office, all I can see is undeveloped land for miles intersected by two roads. I use the peace and quiet to run through the lyrics of my bravado rap, "Girl in Effect." Just in case.

Half way through, a lifted black Toyota 4runner with tinted windows pulls up. The driver's side window comes down. It's Pono.

"MC Sutra," he calls out, his arm resting on the chrome window sill. He gives me a chin-up.

"Pono?"

"Naw, call me Prof. Short for Professor P. Get in," he says, motioning with his hand.

Pono usually gets dropped off at school because his mom's a teacher at Kualapu'u Elementary School near MHIS. I've never seen him driving. I'm impressed. His sweet ride is tricked out. The powerful headlights provide enough illumination to catch a glimpse of the chrome-plated suspension, rims, and foot rail. I spring up and climb into his truck. The inside's immaculate. And the bass is kickin'. L'Trimm would approve because they like the *Cars That Go Boom*. So do I. He's got the new Public Enemy CD cranked up. He turns on the dome light and fiddles with some buttons on the center console. The bass gets heavier. Bobbing my head to the wicked beats and rhymes, I inspect his bumpin' stereo system. I envy the bobblehead doll on his dashboard. I look back and notice a small Hawaiian flag sticker on the lower right corner of the rear window.

Clearly he's spent much of his hard-earned cash on this truck. But thankfully not on naked woman silhouette stickers or fuzzy dice.

"Surprised?" he asks with a mischievous smile as he flips his black L.A. Raiders snapback. No board shorts. No tank top. No slippahs. I didn't think he could look any better, but woah. In his oversized black hoodie with the sizable image of an ali'i crowned in a red and yellow mahiole, baggy jeans, and Timberland boots, the boy looks super fly. Super duper fly.

Did I mention he looks really good? And I'm feeling all tingling, like someone's tickling me under my skin. The same way I feel when I hear *Push It*. Rubbing my sweaty palms on my jeans I recall the words of my lyrical muses, Salt-N-Pepa.

I want to giggle! I roll my eyes instead and reply, "No, not at all. An underground hip hop crew on Moloka'i? That makes perfect sense. And you in it? That's a no-brainer."

He laughs. "But fo' real, this was the hardest secret to keep. At school, I wanted to holler, 'Yo Sutra, I'm an MC too!'"

"And to think I wasn't going to show up," I say, shaking my head.

He reaches up to turn off the dome light. His fingers brush my shoulder.

"You won't regret it. Guaranteed." Now the light is off, and we're sitting in the dark. The moonlight hits his face at the right angle. He's looking at me and his eyes *Stir It Up* Bob Marley style. My heart beats a little faster. I turn my head towards him but he looks away real quick, focusing out the windshield. We pull out of the parking lot onto the main road.

"Where are we going?" I'm working hard to not let myself think about his eager eyes.

"The A-frame at Pala'au. There'll be about ten or so other 4eva Flowin' crew there tonight to judge. You nervous?"

"This new jack is hella nervous."

"No worry, you get 'em. Besides, MC DVus told me your slam

poem was something else. Your rap can't be that bad," he says. I'm pretty sure he winked.

Who's MC DVus? And how does he know about my slam poem?

"If you make it onto the crew, you'll get to perform at the monthly 4eva Flowin' hip hop jam at Mo'omomi."

"Cool," I say, trying to be just that. But my excitement is growing like Jack's beanstalk.

"You ever been to Mo'omomi?"

"Over a year ago, with my dad on a Nature Conservancy hike." I pause, contemplating how on earth a hip hop event takes place on a 921-acre coastal dune preserve. "But isn't Mo'omomi considered sacred by Native Hawaiians?"

"Yeah. But DVus got permission from the dude in charge of the Moloka'i branch of the Conservancy to use the pavilion area only. As payback, 4eva Flowin' members do volunteer work for the Conservancy." In the dark, I think I see Pono's bright ivories so he's probably smiling big. He captures my hand and adds, "I really hope you get to see the pavilion all hip hopped."

"Me too," I say staring at his hand over mine, my eyes widening. In that instant, I'm jealous of Emily because I bet he does this to her all the time. And means it. He lets go after a couple of seconds. I slide my hands under my thighs. They need to be trapped so I don't grab his hand back. But I can't stop my lips from curving up in the dark.

Prof turns left onto Kala'e Highway and begins the drive up to Pala'au. I'm sitting there with my dippy grin. I listen to the 411 on 4eva Flowin's inception. DVus started it about a year ago to give Moloka'i youth a creative outlet. And for some, a way to stay out of trouble.

"DVus grew up with some hardcore family problems," Prof says.

"And he was addicted to coke and heroin for years. Flowin' got him sober." Prof stops. Then with indifference in his voice he adds, "I think you know DVus already. It's Mark."

"Not!" I exclaim, trying to fathom how it is that both Pono and Mark are MCs. I let my thoughts wrap around the newfound fact that Mark—I mean DVus—and I share two things in common. He'd said he could relate to a line near the end of my slam poem. I wonder if he had to save his mom too. Plus rap's our savior. I blurt, "Rap saved his life yo!"

"Yeah for sure," Prof says.

But doesn't alcohol count as drugs?

Do good intentions trump full-blown sobriety? I mean he started 4eva Flowin' to help youth on Moloka'i. That's pretty darn altruistic. I think about the day I read my poem to Mark. It was a pre-audition. Only I didn't know it. More upward lip curving. Yep, good intentions trump full-blown sobriety.

I turn to Pono and inquire, "So, what's your story with 4eva Flowin'?"

"MC Irraz was my in. He and I spent hours rhyming last summer."

"Nice."

"By the way, MC Irraz is Omar."

"Et tu, Omar! Nooooo waaayyzzz!" Now I'm completely blown away. To da max. My three favorite people are MCs. This is the best day of my life.

"Yeah and his flowin' is off the chain. He's been doing it for years. He said it helps him deal with his dad being in lockdown. Sometimes he sends his dad rap instead of regular letters."

I nod, imagining his dad's reaction to reading the rap.

"Speaking of Omar, did I ever tell you that the first time I noticed you was last year when he was clowning you. And you threw your head back in laughter. Your laugh. It was so real." I swear I see him licking his lips, all LL Cool J.

I tilt my head to the side, my eyebrows contracted and my lips pursed. I eye him like he just declared that he saw blue and purple polka dot pua'a flying. I think Pono picks up on my puzzlement because he clears his throat like he's nervous. Then he backtracks lickety-split. "Anyway, Omar and Mark are next door neighbors so they used to collab all the time."

"Cool. So much talent on Waieli Street." I peer out into the darkness, ignoring images of Pono's inviting tongue and lip action. Redirecting the convo to him might help. So I prop my elbow on the gleaming window sill and lean my head on my hand. "Ok Pono—I mean Prof—you gotta help me out here. Ukulele makes sense. But how the heck did you, a Moloka'i boy born and raised, get into MCing?"

"I've been listening to hip hop for as long as I can remember. But anger got me to write my first rhyme. You know, the activist meetings." I nod because I get it. Then what he says next throws me off again. "That was the second time I noticed you. When you were testifying at a water meeting last year. I thought..." He cuts himself off. He coughs, then backpedals again. "I wanted to make my words about Native Hawaiian rights more powerful. Turns out rhyming helped me do that. The rest is history."

"Word."

"How about you?"

"Writing rhymes gets me through the fights my parents have—" I stop. Reality hits. Reality sucks. "Had," I correct.

"Is that why you ran out of the EPA meeting? Because your dad showed up?"

"Uh-huh."

"I ran after you, but you were already driving away." He pauses. "After you left, your dad gave his testimony. And it was really good."

"Yeah, I'm sure it was. I think he has good intentions. But don't you think it's hypocritical to care so much about the water but destroy your own family?"

Good intentions don't trump full-blown family destruction.

"Is that what's going on?"

"Yeah. My mom kicked him out the other day because he's got another woman." I scoff. "I mean, another girl. Wendy Nagaoki. The girl who came to the meeting with him."

I glance at Pono and despite the dark I can tell he's pensive. *Can't Truss It* starts, and the unforgettable intro fills the brief silence. Then Chuck D starts rapping.

"The roses were for Wendy?—you know, that day at Moana's?" Pono's putting two and two together.

"Yeah." I'm surprised Pono remembers. I stare out the window with my head resting on my palm.

"Yo Sutra, you ok?"

Hearing Pono call me Sutra evokes a sense of righteousness in me. Or maybe it's Public Enemy's defiant rhymes. I face Pono and slowly expound, like I'm testifying at a public hearing. "You know, my dad's not some perfect advocate of Native Hawaiian rights. He's not thinking about them when he sells them cigarettes and alcohol at the store." I'm picturing La'akea. "I mean everyone knows that booze and smokes totally ruined their pre-Western contact good health."

"Absolutely."

It's comfortable up here, on my moral high horse. I'm about to say more. To gallop into righteous neverland.

But Pono changes the subject. "Sorry I brought up your dad. Don't think about him anymore right now. Tonight you've got to bring it."

I nod, let go of the reins, and watch the noble stallion ride away into the recesses of my mind.

"There's a killer DJ in the crew, DJ Skittles. He'll be there tonight. Talk to him when we get there. He's a sick beat maker and he'll lay one out for you."

"Nice." The thought of performing "Girl in Effect" to a beat makes me dizzy with excitement. My naked rhymes will finally get a phat outfit.

We pull into the parking lot at Pala'au. Pono stops the truck but leaves the engine on. "You ok?"

"Chillin." I'm trying to hide that inside I'm buggin' out.

"Ok, let's do this."

He shuts the engine off and we step out into the cool Moloka'i night. I glance up. The ironwoods look like fluffy giants floating in the night sky. We walk across the damp grass towards the dimly lit A-frame. It's the only evidence of human existence at Pala'au.

Pono asks, "What's your rap about?"

"Bravado."

"Really?"

"Yeah. Confidence and me—we're not friends. So in this rap I pretend..." I stop and push my glasses back up my nose. I decide to give him a little spontaneous taste instead. A morsel to help him understand why I wrote a bravado rap. The words come together easily and I spit.

It's the me

I want to be.

The large and in charge person

I want the world to see.

So I MC, and throw down

my self-confidence decree

and strive to be

my own queen bee.

"Damn skippy! I can't wait to hear it." We walk in silence the rest of the way. When we get near the A-frame steps, he says, "You know, Sutra, I've always thought you're amazing."

I hear the words but they don't register because right when he says it, my ears get flooded with heart-thumping bass.

FAKE ASS BRAVADO

Last time I was at Pala'au, it was the sound of roosters crowing that got my attention. But as we ascend the steps to the A-frame tonight, it's the 808 from the blasting speakers that slams us. In a good way. 808 in the 808 state.

Pono and I enter the wooden A-frame. A strong, dank smell hangs over everything.

Who's lighting up?

We cut through the haze. DJ Skittles comes into view. He's standing behind a narrow table against the copper-brown planks of the back wall. Almost immediately I forget about who's toking because Skittles transitions to Black Sheep's *The Choice is Yours*. The catchy opening is an astringent that fills my pores and refreshes me. I stare wide-eyed at his DJ gear: turntables, mixer, drum machine, a stack of vinyl, and a bunch of complicated-looking musical gadgets.

Then Mark walks over and distracts me from sizing up the DJ's effects. "If it isn't MC Sutra and Prof."

I'm about to say, "Yo wuzzup," still flying high from Black Sheep. And maybe a little from all the Mary Jane smoke. But then I see Mark's fresh outfit and I smash into Mt. Oh-My-God-He-Looks-So-Hot. Red Kangol bucket hat. Bright red Nautica jacket. Baggy jeans. Red and black Air Jordans.

"Yo," Pono says.

I shove my hands in my pockets and shift in my stance several times. Standing there between the two flyboys makes me a little woozy. I have to focus on keeping my knees from buckling under the weight of my nervousness. So all I can manage to say is an unoriginal and pitiful, "Hey." My eyes sweep the room. I count twelve people, all guys. Except me. Remarkably, I know about a third of them. Mark, Pono, Omar, and Stan Lee.

Mark notices me looking at Stan Lee. He rests his elbow on my shoulder and gives a chin-up in Stan's direction. With his lips close to my ear, he whispers, "That's Black Seoul."

I nod without changing my blank expression. But inside there's a mix of giddiness from having Mark's lips practically on my ear and apprehension from the Stan Lee sighting.

It's sinking in. The reality of the audition. The reality that I'm going to have to get myself up there in front of all these guys and rap. So I don't freak out, I divert my attention to working out who the other guys are. I recognize several of them from around town. The rest I've never seen. For sure they aren't MHIS students.

Stan Lee marches over and plants himself directly in front of me. My eyes start at the floorboards where he's standing and work their way up. His feet, in killer dark blue and tan Puma's with fat dark blue laces, are firmly planted. They're a little farther than hip width apart and slightly out. He's wearing a dark blue Puma tracksuit. His shoulders are hiked and his arms are tightly crossed. He's leaning his body back a bit. His expression is a subtle frown. The hardcore b-boy stance he's giving me tells me he doesn't like that I'm here.

"Wassup, Stan Lee," I mumble.

No words. Only major stink eye. Like he's trying to use The Force to put me six feet under. I take a step back. But Stan Lee steps up to me and glares. He's so close I can smell cigarettes. He snaps, "Sure you can keep up with the big boys?"

Hate emanates from him. I can't for the life of me figure out why he's so pissed. I'm startled and my fear is the glue that seals my lips.

"Are you deaf?" he asks, inching forward and stopping only when he's totally in my face.

"No," I finally stammer. I avoid his eyes.

Pono steps between Stan Lee and me. He opens his mouth to say something. Mark beats him to it. Throwing his arm around my shoulder, Mark says, "Sutra's gonna be in full effect tonight."

I breath a sigh of relief as Mark leads me away. I turn my head back to spock Stan Lee's reaction.

He spins around and stomps off, muttering, "You don't belong here, little girl."

Before I look forward again, I notice Pono. His head is sagged down, his nose wrinkled, and his lips are in a slight pout.

Is he disappointed?

I'm about to call out to him to see if he's ok, but Mark starts talking.

"Forget about it, Sutra," he consoles. Pointing to Skittles, he says, "You'd better get over there and figure out your beat.

I walk over to Skittles and Black Sheep's beats and rhymes mollify my uneasiness from Stan Lee's intimidation. I walk a little taller. By the time I get to Skittles, my game face is on.

"Sup." I say, greeting him with a chin-up.

He gives me one back and smiles. Then he asks me to spit a verse for him. I rhyme about a third of my first verse and he stops me. I watch him work his magic. Fingers pressing buttons, turning knobs, sliding levers, and flipping switches. His long, straight blonde hair is tied back in a low ponytail. I'm guessing he's about twenty. He's wearing low-riding boardshorts. Nothing else. I'm envisioning washing some clothes on his abs when he passes me the headphones.

I give him a goofy smile and listen. I guess I figured beatmaking is his part-time gig and that he's probably laid out some disco and funk samples over a simple drum beat. But what I hear is beyond expectation. Way beyond. "No way," I whisper, gripping the earpads and nodding my head. Kinda like Prince Paul, Skittles layered unexpected musical samples onto a combination of different drum hits. I recognize some of the samples. But what amazes me the most is his use of some of the melody and bass line from Queen Latifah's *Fly Girl*. And then there's the drum sounds. So complex. I'm sure he's used the drum machine and individual drum hit samples from records. A snare and kick, for sure. I muffle an ecstatic "yeah!" listening to his one-of-a-kind musical collage that'll be the background for my rap.

Still savoring the beat, I hear Mark's mic check. I give the headphones back to Skittles.

"Mic check 1-2, 1-2. Yo, it's audition night. We've got four MC's throwin' it down," he says, with the confidence of Ed Lover from *Yo*

MTV Raps! "Rules are simple. Perform one rap. That's it. You'll be judged on your content, flow, and crowd skills."

Mark walks closer to the back wall where I'm standing and catches my eye. I hold my breath. He's got this Color Me Badd look. I restrain myself from crying out, "*I Wanna Sex You Up*, Mark!" Mark keeps eye contact with me and says, "So bring it hard." Then he moves in the other direction and says, "MC Kanaka, you're up first." I exhale and fan myself with my hand.

Kanaka takes the mic and gets right to it. I become drenched in self-doubt. His lyrics are riveting and complex in meaning. Similar to Paris. But it's Kanaka's delivery that especially astounds me—super fast, like a tornado. I'm so juiced up by it that I wish I had closed captioning so I could rap with him. It feels like I need to release this combo of excitement and uncertainty bubbling up in me.

Stan Lee must have picked up on my jitters. With uncanny timing, he stands behind me. "Sure you can handle it?" Then he moves next to me. He's got this scowl that unnerves me. I look back at Kanaka and make like Stan Lee's not there. But his question echos in my mind. I answer it.

No.

MC Kanaka finishes and throws up a peace sign. I'm covered in a veil of cold sweat.

Riz-Al's up next. He raps about his Filipino family, giving them props for how they "raised right" him and his three brothers. His feel-good rhymes, mellow delivery, and steez are impressive. Reminiscent of Q-tip. The vibe he brings is chill. Like a lazy Sunday afternoon. Like I'm at his family barbeque and his mom's serving up some delish lumpia. I smack my lips at the thought and feel calmer.

Kamikaze's turn. He grabs the mic and comes on strong. He rocks the room with his rhyming social commentary on modern day racial oppression. I can't help but think of KRS One and the *By All Means Necessary* album. His tight lyrics make his message undeniably compelling. They rile me up like we're at an activist meeting. Kamikaze wraps up and I watch him hand off the mic to Mark.

That means I'm next. My stomach curls in on itself. Then my throat tries to choke itself. I clasp my clammy hands behind my back.

Run away while you still can!

But anxiety's a trickster and it won't let my legs move. Worse, I'm sinking into quicksand.

Mark gets on the mic. "The final MC is the first girl to audition for 4eva Flowin'."

Too late. I shut my eyes and go to my memory palace, caging the apprehension in the dungeon. From the palace's lyrical lab, I retrieve my rap from one shelf and the relevant feelings from another. I weld together the emotions and rhymes. I open my eyes.

You can do this. You're in the zone. You're ready.

Then I hear nothing except my breathing. Air in. Air out.

I take the mic from Mark. His mouth is moving. His lips read, "Knock 'em dead, Rani."

Without warning, my hearing returns to normal. Something clicks and the fake courage I've written about seeps from the depths of my wanna-be MC soul. So much so that an impromptu introduction easily flows from my mouth, shocking me. I go with it.

This was my evolution

into rap elocution.

Nonviolently battling persecution,

putting misogynists in verbal correctional institutions.

Call my solution a female revolution,

retribution in the form of rhyme electrocution.

My underground contribution

calling out mainstream rap—counterrevolution.

instead of rap about bitches and hoes,

wish the radio would overflow

with my kind o' flow,

so here goes.

DJ Skittles drops my beat and I spit.

You be judgin' this book by its cover,

killing this mockingbird only to discover

at its core a fascinatin' soul,

changin' yo life like an ancient scroll.

I'm a kung fu master

kickin' your small-minded game,

recipe for disaster.

Your school's headmaster, throwin' a wrench

in your man's plan, clenchin'

my fists as I drench you in my

lyrical flow and drop you into the trench

with your woman-hating stench.

I'm the contraceptive

prophylactically preventin' your

assaultive mind conception and

deception.

What did you expect?

That I'd be like all the rest?

Well, you best come correct

cuz this girl is in effect.

I maneuver around with my mask of self-assurance. All that's going through my mind is *Keep on frontin', Rani. Keep makin' 'em think you got guts.*

Indian girl trekking this lyrical mountain.

I be in effect when my rhymes be flowin' like a fountain.

I'm the verbal architect leading this rhyme expedition.

Startin' a new female tradition.

And what I be sayin' got you weighin'

and considerin' alternate views, conveyin'

my message while slayin' your close-minded prayin'.

Usin' my mind to define my own shine.

Blowin' up your unkind words—landmine.

Mastermind in my own life.

This ain't no blind leading the blind.

I got an ax to grind with your maligned mind,

don't need your praise to phase how I self-appraise.

I be settin' ablaze your trifling ways

and seeing better days filled with majestic sun rays.

Finding my way out of the maze.

And boy, I see you gaze

wit' yo eyebrows raised.

I'm astonished at what's happening. The potent effect of the delivery on both me and the crew. They're feelin' it. Their eyes follow me as I move. Only it's not really me. My alter ego spits another two mad verses keeping the crew engaged the entire time. Even Stan Lee.

As soon as I'm done, nervousness flings itself on me again. I shove the mic into Mark's hand and run outside. As I'm escaping I think I hear someone say, "MC Sutra in da house!" I hide behind the A-frame and lean against the wall, taking deep breaths to collect myself.

Mark appears from out of nowhere. Engulfing me in his arms, he kisses the top of my stubbly head, then angles to the side. His lips graze my ear as he whispers, "That's my girl."

I'm dazed. And a little breathless. XO from Mark? Never had an XO from any non-related XY. Before I have a chance to say or do anything, Mark disappears back inside the A-frame.

MY HERO

What would full on making out with Mark feel like? Because if his purely platonic XO feels that good, first base might feel like a home run. Five days of XO constant replay has been exhausting. In a good way. Yeah, yeah, I've been wondering if I made it onto the 4eva Flowin' crew. But that's taken a back seat to the close encounter of the Mark kind. I don't mind. Hey, it's better than feeling sorry for myself about my disintegrated family. Mark's XO even inspired me to write my first rap about a guy. I laid out a rough verse last night.

> Hey boo, I've been thinkin' bout chu.
> When I saw you in the Kanemitsu queue,
> I couldn't help but take a fancy to
> your blue eyes and dreamcatcher tattoo.
> Didn't need a camera cuz I had a mental scar,
> like a cerebral burn from a cigar.
> That was it,

like a junkie's nightmare, just one hit.

And when I turned around

there you were, asking me to hang out in town.

Said you liked my Indian eyes, reminiscent of a queen.

Overstimulation of my senses—intoxication—caffeine.

Boy, you got me wrapped—tur-ban.

You the anchorman,

keepin' my line steady,

with your sweet support at the ready...

No time to write today though. It's freight day at the store and that means I have to haul a ton of boxes from the truck, then stock all the products in the right places. I finished loading the chill items first. Then the canned items. Now I'm down to the candy and the cigarettes, daydreaming meanwhile about Mark.

Footsteps interrupt my thoughts. I place the box of Smarties on the shelf and turn around.

Oh my God.

Dad looks so old and small.

Oh my. God shrunk.

And looks to have aged ten years in a month. Standing next to him is Wendy. Dad looks old enough to be her father. Maybe even her grandfather.

Ewww.

So there I am. My hands on my cheeks. My eyes wide. My mouth gaping. Totally Macaulay Culkin in *Home Alone*. But then my hands drop and I feel fists forming behind the counter. "Dad, what are you doing here? Mom said not to..."

He throws his palms up in midair and rolls his eyes. He reaches into his pocket and pulls out two white medicine bottles with child resistant caps.

"This is why I'm here." His eyebrows ski slope down towards his nose.

The pills jostle as he flings the bottles onto the counter. I watch them roll around before finally coming to a rest. "What are these?" I avoid looking at Wendy.

He breathes out a long, embittered sigh. More eye rolling. "Look!" He points at the bottles.

One at a time, I pick up each bottle and inspect its label. One reads Zoloft 100 mg tablet. Take 1 tablet every morning. Prescribed by Dr. Jeriss. Refilled about a month ago. Dad's supposed to take one pill a day. So shouldn't the bottle be almost empty by now? The other reads Xanax 2.0 mg tablet. Take 1 tablet each day as needed for anxiety. Also refilled a month ago. Only a few pills bounce in this bottle. If he's only supposed to take it as needed, why is this bottle almost empty?

"These are for anxiety?"

"For my depression and anxiety," he says, leaning one arm on the counter.

Hold up. Let me double check that. Because in the universe that is my dad, depression and anxiety are "a weakness" and "a character flaw." And medicines for said weaknesses and character flaws are like drinking alcohol or doing drugs. An excuse for getting high. At least that's how he explained it to me after we moved to Moloka'i. In Connecticut, it was a different story. Probably because he used to work at a large pharmaceutical company.

Dad says, "They've helped me a lot."

"Really?" I must look surprised or something because Dad straightens up fast and crosses his arms.

"Yes." He inhales and exhales loudly to demonstrate his irritation.

Well, maybe those poor rats didn't die in vain. I bite the side of my lower lip as I remember the first time I went to work with him when I was eight. The bright, sterile hallways. Crisp, white lab coat-clad scientists towering over me. I felt so proud of my dad. My hero.

"Rani, are you listening?"

Dad's voice brings me back to the present.

"Yes."

"I'm in debt to Dr. Jeriss. These pills saved me. Helped me deal with those Ranch jerks."

I'm confused because I don't think he's taking the meds in the right way. I mean he's taking more Xanax than Zoloft. From what it says on the bottles, it seems it should be the other way around. Is Dr. Jeriss ok with that?

Before I can ask my dad about this, Wendy chimes in. "Yes, your father was having a very difficult time before the medication."

I look at her like she has three heads.

Why is she talking to me like she knows anything about my dad?

I flash lightning at her with my eyes. I consider seizing the cash register and hurling it at her. I don't have a chance to imagine more inflict-pain-on-Wendy tactics because Dad shakes his head and stammers, "The leases will be up soon. What'll we do for income?"

We?

He drops his head and his voice. "It was..." he whispers.

I wait.

"It was..." His eyes are narrowed. I rub my eyes under my glasses because I think I see the whites of his eyes turn black. My blood drains and my heart tries to keep pumping whatever fluid remains.

That's when I see Mark and Omar come into the store. My heart beat steadies. I thank my lucky stars. I glance at Mark. He puts his finger to his lips and mouths, "Shhh." I guess he can tell something is wrong. He and Omar move to the back of the store before my dad or Wendy notice them.

"It was what, Dad?"

"The pills also made me do things I didn't plan on," he spouts.

"You mean, have an affair?" I blurt out.

Wendy shifts uncomfortably.

Dad slams his hands on the counter. "Wendy needed my help. She doesn't have a father," he yells. He snakes his arm around her and pulls her forward to the counter.

My skin is crawling.

Crawling skin. Yeah, I'm sure you know what that feels like, Wendy. Being an ex-batu addict and all.

I frown at her but then turn to my dad and say, "I don't want to hear this, you need to…"

He interrupts me and shouts, "Rani, you owe me this! All this—," he says, propelling his hands in every direction. "All this is for you. Everything I've done is for you." He seems to catch himself and settle down. "Now, go tell Mom that Wendy and I can move in."

Oh. I get it now. That's why he's here. He wants me to feel sorry for him. That he's depressed and anxious. That he has to take pills. And the pills messed him up and made him have an affair. And that, since it's not his fault, I'll agree to convince Mom to let him move back in. With Wendy.

Where has he been for Mom all these years? You don't have to be Freud to figure out that she's been depressed and that the head banging, knives, and half gallons of Breyers were sadness and desperation. Even as a kid, I knew something was wrong.

I don't say a word.

"Rani, you know I love you," he adds, but his eyes are about to breathe out fire.

His verbal magic isn't working. And really his words sound absurd with his crazed look. Practically hilarious. I laugh out loud. Liberation finds me and swathes me in its embrace.

Free at last, free at last. Thank God almighty we are free at last.

Obviously, Dr. Martin Luther King, Jr. was referring to more noble issues when he said this, but it's what gets stuck in my head. Because I'm about to cut the last thread of hope that Dad will dump Wendy and come back to us.

But faithful concubine Wendy tries to do her part to help convince me. "Yes, Rani, your father really loves you."

I stare at her with my face frozen in a "whatchu talkin' 'bout Willis" look. Then I snap out of it and give her the cold shoulder.

I say, "No, Dad. You only love yourself. Get out. Mom already told you not to come here." Under the counter, my fingers are in a sideways V and I make a cutting motion. I snip the last of my hope about Dad.

He leans in but then changes his mind and heads behind the counter. "What did you say?"

It's like he's Medusa. His anger turns me to stone. I can't move. Right then Mark steps forward. "Hey, Pradip, let's go outside."

Dad turns his head to look at Mark. "Stay out of this!"

126

Omar says something in a soft voice to Wendy and tries to lead her outside. Wendy hesitates and gives my dad a distressed look.

"Come on, Pradip, let's talk about this outside. It's cooler on the porch."

Mark's suggestion infuriates my dad more. Dad's not used to anyone interrupting him when he's manipulating me. I can't help but wonder—would Dad have reacted the same way if Mom had gotten between us in the past?

"Mind your own business, Mark. I'm warning you," Dad barks.

What happens next is surreal. Like we're in *The Twilight Zone*.

Dad lurches toward me, grabs my shoulders, and starts shaking. Mark whisks behind the counter and pulls him off me. They struggle. Dad takes a swing at Mark, misses, and knocks over the stack of candy boxes on the side. Mark darts back to the front of the counter and Dad follows him. Dad lunges at Mark.

"I warned you," Dad shouts. He takes another swing at Mark.

Mark jumps back, avoiding the blow. Then quick as a wink, Mark's behind my dad. He grabs my dad's arms.

Wendy cries out, "Pradip!"

Mark pins Dad's arms on his lower back. Dad's immobilized like a handcuffed criminal.

I look over at Wendy. She's crying. Her face is in her hands. I like seeing her suffer.

"Time to get out of here, Pradip," Mark says.

Dad jerks. Mark tightens his hold.

"You should've stayed out of this, Mark."

"Mrs. Patel told you not to come here, so don't show up anymore," Mark asserts.

"Let go of me! I'm leaving!"

Mark and Omar escort Dad and Wendy to the Cressida. After they drive off, my boys sit with me on the front porch.

"You ok, Rani?" Mark asks, cracking his knuckles then leaning back against the porch railing.

"Yeah. A little shaken, but ok," I say. I shift my eyes to the long road leading out of Maunaloa and watch the Cressida get smaller and smaller. "Thank you, guys."

Then Omar says, "Oh man, your Dad is like Dr. Jekyll and Mr. Hyde. I'm so used to seeing him friendly and calm at the store. But now I've seen him pissed off twice. And both times at a woman. That ain't right."

I nod.

Omar scratches his head. "Rani, girl, I'm not superstitious or anything, but I'm getting this bad feeling that maybe there's gonna be trouble." He drops his eyes. "I don't know. Your Dad seems unstable." Then he lifts his head and gives me this serious look. "Bad things can happen to good people. Like what happened to my dad. All I'm saying is be careful."

Omar's no-nonsense words of caution are more unsettling to me than thinking about my dad. I'm not sure what to say.

Mark jumps in. "No worries. Everything's gonna be ok. We got your back. Right, Omar?"

Omar brightens up and nods. Then he gestures all thug and says, "Hey, Rani, great rhymes comes from hard times. So I'm thinkin' yo' flow about to blow up."

"Word," I say.

Mark gets up from his side of the porch and sits down next to me.

He puts his arm around me and gently squeezes. Our eyes meet. I'm mesmerized. So much so that it feels like his larger than usual pupils are an abyss I'm falling into.

"We're like family now, Rani. Family always looks out for each other." He smiles. And winks.

My new hero.

CRUSH MY CRUSH

A wave of Chaka Khan pours over me like warm jasmine hair oil. I step into the lobby of the gym and *Ain't Nobody* induces inescapable head nodding. It holds me under its spell. It's a love spell. The smooth groove and lyrics arouse my body and mind. This is what being in love feels like. I'm sure of it. I get chicken skin every time I hear this song. I touch my bare arm. Yep, there it is.

The dance floor is packed. Sporting my short denim overalls, red tube top, red, white, and black paisley bandana (do-rag style on my head), red Adidas high tops, and big silver hoops, I make my way through the gyrating bodies to the bleachers. It's a fact that no one has ever asked me to dance. Plus I'm too much of a wuss to ask anyone. This turd of a nerd isn't looking for more rejection. Climbing to the fourth bleacher on the right side of the gym, I park myself.

The only reason I'm here is business. Strictly business. All the class reps have to show face since we organized it. I'm still amazed that we got everything done in less than two weeks. Pono and I handled the posters, flyers, and gym decorations. Tiana, the treasurer, took care of the budget and ticket printing. Gerry, the secretary, has a cousin on Maui who's a DJ and agreed to give us a huge discount to spin a mix of 80's and 90's R&B and hip hop. Secretly, I wish DJ Skittles could throw it down tonight. I smile thinking about the audition. I still don't know whether or not I made it onto the 4eva Flowin' crew. But either way, I'll always have Mark's hug and kiss.

The unobstructed view from the bleachers offers up an almost cinematic experience of the cool kids dancing to the surround sound of *Ain't Nobody*. It's like I'm in the middle row of the Consolidated Theater in Waikiki watching *Breakin'*. Tapping my kicks, I imagine I'm Kelly, Pono is Ozone and Omar's Turbo. Ozone's trying to teach me the nuances of hip hop dancing despite Turbo's reservations. Within the span of the song, I'm a pop-lockin, break dancin' pro. And, after a little popping, wrist twirling, pointing, uprocking, and knee spins, Ozone and I fall in love. And Turbo and I are buddies for life. It could happen. Really.

For one thing, I can dance. Back in Connecticut, I spent so much time alone that when I got sick of finishing more than one book a day, I started watching a ton of MTV and breakdancing movies. I picked up some moves. Full on Janet Jackson *Nasty* style.

And then there was the shout out to her bro when I danced and lip synced *Billie Jean* at a school talent show. Red zippered jacket, white sequined glove, gelled curly hair—check. Moonwalk—oh yeah. After the show, a kindergartner asked me for an autograph.

"Can you write 'To Sally, love Michael,'" she asked politely.

I obliged.

Sadly, reality slaps me silly. My *Breakin'* fantasy fades away when I see Pono and Emily grinding to the Stevie B mix the DJ just dropped. Pono's got his hand on Emily's waist and their pelvic regions seem to merge as *Party Your Body* merges into *Spring Love*. My face merges into my palm. When I look up, everything's cloudy. I realize I smudged my glasses.

I'm such a loser.

I take my bandana off and wipe my lenses clean. I retie it and slide my glasses back on, appreciating the clear view. Then I pick my sorry ass up and move ten paces to the left so I can gaze at cool kids I've never crushed on.

The DJ fades into Oran "Juice" Jones' *The Rain*. The less than cheerful lyrics seem to be amplified in my ears for some reason. Is it coincidence? I think not. Nope. It's naseeb reminding me about my dad. Then as if naseeb really wants to stick it to me, it orders my eyes to wander to Pono and Emily. Apparently they don't care that this is the classic hip hop break up song. Because they're still freaking like they're together until death do them part.

Stop torturing yourself!

Ok, naseeb. You win. I'll give up my crush on Pono once and for all. I really should anyway. I mean let's face it, he's obviously happy with Emily. And I'm just tormenting myself every time I venture down the I love Pono path.

The DJ transitions to *Poison* and immediately I feel better. My elbows are resting on my thighs and I'm leaning forward, head down. I can't stop my upper body and head from moving to the beat, even though I'm still sitting. Remaining stationary to Bell Biv Devoe is impossible. And BBD's hook gets me in a different way today.

Because instantly I think of Mark. Fully in my Mark zone, I don't notice Pono making his way up the bleachers. He sits down next to me and starts moving his upper body and head synchronously with mine. I look over and give him a chin-up. You don't need words when you're hopping to this hip beat.

The DJ spins The KLF's *3 A.M. Eternal*. I'm thinking about how cool it is that the DJ's playing a British acid house band, when Pono says, "Our hard work paid off, right? This place is packed!"

"Yeah, we're gonna have one classy senior luau now," I say, determined to put Pono in the friend zone.

We watch the crowd for a few minutes. Then Pono asks, "How're you doing, Rani?"

"I'm ok. How are you?" I ask back, feeling proud that I'm actually keeping the butterflies away.

"I'm good," he says. He bumps my knee with his. "I meant, how're you doing with your family stuff?"

I give him a thumbs down. And a half smile. "But let's not go there. Don't wanna kill your Emily dirty dancing vibe."

He chuckles, then gets quiet. He stares at his black and white British Knight high tops. "It's not like that," he says. "But anyway, I'm here if you wanna talk. Ok?"

"Ok. Thanks." I'm not sure what to make of the *it's not like that* comment.

Pono taps his BK's to the beat and leans his head on his hand. He drums his fingers on his knee. His eyes dart around. I'm about to ask him what's up, when he opens his mouth. "After the audition you ran out. I saw Mark follow you. What happened?"

Something I can't stop thinking about, Pono.

But there's no way I'm telling Pono about Mark's XO. Hey, it's about time I put my own skeletons in my closet. How boring to have only family skeletons, right? Luckily I see Emily because it lets me steer clear of Pono's question. I stop for a second shocked that the words "luckily" and "Emily" were in my mind at the same time. Emily's standing on the first bleacher, her hands on her hips, throwing daggers at me with her eyes. I turn to Pono and say, "Hey, you better go check yo' girl, she about to go postal," motioning in her direction with my chin. Her stink eye shifts to him.

Pono looks down at her and rolls his eyes. "Sometimes I feel like I'm Emily's he-bitch."

I snicker but quickly cover my mouth with my palm, for fear that she'll think I'm laughing at her. Which I am. Pono gets up and starts down the bleachers. Looking back at me, he flashes a killer smile and says, "See ya around."

After a few more songs, I conclude I've done my duty and that I can go home guilt free. I stand, stretch, and head down the bleachers. This time I stay on the edge of the dance floor, to avoid brushing up against sweaty bodies. When I reach the hallway I see Omar rushing in.

"Yo, Rani. What's up, girl?"

"Not much. Just heading out. You're fashionably late," I say, raising my eyebrow and crossing my arms.

"Yeah, you know me. Gots to handle my biz. It ain't easy bein' MC Irraz. I don't get no rest from da game."

As usual neither of us can keep a straight face. Almost immediately we burst out laughing. Omar says, "Naw. I helped my mom clean the rooms at Kaluakoi so she could finish work early."

"You're such a good son!"

"True dat," he says holding out his fist.

I bump it with my fist and say, "Well, have a good time. I'm outta here."

"No way, Jose! You gotta dance with me once," he says, grabbing my hands. "I just got here!" He drags me back into the gym. *Bust a Move* comes on and Omar turns his head back as he pulls me, nodding and smiling, because we both love us some Young MC. I let him tow me into the thick of the moving bodies. I'm diggin' on the sights and the sounds of being on the dance floor with the sole purpose of shakin' my thang. For the first time.

As it turns out, we're next to Pono and Emily. I risk a peek at Emily and she gives me another hostile stare. I frown and resolve to show her how it's done. Young MC raps and I follow his advice.

That's when Pono's eyes widen.

And Emily's jaw drops.

ROYAL ELEVATION

"Rani?" Mark gives me that electrified Danny Zuko look. The one Danny gave Sandy at the carnival the first time he saw her after Frenchie's makeover.

I tilt my head up. "Hi, Mark!"

"I like it," he says, nodding. "Oh. And a pack of Salem Lights and some matches por favor, Blondie."

I can't wipe the sappy grin off my face. I search for his smokes through the open cartons of cigarettes that I'd been in the middle of loading. With his poison pack in my hand, I resist the urge to jump up, like one of those bouncy, yippy little dogs that go all bonkers when their master gets home. Instead I buy myself some time to calm down by pretending to search for the matches.

"Where oh where did I put those matches?" I ask myself out loud to add credibility to my act. I fake forage the shelf below the counter for a bit. When I'm composed, I grab a book of matches from the box that's exactly where it should be, and stand up. I slide the cigarettes and matches across the counter towards him.

He takes a step back and crosses his arms. "Turn around. Let me see the back."

I turn and rub my palm over the soft, newly bleached stubble. "Yeah, after all that drama with my dad on Thursday..." I pause. Then I decide not to mention that later that night when I told my mom about Dad's combative behavior, she didn't bat an eye. I asked her what she thought, trying to get her to commiserate. But she didn't say one word. She didn't even look at me. She kept her eyes anchored on the thali as she scanned the urad dal one by one for tiny pebbles. There was a small pile of pebbles and misfit urad dal in a bowl next to her. Maybe I could have picked a better time to get her attention. But surely Dad's physical violence surpassed me shaving my head. Surely she'd put down the thali and talk.

Nope.

The victory I'd felt at cutting the cord with Dad turned into a bitter, lonely defeat with Mom. And my hair paid the price again. It came down to either re-shaving my head clean or bleaching it. Bleaching won. After the dance last night I stayed up late to do it. Secretly, I hoped my bleached head would have the same effect on Mom that my shaved head did.

It didn't.

Leaving all that out, I face Mark again. All racy I say, "If I've only one life, let me live it as a blonde."

"Gentlemen prefer blondes." He hands me ten bucks.

I giggle. "Thanks again for rescuing me the other day." I stretch my hand out with his change.

"No problem." He grabs the change. And my hand. "Come hang out on the porch."

The touch of Mr. Thunder God's hand sends a pulse-quickening thunderbolt through me.

"Ok, sounds good," I say, trying not to give away that I'm having flashes of us strutting through the "danger ahead" tunnel in *Grease* singing *You're the One That I Want*. I also hope he won't notice that the jolt of his touch hurtled down my spine and came to a screeching halt in my yoni. I have to walk kinda bowlegged around the counter. He follows me onto the porch. He's staring at me. I fidget and tug at my fitting tank top and short shorts, wishing they'd somehow miraculously convert into a turtleneck and jeans.

Get off it, Rani. There's no way he's checking you out. A guy like that—only in your dreams.

It's time to come clean. To myself. I've reassigned my crush from Pono to Mark. Mark's hot. He's single. He's community-minded. And, of course, he's my new hero. When we did the Greek unit in AP lit, I remember we learned that the word heros can mean demi-god. *Hmm.* Mark is like...Krishna. Yep. Definitely Krishna. And I'm a young gopi following him around, unconditionally devoted. Suddenly, I'm Sandy again. *Hopelessly Devoted to You*, Mark. I ignore the little voice in my head that screams, "But he's at least ten years older than you!"

"How old are you anyway?" I ask.

"Old enough to smoke and drink." He laughs.

"No, really, how old are you?"

"Thirty-one."

My eyes widen. "You're officially the oldest friend I have," I say.

"Well, you're the only blonde burr-skinny-beautiful-smart-rapper-Indian friend I have."

Beautiful?

"Thanks. You're not so bad yourself. But I think you might need to eat more. Looks like all that hard Ranch work is taking its toll."

"You think?" He stands up, stretches his arms out, and inspects himself. He pulls at the waist of his cargo shorts and there's a lot of room. "Yeah, I think you're right, Rani. I'll get chowing." He sits down close to me. So close that my bare thigh and knee lightly press up against his.

Holy crap! Am I up to bat? I let out a long, slow breath.

Mark pivots on the bench to face me, but the touch of his leg is gone.

Come back, my burly leg!

With a businesslike expression, he asks, "So what'd you think about the audition?"

"It was unreal. Never thought I'd perform a rap in front of people. And with a beat," I say putting a lid on my urge to get to first base.

Keep your cool, Rani. Gotta keep your cool.

He nods his head and lights up. "Smoke?"

"Me? Cancer sticks? No way. I've never even tried alcohol." I shove my palms under my thighs. "Bet you think I'm a total loser, right?"

"Nope. Just makes you smarter than me." He takes a long drag then exhales a ring of smoke.

I zero in on his carcinogenic smoke magic.

Why is that like the sexist thing ever?

"What was it like performing?"

"A rush," I report. I press my thighs down hard. Now there's something I could get addicted to.

"Bingo," he says, with a satisfied look.

"Pono told me you got into rhyming because of personal stuff."

"Yeah."

"What kind of stuff?"

Suddenly Mark's golden demi-god aura is gone. A shadowy gloom replaces it. He stares at the porch floorboards. "It's kind of intense." He wavers. Then he raises his head and smiles. "I'll tell you some other time, ok?"

"Ok, no worries." I try to get things back on a flirty note. I catch his eyes and grin from ear to ear. "By the way when will I get to hear you rap, DVus?"

He shrugs. "I don't know. Haven't had much time to write these days, with work and planning 4eva Flowin'."

"A girl can hope."

He grins. "Maybe." Then he moves his head close to mine. His smoky mouth skims my ear and he whispers, "Sutra, the 4eva Flowin' crew thinks you've got it goin' on."

Afraid I might turn my head towards him and hit his lips with mine, I let my head drift slightly away from his tantalizing face. With my index finger I push my glasses up and say, "Nah, nah. They're just being nice. Anyway, Stan Lee wasn't happy I was there."

He sits upright. "He's stressed about his mom. Her boyfriend beat her up again. I'm sure that's why he's been trippin'."

"That's terrible."

"Don't worry. His mom's ok. I'm sure things will work out between you two," Mark says. He pauses, clears his throat. In an official voice he announces, "MC Sutra, it's my pleasure to inform you that you've been accepted as a member of the 4eva Flowin' crew."

He changes his voice back to regular and gifts me his sexy smile as an added bonus. Then in a sweet almost shy way that surprises me, he says, "If you want it, that is. You in?"

"Heck yeah. All in," I say, beaming.

"Cool, my rap queen. Start preppin' for your first performance at Mo'omomi." He gets up and crams the cigarette pack and matches in his back pocket. He turns and heads down the porch steps.

Queen?

A few weeks ago, I would never, ever, ever, ever have imagined this double whammy jackpot. I don't know what to feel more excited about—being a member of the 4eva Flowin' crew or getting my royalty status elevated from Dad's princess to Mark's queen.

Stop frontin', Rani! You know what you're more stoked about!

Queen beats *crew* by a landslide. And my oh my oh my how I've missed this feeling. It's as if Mark injected my vein with a needle full of praise and it went straight to my brain. And unleashed all my feel-good neurotransmitters in one shot. Exactly like what my dad's words used to do. Who needs scary drugs when you can get naturally high on a man's attention?

I don't need you, Dad.

I got a new man. Sort of.

Mark stops on the bottom step and looks back at me. "Oh and Sutra, let's hang out tonight."

Methinks me just OD'd.

LOVE DRUG JUNKIE

I'm home. My skin, muscles, and bones feel it. My beating heart feels it. Every single individual neuron and blood cell in my body feels it. Inside and out, every part of me is being swaddled by a downy blanket of happiness. Comfort. Safety. I'm snug as a bug in a rug gaping at the richest confections. My salivary glands exude excitement and desire.

This is how I felt with Dad for as long as I can remember. He was my home. Then he left me and found a new home. With Wendy. I've been lost since then. Drifting aimlessly among people. Searching for a someone I can call home.

I've found home again.

It's a clear, lovely Kaunakakai night. Hotel Moloka'i is jam-packed mostly with tourists getting their drink on. And they'll be boisterous in no time. I watch the coconut trees slow dance in the breeze. Guilt about hanging out with a man in his thirties tries to lure me out of my home. But in a flash I slam the door shut on guilt. What's the big deal? When home was my dad he was obviously older than me. Dad and I used to hang out here at Hotel Moloka'i all the time. In fact, we've sat at this same table overlooking the ocean. I take a look at Mark. His eyes are on the ocean.

As far as I'm concerned, this is all legit.

"A tequila for the lady?" Mark asks with his deep and confident voice.

It crosses my mind that Mark's probably sat here with many girls before. I'm sure he's asked them the same question in the same alluring way. But I don't care. Because right about now he's making me feel like I'm the only girl on the island. No, wait. The only girl in the world.

I open my mouth ready to say sure because I'm ready and willing to do almost anything he asks. But then I realize what he actually asked. I panic inside. Alcohol hasn't been part of home for me before. Plus I took D.A.R.E. very seriously in school. So I turn it into a joke because I don't want to come across as too nerdy. Or difficult. "What? Me?" I shake my head. "No way. I'm not twenty-one and I'm a law-abiding citizen."

I guess if we're getting technical there was alcohol in the chocolate rum cake that Auntie Maile made a few months ago for Mom's birthday. But I'm pretty sure most of the actual alcohol got burned off in the baking process.

Mark holds his stomach and leans forward a bit, cracking up like he's vomiting laughter. "Ok, ok, Officer," showing me a vertical palm in acknowledgement. He orders a shot of tequila with a beer back. I'm not sure what a "beer back" is, but I'm too embarrassed to ask. I order a Sprite.

Our drinks arrive. I take a sip of my Sprite and attempt to hide how easily I've fallen into a comfortable rhythm with Mark. That I'd be overjoyed to continue this. Forever. "It would be cool to hang out with Omar and Pono next time."

I totally don't mean that! I want to hang out with you alone all the time!

"Not Stan Lee?"

"I wish. If we got to know each other, maybe he wouldn't hate me. I wish he would give me a chance."

"He doesn't hate you, Rani. Like I said, he's stressed out. And yesterday he told me..." He stops and downs his tequila shot. Then he takes a swig of beer.

"What?"

"He likes me."

"Likes you?"

"Yeah, you know. Likes me. As in he likes me, likes me."

"Oh." *What are you talking about?*

"He says he hates that I talk about you all the time."

"Oh." *Mark talks about me all the time?*

"I told him I'm straight as an arrow."

"Oh." *OH! Duh. I get it.* I let it sink in, taking another sip of Sprite. "Poor Stan. Now I feel bad for him. Unrequited love. That sucks..." My voice and eyes drift off.

"Yeah, give him some time. He's only been on Moloka'i for six months. And he doesn't have any friends besides me and a couple of the 4eva crew." Mark takes a gulp of beer. "He'll warm up to you."

"I hope so."

"He will. By the way, keep all that info on the low. Moloka'i's so small."

I nod.

The waitress asks if we want another round.

"I'm ok, thanks."

"I'll have another shot of Cuervo. Oh, and can I get a Kahlúa on the rocks?"

Right when Marks gives his order, there's a boom of laughter from the group of tourists sitting behind him. I tilt my head to the side to sneak a peek at what's so funny. Eight middle-aged guys are sitting around a table covered with beer bottles. They're all wearing the same tacky aloha shirts. Navy blue and white. The design—coconut trees with the word aloha. One of the guys stands up and makes a toast. Something about "the good ole' fraternity house days." I roll my eyes, because if they're the Alpha Betas, I'm Gilbert.

The waitress says, "Try say 'em again."

He repeats the order to her.

I'm confused. "You drink Kahlúa, tequila, and beer at the same time?"

He chuckles. "No, silly. The Kahlúa is for you. You gotta try it. It tastes really good."

"Ok," I say, pushing my glasses up by the bridge.

Ok? What the heck, Rani?

What just happened? For a second, I wonder if Mark was even listening to my strong underage anti-alcohol stance. It shouldn't matter that I tried to minimize it by being humorous. I still said no.

They don't take a woman's words seriously.

But there's no way I want to put Mark in the same category as my dad or Gautam uncle. Fast as I can, I choose a more likable explanation. I got enchanted to say ok by Mark's gorgeous eyes.

That's my story and I'm sticking to it.

The waitress brings back the drinks. As soon as she leaves, Mark pushes the glass of Kahlúa towards me.

"That seems like a lot." I raise my eyebrows.

"Try a sip."

I take a big sip. "Ooh." It's cold and sweet. "Yum. Like drinking coffee candy." I take another gulp.

"I knew you'd like it." He holds up his shot glass. We clink glasses and I polish off my first drink. He shoots his tequila. "How about one more?"

"Ok!" *Who am I?*

Mark orders another round as I try to figure out what parallel universe we're in. When the waitress brings our round, I can't help but question why she doesn't notice that underage me is actually drinking the Kahlúa. Maybe as long as the customers tip well they can do whatever they want. We throw back our drinks quickly. My head starts to feel a little dizzy.

Mark narrows his eyes and smiles. "Ok, it's my turn to spring this on you. How come you don't have a boyfriend? Like Pono or Omar?"

"I've never had a boyfriend. Boys never like me like that." I sigh. "You know, I can relate to Stan. I used to like Pono. But he has a girlfriend. So I've admired him from afar."

I keep going, trying to keep my face unreadable. "Pono's got a really good family. He's super smart. He plays ukulele like a master. He surfs like a pro. And he works hard. Did you know he works at Kaluakoi as a busboy?"

I'm talking faster now.

"Plus, he raps! Total renaissance man. But, he'll never like me, like me. So I gave up. You gotta know when to quit, right?" I peek at Mark. His expression makes me think he's at least kind of entertained. Suddenly I want to profess my undying love to Mark. Tell him that I shifted my crush from Pono to him. But I decide that's probably not the best idea because what if he totally rejects me? I keep my buzzed trap shut and focus on not saying what I really, really want to say.

But now I love you, Mark!

I laugh nervously. "Sorry, I'm rambling."

He doesn't seem bothered. He gets this tough, hold you down expression. Like he's Mark Wahlberg in the Calvin Klein underwear commercial. "All I have to say is, his loss, Rani. If only I..." He stops. His spellbinding eyes glimmer.

If only he...what?

I'm light-headed and I don't want to keep making A with more chattering. So I try to flip the script and put him on the spot. "Wait a minute, how about you? I still don't get it. You don't like guys. You don't have a girlfriend. And you want to hang out with me?" I pause and shake my head. "Something doesn't add up." I put my elbows on the table and massage my temples.

"You ok?" Marks asks.

Before I can answer, someone taps my shoulder. I look up.

Oh no.

The beer-belly-balding-okole-grabbing-drunk-ass-creep from that night at the Cafe is standing next to me. He's hovering like a predatory animal. Tonight it's not just like he's the hunter hoping to get a deer, but more like a tiger closing in on its prey. I notice he's wearing one of those matching gaudy aloha shirts!

"Well, well, well. If it isn't the crazy bitch," he slurs reaching out and brushing my stubbly head with his gross, calloused hand. "Crazy blonde dyke I should say." Before I know it, his hand reaches the nape of my neck then switches course and moves over my collarbone and down into my shirt.

Mark doesn't hesitate. He shoves his chair back and yanks Mr. Drunk-Ass-Creep's hand off me. Then he gets up in the drunk's face. "What did you say?"

The guy doesn't seem to understand. "Watch out for this one," he tells Mark. "She's a tease." He snickers and points at me with his thumb. "Last time all I got was some ass over clothes. No skin." He shifts his eyes to me and I quickly look away. "But I got me some skin today."

That's when Mark turns into Smaug.

I almost feel sorry for the drunk because I know what's about to happen.

And it does.

Mark cold-cocks the drunk. He ends up sprawled on the ground. He lays still for a couple of seconds. Then he comes to and moans, holding his nose and cheek. Blood is dripping between his fingers. I think it's coming from his nose. I wonder if it's broken. Mark cracks his knuckles. He glances at me, then marches over to the frat-man table. He says something in a hushed tone to a couple of the guys. Two of them hustle over and help their drunk friend up.

I feel like I'm watching the last scene from *Revenge of the Nerds*. Queen's *We Are the Champions* automatically starts playing in my mind's boombox.

Ha! *Revenge of this nerd*.

Mark pulls up his chair and sits back down.

"Is your fist ok?" I draw his right hand toward me and inspect it.

"It's ok, don't worry." He takes a deep breath and exhales. "Where were we?" he asks, locking eyes with me and smiling. He seems calm and composed. As if nothing happened.

But I'm going crazy in my mind. I can't believe what he just did. My hero! My knight in shining armor defended my honor. Again! I manage to erase the ridiculously mushy look off my face and say, "Thanks, Mark. No one's ever..."

He interrupts me. "No one disrespects my friend."

Now I'm about to explode with giddiness. I don't know what to do with myself. Mark takes care of that.

He smiles mysteriously. Reaching across the table he grasps my hand. He strokes it with his thumb and says, "Hold up. Let me rephrase. No one disrespects my girlfriend."

Girlfriend? I'm his girlfriend??!!??

There is nothing I can possibly say to describe how insanely good that makes me feel.

I'm really home. Home sweet home.

EVOLUTION

I'm still high on Mark when I get home. I'm envisioning him as the snake charmer and me as the cobra. Must be so because he charmed me. With his eyes. With his words.

My lips curve up until they can't go up anymore and my face muscles hurt. His words make me feel like I'm worth something.

I'm addicted to Mark.

You've been replaced, Dad.

Then I see Mom. She's in her usual late night place in front of the TV. Her eyes are glazed over in a narcosis of Bollywood and butter pecan. My lips start their descent. I take my usual spot in the doorway of the den with my usual longing for connection. I fake cough trying to get her attention. She doesn't flinch. So I say, "Hi, Mom."

She mumbles, "Mmm."

I decide not to go through my usual questions. So I don't have to get her usual lack of response. I want to stay high on Mark. Anyway I'm kinda over trying with Mom. I decide right then and there to give up on her. If I can give up my crush on Pono, I can give up on wanting a relationship with Mom. I head back to my room. Marching like a woman on a covert mission. Operation Mark.

That's when I hear Mom's voice. I freeze faster than a wart sprayed with liquid nitrogen.

"Rani, come here," she calls out.

For a second, I can't get my body to respond. Mom calls my name again. "Come here."

I walk back, taking my time. *What could she want*? "Yeah?"

She doesn't look at me. "Where were you?"

"Um...out."

"Where?" she asks.

Don't lie! "Hotel Moloka'i."

"With who?" she asks.

Don't lie! *Well, try not to lie*! *Oh heck, just lie already*! "Pono and Omar."

"It's 12:30. Next time I want you home by 10:30," she decrees.

I stand there like a fish out of water. I can't figure out what I should feel.

1. Scared. Because I'm busted.

2. Angry. Because now that I'm feeling better, she's going to cramp my style.

3. Overjoyed. Because she's noticed me.

"Ok." I tip my head and scan her expression. Though she hasn't moved from her seated position and isn't looking at me, I can tell she's smiling, just a little.

PLAYING WITH FIRE

Pono's standing with his back propped against the wall. The contrast of his virile body in a Bob Marley tank top and board shorts next to the painted caricature of our school mascot—a portly farmer in overalls wielding a pitchfork—almost makes me burst into laughter. Pono's got his arms crossed high on his chest with both thumbs up. But it's the brooding look in his eye that keeps me from guffawing. I'm not sure what to expect.

"Hi, Pono!" I call out, trying to be peppy.

He gets right to it. No exchange of pleasantries. No comments—mocking or otherwise—about my blonde head. His voice is tight. "I was at Hotel Moloka'i on Saturday night for my auntie's birthday dinner."

Uh-oh.

"I saw you and Mark. He was holding your hand." He kicks a rock with his slipper and follows its trajaectory with his eyes. "Just wondering what's up with that," he mumbles.

My palms and pits are suddenly sweaty. I stall. A couple of

seconds adjusting the books in my hand. A few more hoisting my backpack to a more comfortable position on my shoulder. "We were hanging out," I say, avoiding his eyes.

"He was drinking. Remember I told you he's supposed to be sober?"

"Yeah, I was wondering about that. But he only had a couple of drinks. He seemed fine."

He shakes his head. "It's weird that he'd be drinking at all if he's sober." Trouble brews on Pono's face. "Rani, there's something else." He narrows his eyes. "I've seen him with Reynold in the Kaluakoi parking lot, exchanging something."

And?

"You know about Reynold, right?"

"No."

"He's the biggest batu dealer on Moloka'i." He stares down at his balled up hands. "Omar said his dad used to work with Reynold. That maybe Reynold framed his dad."

My thoughts gallop as I try to put two and two together.

Mark's not an alcoholic or druggie. If he was how could he function? I've seen junkies around town. They look dirty, wasted, and they talk to themselves. Mark's not like that. He works hard at the Ranch. So hard that he's losing weight. And how can a junkie organize 4eva Flowin' jams?

"Huh? Th-there must be a misunderstanding."

"Mark might be using batu. He's definitely drinking. He's way older than you. Why does he need to hang out with you outside 4eva Flowin'?" Pono asks.

But I've already resolved that there's no way Mark is using batu or any other drugs. And I'm excusing alcohol. It doesn't count.

Pono's angry. "You and Mark were a little too..." He stops, like he's searching for the right words. "...a little too close."

I can't stand the thought of not hanging out with Mark. I take a deep breath and say, "Pono, you're so sweet. I get why you're worried."

His lips are tight.

"Look, everything's ok. That was the first time we hung out away from the store." Half smiling, I gently elbow him in his side.

He relaxes. "Listen, Rani." He steps a little closer, his milk chocolate eyes tempting me back to Pono crushville. His strong hands softly grip my shoulders. "Be careful. We're family now and I got your back."

We're family?

I like the sound of that. My smile grows and I get this familiar tingling in my body. Surreptitiously, I graze my arm with my fingers. Chicken skin.

But then I think about Mark and how he said it first. That drives me out of Pono crushville. My body stiffens. Then guilt looms. I should tell Pono about the butterflies I feel when I'm near Mark. About the flirting. That Mark bought me a drink. That it got me buzzed for the first time and I liked it. That Mark said I'm his girlfriend. That I know I'm playing with fire.

But I keep all that to myself. Instead, I smile and say, "Thanks, Pono. I really appreciate that."

HOLD UP, LEMME TAKE MY HOOPS OFF

The reverberating ring of the vintage silver-finish, wall-mounted school bell demands a vote in my mind—yes or no: power through and finish the yearbook senior class layout or chill near the banyan. Banyan chill time wins by a majority. In a hurry, I file away the photos and grab my books. I stroll down the open hallway dreaming up a sunny, expansive field. I'm lying in the tall grass holding a perfect white and yellow plumeria. Picking off one petal at a time.

He loves me, he loves me not.

With it's five soft petals, Mark's always going to love me. That's when my beloved rides up shirtless on a white stallion...

By chance, I catch my reflection in the large window near the gym. My goofy face makes me look like Dopey. Lovesick Dopey. Who turns into Clumsy Dopey and runs into Emily Angara. Literally.

"Watch it!"

Our books fall into a mixed-up, jumbled heap. I kneel down real quick, separating the books, stacking Emily's in a neat pile. I look up and notice we're both wearing big gold hoop earrings. She looks pissed.

She smacks her gum. "Watch it, you butch slut."

Butch. Ok. Whatever. But, slut?

I look up. "What're you talking about?"

"No make like you don't know."

"No. Really. I don't." That seems to infuriate her more.

"Pono broke up with me because of you!"

He broke up with her? "I don't know what you're talking about." I'm amazed.

She looks like a raging bull ready to charge. "No ack! I see you flirting with him."

"Emily," I appeal, "I'm not. We're just friends." I hold out her books hoping she'll take them and hele aku.

"Shut up, you two-faced skank." She knocks her own books out of my hands.

I can't think of any good comebacks. And I can't stop my eyes from filling with tears. I pick up my books ready to walk away in shame. I keep my head down hoping she won't notice the watery evidence of hurt and embarrassment in my eyes.

But of course, she notices.

"Yeah, go on and cry. You think you so innocent, but you really jus' one slut."

I wipe my eyes under my glasses with my free hand. Her anger flares up again. She pushes me. My books drop, scattering. I'm stunned. She pushes me again. She takes off her hoops and crams them in the pocket of her tight jeans. By now I realize she's ready to scrap.

I've never been in a fight before. I beg. "Come on, Emily. I'm sorry Pono broke up with you. But I didn't do anything." I back away from her. "Let's not..."

Charging forward she shoves me hard. I stumble back. My back slams into the concrete wall. She rushes forward and rips my glasses off my face and flings them to the ground. I shield my face. She slaps and scratches at my chest and arms. I slide down the wall, trying to protect my face. Next thing I know I'm on the ground. And she's on top of me, choking me with her small hands. I catch a glimpse of the growing semicircle of students around us as my breath and vision diminish.

"Geev 'em, Emily!" I see a fist in the air. More yelling. "Give her dirty lick'ns!"

The crowd's encouragement fuels Emily's beat the crap out-of-Rani-fire. I'm about to be incinerated when out of the corner of my eye I see the crowd part. Like the Red Sea in *The Ten Commandments*. Pono emerges all Charlton Heston. He pulls Emily off me. I gasp for air, clutching my tender throat.

"What're you doing, Em?" He holds onto her hands so she won't hit me again.

"Giving her what she deserves!" she screams. She struggles to escape. "Get off me, Pono!"

He lets go of her. She catches her breath and smoothes her hair back into place. "You broke up with me for that?" she shouts, pointing at me.

"Emily, that's not—"

"Forget it. I'm glad it's ova!" she yells, gathering her books. She turns and flips me off. "SLUT!" she hollers at the top of her lungs, then sprints away.

The crowd dissipates, disappointed. I sit up and cough.

"Rani." Pono puts out his hand to help me.

In one swift motion, he pulls me up. His head is angled down and for a second, our lips are like a millimeter or two apart. I take a step back feeling flushed. Random words stumble out of my mouth "Um, wow. Yeah. Woah. Like..." Finally I manage to say, "Thanks, Pono." I stroke my neck and flinch. "Ouch."

"That's gotta hurt."

"Yeah, but I'll be ok." I dab at the blood on my arms.

"Your glasses," Pono says as he crouches down and picks them up. Holding them straight out in front of him, he examines them. "They're a little bent."

"That's ok, I can fix them later." I take them from him. I slide them on and they sit uneven on my face. "Well, this completes my nerd look. Thanks, Emily."

Pono snickers. He reaches for my glasses and says, "Here, let me."

"Don't worry about it," I say, not before his fingers brush my cheek. I swear it's as if he pressed a button on my face that caused instantaneous blushing. Flustered, I take another step back. It's strange because my body's still getting fired up around Pono even though my mind let go of the crush. I grasp the hinges of my glasses and pull the lopsided frames up the bridge of my nose. "At least she didn't crush them in her rage, right?" I laugh. Then I lean over and whisper, "I think Emily has claws."

Pono chuckles and whispers back, "And she breathes fire." He sits down on a concrete stair and motions for me to sit next to him. "By the way," he says pointing to my head, "I like the blonde. It's a good look." He runs his hand over the back of my head.

"Thanks," I say, keeping a straight face, but I'm really glad Pono noticed. And that he likes it.

Stop! *Why do you care what he thinks*? *It only matters what Mark thinks*.

We sit in silence for a minute, both of us staring at the ground. Then he bumps my knee with his and says, "Sorry about all this."

"Not your fault." Then I remember what Emily said. "I didn't know you two broke up."

"I was going to tell you but then—"

"'What?"

"Nothing." He shakes his head.

"Come on, Pono. Tell me."

"Nothing, nothing. Don't worry." Perking up he says, "You need a bodyguard. Omar told me about your dad. That's two attacks in less than a week."

I don't correct him and tell him that it's really three attacks if I count Mr. Drunk-Ass-Creep's grab at the Hotel Moloka'i because that would mean bringing up Mark. So all I say is, "Yeah, a bodyguard. Ha ha, very funny." I roll my eyes. "But seriously, thanks for saving me from your crazy ex."

He nods. "No problem. Anything for you."

I smile. And this time I manage to negate my primal response to him and feel nothing but grateful.

I can do this.

The bell rings and we make our way to AP Physics. My hankering for Pono has passed.

SPITTIN' DA TRUTH

In the dark I can barely make out the sign for the Hawaiian Home Lands. Pono stops his truck on the last bit of asphalt. "Mo'omomi's gonna look unreal tonight."

I'm pumped up as we begin the drive down the long, unpaved road. Only four-wheel drives can handle this choppy passage. But with the Beastie Boys' *Shake Your Rump* on blast, the unpredictable jarring doesn't phase us.

We arrive at a clearing and park beside a bunch of other trucks. I smell the ocean, salty and fresh. In the bright glow of the 4runner's headlights, I notice the eerie, windswept kiawe. These invasive trees are everywhere they shouldn't be. Especially at Mo'omomi. They're all bent the same way—as if Mo'omomi's mana tried to sweep them off the land—their trunks windward and their branches and leaves leeward.

Pono and I walk side by side down the trail, makai, following several other stylin' crew members. Then the bass hits us. Pono prods me and our eyes meet. We hail the *Check the Rhime* beat in unison. The path narrows. Pono is walking behind me. We quicken our pace, excited. It's Saturday, October 5, 1991 and so begins my 4eva Flowin' quest—to *A Tribe Called Quest*. We reach the end of the path. I stop abruptly, because what I see makes my retinas overdose.

Pono runs into me from behind. "Woah!"

There in front of us is the stage, like a luminous hip hop oasis in the night. I realign my glasses and take it all in. Four portable lighting stands, each with four par can lights, are spread out across the stage. Mark is tinkering with a couple of them. On the floor of center stage sits a borderlight. Colorful graffiti covers the walls of the pavilion. And huge speakers deliver the precious gift of bass and treble. Mostly bass. Feasting on the sight, I can almost see Queen Latifah spitting her rhymes on this souped up stage.

Suddenly I get cold feet. "I don't think I'm cut out for this."

"You got this. Trust me." We stand there as the hip hop splendors fill our senses. "Let's go check it out."

I'm blown away again. Queuing the next song, DJ Skittles reminds me of a mad scientist. One hand holding up enormous headphones to his ear, the other on the crossfader. I take some time to check out his gear. Equipment spread out all around like a bubbling lab setup. Two turntables. A mixer. Vinyl everywhere. An E-mu SP 1200 sampler/sequencer. An amp. More speakers. A Roland T-808 drum machine. A keyboard. My eyes are about to get lost in the levers, buttons, and switches.

Pono elbows me. We go around the side of the pavilion, making our way through the growing crowd of done up young hip hoppers. There must be at least fifty of them. Hellafied hip hoppers on

Moloka'i. Unreal. It's like *Yo! MTV Raps*, the Mo'omomi episode. I see Tim, Jay, and Keoni from school. I recognize some guys from Maunaloa and from town and a couple of guys from water meetings. I spock the crowd looking for Auntie Hannah and Auntie Lani. Seems only natural they'd be here. I don't see them. That's when I realize there aren't any other girls here. Before this fully registers, Pono and I are walking up a couple of stairs onto the stage.

Mark calls us over. He's having some technical difficulties with two sets of lights.

"Hey, hey. How are you two doin'?" Mark's eyes are on me. He gives me a come-hither look, then winks.

"Good," I say, trying to suppress the urge to go-hither, push him down on the stage, and give him some mouth to mouth. I drop my head because my face is pretty much one big kooky smile. I peek at Pono to see if he's noticed the sparks between Mark and me.

"Ditto," Pono says. His eyes shift back and forth between Mark and me.

Shoot. He noticed.

"Favor, please. Can you two go back to my truck and get the extra light stands?" Mark requests. "Some of these lights aren't working."

"Shoots," I say, thankful for the excuse to get out of this awkwardness. I turn and start walking away. Fast. Pono catches up. His nose and eyes are scrunched up and he's frowning.

"Yo Sutra, did I just miss something?"

"Naw, Pono." I don't say anything else. I take a quick look at Pono as we hustle down the path. The faint glow from the moon rests on his face.

When we reach Mark's truck, Pono seems to get distracted with hauling the lights. But as we're grabbing the lights, high beams blind me. A navy blue Ford pick-up truck pulls up.

It's Stan Lee. I panic until he steps out of the truck and I see his gray, white, and silver Adidas high tops. I've got the exact same pair. My lips start to curve up in commendation but quickly go the opposite direction when I get a load of his stinkface. He slams his door shut. I'm feeling daunted but something about seeing him in the fresh sneaks motivates me to try to contend with his antagonism.

"Hey Pono, go on ahead of me, I gotta talk to Stan Lee," I say.

"K'den," Pono says. I watch him as he drops out of sight down the path.

I shift my attention back to Stan Lee as he hustles to the trail. I adjust the light stand in my arms and follow him, thinking how different can we be if we floss the same Adidas?

Still I know I'm shooting in the dark here.

The only times I've directly confronted anyone was last month. And two of those times my hair succumbed to the messy emotional aftermath. I'm scared. How am I supposed to handle this tension with Stan Lee? I sort through the mishmash of competing ideas, trying to figure out what to say first. I dig deep but I can't come up with anything. And with all the thinking I've been doing lately, I've become tuned in to what I shouldn't say.

I happen to be an expert on what not to say. That's what I've done with my parents since way back. See they never talked about what was really bothering them. I followed suit. You live what you learn, right? It was the worst after their fights. I bottled up how much it frightened and hurt me. Plus they never asked me how I was doing. Instead, after breaking up the fight, I cheered them up by steering the conversation to light topics. They got away with never addressing the reasons for the fights or how they felt. Then Mom would be more icy than usual towards me because she was really still mad at Dad. And Dad would be extra nice to me because I saved his ass from having to talk to Mom. This would piss Mom off more as if it was me and Dad against her. Her silent hostility towards me would grow. I'd be walking on eggshells around her, trying to be super sweet and accommodating. Then they'd fight again. And the cycle repeated. Over and over for the past ten years.

None of that is helpful right now. I don't want to kiss Stan Lee's ass to slow his roll. I rack my brain some more. Maybe if I start with small talk...

He's about ten feet ahead of me on the trail. I call out, "Nice kicks."

He keeps walking.

That didn't work. Maybe I should do what he does—get right to it. "Hey Stan Lee, wait up," I say. I get to a toned down version of it. "I think we got off on the wrong foot. Can we start over?"

"No," he says. He doesn't look back and he doesn't stop.

He doesn't sugar coat it, that's for sure. Ok, let me dust the sugar off my words.

"Hold up!" I half-shout.

He stops and whirls around. "What?"

For a second I'm really scared because the moonlight makes his frown white-hot. I almost back down. I shudder then force myself to match his glare. "Why are you so rude?"

Booya. Props to myself for spittin' da truth.

"Listen Sutra, stay in your little sheltered, entitled world. Leave me alone."

Oh snap. Props against me cuz he just drew the line.

It feels like he stabbed me in the back of my heel. My Achilles heel, that is, of being misunderstood as some kind of haole snob.

Oh. No. You. Di'int.

That's when I find my words.

"Wait a minute. How would you know anything about my world? It's not like we've ever talked about anything other than how much you owe for cigarettes. I'm trying to make peace here."

He doesn't say a word.

"What's your problem?" My hands are pressed into my hips and my torso's tilting slightly forward.

"Let it go, Rani." He pivots and marches down the path.

So that's it. No mixed messages. No reading between the lines. Straight up rejection. And there's nothing I can do to fix it.

Eh. I stand alone on the path for a few minutes. I collect myself and strong-arm my tears to stay in my eyes. When I'm simmered down I make my way back to the stage. DJ Skittles is playing Run DMC's *It's Tricky*.

You can say that again.

My thoughts shift to the night to come. Anticipation of performing covers up the let down of Stan Lee's rejection. I help Mark and Pono set up the lighting stands. Then I decide to take a short solo break to mentally prep for the performance. I find a quiet corner behind the pavilion. The night softens the view of the rough, wide ocean expanse. The sound of the waves breaking on the shore is hypnotic. I sit on the coarse sand, enjoying the serenity of this Mo'omomi moment.

Hmm...

My mind fills with ideas for a new rap.

In this Mo'omomi moment,

my body and soul are content

in the gentle throes of my lyrical flow.

And I'm ready to go.

Gimme that mic

and I'll strike

ya'll with my verbal spike.

Someone taps my shoulder. I look up. It's Mark.

"Yo Sutra, I was looking for you. It's almost time to start. You ready?"

"Most definitely." I push myself up and wipe the sand from my jeans. "Ready."

Mark holds out his arms. "Hug it out for good luck."

I move closer. He locks me in his strong arms and holds it.

And holds it.

And holds it some more.

He seems stuck like I'm a magnet and his body, iron. Starting at the nape of my neck, his fingertips glide down and come to rest on the small of my back. His embrace starts a chain reaction of tingling all over my body. I don't want him to stop.

"We'd better head back," he says softly, taking a little step back.

No! Keep going!

"Ok," I manage to utter, a little winded.

By the time we get back to the stage area, it's packed. DJ Skittles cranks some Public Enemy, *Don't Believe the Hype*. I catch sight of Pono and Omar and head over to them. I have to fan myself with my hand. Like that'll really cool down my Mark blaze.

Mark hops on stage. "Mic check 1-2, 1-2, yo, yo, yo, you ready to get this party started?"

The eager hip hoppers congregate around the stage, juiced up. The vibe is ill and my chicken skin is inevitable. Skittles pumps Afrika Bambaataa, *Planet Rock*. Two guys I recognize from around town jump onto stage and throw down some coordinated top rock, 6-step, one-handed pikes, and stabbed windmills into back spins. Then one goes into b-boy stance while the other launches into a breakdancin' solo. I'm speechless. They tag team and the other drops into his solo. All I can think is how much I never want this night to end. And how long I've waited to experience a live hip hop production. They go into another set of matched moves culminating in headspins that end in baby freezes. The crowd claps and hollers as Mark exclaims, "Give it up for our 4eva b-boys!"

He lets the cheers die down before announcing, "Tonight we've got nine outstanding 4eva Flowin' MC's performing their original rap. Ya'll ready?"

The crowd roars.

"Let's get things warmed up with MC Irraz. Give it up!" Mark hands over the mic.

"Yo yo 4eva Flowin'," Omar calls out. "Lemme take you on a little journey."

Skittles drops the beat, and Omar starts rapping. I get lost in his delivery. Like everyone else in the crowd, my head's bobbing and my hand waves high. I study Omar's face as he struts around the stage in full form. Everything about him—his eyes, his body language, his potent lyrics—emanates passion, determination, and survival. His style is kinda like Guru from Gang Starr. My eyes well up because I feel uplifted by his words. I've never seen Omar so out on a limb with his soul. I smile and make a mental note to ask him if the rap is about his mom. His performance ends. The crowd goes wild.

Mark gets back on the mic. "Next up is Professor P. Give it up!"

Pono takes the mic and nods at Skittles. As the beat starts, Pono transforms. Optimus Prof. Enthralled by his lyrics about Native Hawaiian oppression, I close my eyes and head nod. Pono uses a simple rhyme scheme with vocal emphasis on certain words, authoritatively getting his message across. Kinda like Chuck D. I swear my brain is getting wiser as Pono schools us in a way that my neurons can't help but form new connections. I'm soaking up his sentiments the way the deep fried jalebi my mom makes soaks up the sugary sweet syrup.

Five more incredible rappers impress the crowd. The fervor grows. Stan Lee's on stage now.

With the beat, Stan Lee takes off lyrically. He delivers fast, multi-line rhymes about some of his family that's stuck in North Korea. His technique reminds me of Busta Rhymes from Leaders of the New School. It's mind blowing. And makes me exhausted. Like I've just sprinted a mile as fast as I can. He's done but I'm still under his abracadabra of beat and his flow. The loud cheers break my trance. I take a couple of seconds to catch my breath.

My turn.

Mark takes the mic and announces, "Give it up for the first girl on the crew. M...C...Suuuutra!"

I push through the crowd to the stage, hop up, and grab the mic. So far, this night's been packed with setting up, getting served by Stan Lee, and a hug from my hottie boyfriend.

Fear about performing hasn't had as much time to get on me. Plus I've got the vapors of the eight MC's who just performed. I'm ready.

Skittles cranks my beat. It blitzes the crowd with a massive hip hop assault loaded with samples. It's like there's a powerful army of funky beats encircling all of us in a curtain of fire. There's even a layer of grunge. He's chopped up and sequenced Nirvana's *Smells Like Teen Spirit* and woven the distinct intro and the saturnine guitar riff into the hip hop mix. The complexity and strength of the beats reminds me of how I felt the first time I heard what The Bomb Squad did on Public Enemy's *It Takes a Nation of Millions to Hold Us Back*.

I hear the beat. I feel the beat. I'm in the zone.

My voice and body break it down one hundred percent. No half-steppin'.

From Gujarat my family hails,

with Hinduism as their excuse to assail

the disease of intolerance they caught,

while Gandhi's liberal consciousness they forgot.

Muslims and Africans they can't stand,

easy now Indian Ku Klux Klan.

Selective amnesia of the Mahatma's plan

who, ironically, is also a Gujarati man.

And Gujarat's Hindu-led government justifies genocide,

bona fide.

Hindu holy writ

like persecuting women and dalits.

Subjugation too legit to quit.

And Gujarati posse wants me to marry

instead of finishing my degree.

One says for each Hindu baby boy I see

ten thousand dollars plus I'll give to thee.

Cuz a flourishing Hindu race needs an installment plan.

They want women uneducated, married, and hidden.

Hindu, Christian, or Islam...religious interpretations

include master plans

for control of women,

who they consider less than

a man.

As I rap the next two verses, I move around the stage like I own the whole damn place. And the crowd's hype. Their energy comes at me. From their hands, eyes, and bobbin' heads. By the time I get to the last verse, I'm wishing I had another four verses.

Out of the oppressive Hindu frying pan

into the catamaran

of good fortune

to the US of A I am orphaned.

Crushing all Gujarati misogynism.

Thankful every day for my Americanism.

Crushing all Gujarati stereotypes.

The stars and stripes

let me be the first woman in my family

to strive for an MD.

To openly choose my own lover.

But I am still trying to uncover
my identity,
so I rhyme about being free.
Cuz I am trying to be
the change I want to see.
Peace.

Through the whistles and applause, I scan the crowd. Pono and
Omar are near the front cheering loudly. I smile at them. Pono gives
me a chin-up. I don't see Mark. Disappointment creeps in. But it's
tempered by the adrenaline still pumping from the performance. I
walk down the side stairs ready to chillax and hang out with my boys.

Then as if out of thin air, Mark appears. He drags me to a
secluded spot on the side of the pavilion. He grips my wrists over
my head with one hand, pinning me to the wall. Without warning his
tongue's in my mouth like warm satin. It happens so fast and feels
so good. I go with it. Our tongues are delicately tangled and I tilt my
head back a little to find the perfect angle to get more. I lift my head
off the wall slightly and press my mouth harder onto his. But then
he pulls away. He looks into my eyes, our foreheads barely touching.
He lets go of my wrists and walks away. Just like that. And my body
is melting chocolate ice cream. It drips slowly down the wafer cone
wall. My eyes widen as I slide all the way down the wall and sit with
one leg extended out and the other, knee up. I realign my glasses
and catch my breath. Then I put my hand on my chest, surprised at
my rapid heartbeat. Mark left me floored by his French kiss.

That's when the icky thoughts encroach. I can't stop them. I can't
lock them away and avoid them like I usually do.

Dad. Hands. Lips.

Hidden images zoom. I'm terrified.

I try to pull my straight leg up, but I can't move it. All at once the muscles in my whole body are tensed. Then I realize my heart is pounding violently. I can't get enough air. It's like I'm choking and meanwhile someone's slowly pulling down thick, black curtains over my eyes. Everything gets blurry. I feel dizzy. I watch myself from above. It's hazy. Unreal.

I'm not here.

My body shakes with sobs as the walls of the pavilion, the beach, and the ocean close in. I want to run away but I can't feel my body.

Am I dying?

I try to endure. To no avail. I feel myself slipping.

PAPOHAKU PLEASURE AND PAIN

Mark points to the crusty scabs on my arms. "Woah, what happened?" he asks.

"Oh these. Battle scars." I was kinda hoping he wouldn't notice. I mean, he didn't make out the scabs at Mo'omomi, probably because it was dark. Even though he did make out with me. And thankfully, unknown to him, the world's fastest make out session resulted in a chain reaction revealing my mental scabs. Scabs adhering to the convolutions of my brain. Scabs that were ripped off by recollections of the past. Instead of blood, panic gushed out.

"Miss nonviolent in a battle? And to think I missed it," he says. His eyebrows arch high and the corners of his lips head south in fake disappointment.

"Yeah, I caught cracks from Pono's ex, Emily."

"What? No way. What happened?"

"Girl was pissed. She said I was the reason Pono broke up with her. Not." Shaking my head I say, "Hell hath no fury…"

"Uh-huh," he says, laughing. He clutches my arms, one at a time, for inspection. His fingers skim the flush semicircular discolorations on my inner arm. "These are older. What happened here?"

I feel my pulse rise. "Oh. Umm. I got them on a freight day last month, I think. You know, all that unloading boxes and stuff." There's no way I'm telling him that I did that to myself. I know I didn't mean to do it. It happened just like the panic did. Because of flashbacks. But I'm not sure he'll get it. He might think I'm crazy.

And that would be a major buzz kill. Not that I'm drinking. Yet.

I pull my arm away and change the subject.

"Yep. Emily did all sorts of beat down on me. Clawing. Slapping. Choking. But Pono saved me in the nick of time," I say with a flat tone. A slight sigh still escapes from my mouth. I scowl inside because though I haven't been thinking about my crush on Pono, my body still sometimes betrays me.

"Good ole' Pono," Mark says making a wry face.

Why's he frowning and being so sarcastic? I want to ask him about it, but my goal is to avoid conflict with Mark at all costs. Best to keep my mouth shut.

My eyes take inventory around the restaurant. It's empty except for a tourist couple ordering lunch. Mark is sucking down a beer. He knows the bartender here at Kaluakoi, so underage me gets to park on a barstool. And drink. I'm waiting for the tequila shot Mark ordered for me. The bartender had to go to the storage room and grab another bottle of Cuervo. A popular poison, indeed.

Mark kills the rest of his beer. His short sleeves are rolled up so his dreamcatcher tattoo is clearly visible. I trace it lightly with my fingertip, lingering on the ink a tad longer than necessary. I watch my finger slowly work its way down the tanned skin of his arm. His hand gravitates down and wraps around my bare thigh. It works its way up. I bite the side of my lower lip. Is there such a thing as a moist fire? Because that's what's going on down there.

He pulls his hand back just when the bartender returns. I steady my breath, watching the bartender pour the shot of Cuervo. The small, forbidden thrills of touch and anticipated taste exhilarate me. The bartenders grabs another beer for Mark and sets our drinks in front of us. Mark grips the frosty bottle. I catch a glimpse of what looks like small burns on his fingers. "Wait, Mark. My turn. Let me see your hand," I say, gently prying his hand off the beer. I study the wounds. "What happened?"

"Battle scars," he replies. Then he raises one eyebrow and gives me this look that says touché.

"No really. What happened?" I ask, persisting.

He rips his hand out of mine. "Don't worry about it, Rani." He's a little irked.

I let it go and stare at my tequila shot.

Are we both lying to each other?

Mark hands me the shot glass. "You have to drink it quick. Don't sip it."

I remember my dad sipped on his tequila. But I take Mark's advice. Putting the shot glass to my lips, I tilt my head back and down the one and a half ounces. It burns in the back of my throat. I gag and cover my mouth with my hands. Wish I had sipped it.

I take a swig of water. I think about his tattoo again. That's when I remember a paper I'd written for social studies last year on Algonquian peoples. "About your tattoo. Why a dreamcatcher? Are you part Ojibwe?"

"No. I'm white as snow. I got this tat when I was sixteen. I'd been having these nightmares about my dad killing my mom. My dad used to beat her up all the time. I had to get in between them so many times. Pull him off her so many times."

He knew exactly when to pull my dad off me.

He takes a deep breath and holds it for a bit before exhaling. "I wanted the nightmares to stop. I tried everything. Nothing worked. Then my mom told me to talk to her friend. A healer of some sort. Anyway, I spilled my guts. The healer told me to get a dreamcatcher tattoo. That it would protect me. It worked. No more nightmares."

"Oh man, that's intense. Poor you. And your poor mom." I reach for his hand and hold it in both of mine. He gives me a meek smile.

All of a sudden he gets wild-eyed. "I could've killed him. I should've." He pauses and looks through the menagerie of liquor bottles on the wall, his expression blank. "If he wasn't beating my mom, he was high or fooling around with other women."

"Oh no." I know his mom lives on Maui. "Where's your dad now?"

"I don't know. I haven't seen him since I was twenty." Then his face turns pallid, like it hasn't seen sun in years. "My guess is that he overdosed on heroin."

"Geez. Is your mom ok?"

He drops his head and shakes it. His eyes and nose are crinkled and his lips are in a slight downward pout. "She got into heroin and coke because of my dad but got clean and sober years ago." There's agony in his voice. He stops and peels the label off the beer bottle. "She relapsed four months ago. It's been so hard. She's been my rock."

I rub my thumb over his hand. "I'm so sorry."

Mark orders another beer for himself and another shot of tequila for me. I think about his parents using hardcore drugs. About what it was like for Mark as a kid. I can't even imagine.

Then without warning, Mark sweeps his hand over his face. It's like his hand has magic powers to change his mood in a split second from down in the dumps to high in the sky. When he drops his hand, he's wearing a nice smile. And I can't help but give him a big smile back. He changes the subject. "What's up with your dad? Your mom hasn't let him back in, huh?"

"Nope. Mom seems happy. I haven't seen Dad since that day you served him." Our drinks arrive. I take my second shot grimacing at the caustic feeling in my mouth. "Maybe I need a dreamcatcher tattoo. I keep having these nightmares that my dad's—" I stop myself. I think he notices that my smile's gone.

Oh no. Why'd I bring that up?

"He's what?" Mark asks. His chin is tucked but his eyes are up. It looks like he's expecting bad news.

"Nothing. Nothing." I spin the shot glass with my fingertips.

"Come on, Rani. Tell me."

I look up. His sympathetic eyes console me. I open my mouth, but all I can say is, "Doing what he's always done to me."

Mark frowns and his eyes narrow. And that tells me he might know what I'm alluding to. "What's he always done to you?"

I've never told anyone.

He shifts to the right on his barstool. Now he's facing me. He looks concerned. "Has he..." He eyes me intently.

I can't talk.

Under his breath, I think I hear him say something like, "I should've kicked the shit out of him the other day." He says something else but I miss it because I'm lost in my head.

I've never, ever, ever let myself really think about it. Because thinking about it made it real. I've never, ever, ever told anyone about it. Because telling someone about it made it real. And what would it mean about me if it was real? I've always thought it was my fault. Like I was the other woman. I figured that's why Mom was always mad at me.

When it happened, I escaped. Not literally. Not my body. Only my mind. In my head I went up the mountain to the Wailau lookout. Machete in hand, I'd hack my way up. Wary of wild pigs of course. The thick foliage all around blocked out the blazing sun above. Alone, I'd trek in the shade of the jungle. Though I was sweating and my breathing was heavy, I'd feel at peace.

Dad hasn't been in my room since last spring. But the memories I've blocked out for years somehow got released after he started leaving me alone. The recollections have been coming in different forms. There's been the recurring nightmares. Then the thoughts and images that pop up when something reminds me of my broken family. But it really hit me after Mark full-on kissed me.

"Rani?" I feel his hand on my back. How long has he been rubbing it?

"Rani?" This time I hear him.

Don't tell him anymore.

I shake my head. My eyes well up. Tears escape.

Mark finishes off his beer. He stands up and moves next to me. He puts his hands on my shoulders. "Hey, let's get out of here."

He drives us to Papohaku Beach Park. The wide, empty road to Papohaku is lined with kiawe. I've often seen deer grazing among the thorny trees. Today only a couple of wild turkeys roam. We don't pass any other cars.

We arrive and he backs his truck into a stall in the empty parking lot. We make our way to the sand. I get why people call it Three Mile Beach. The sand seems to stretch for miles. There's no one around. I delight in pretending we're the only ones on the island. I tread carefully over the warm, soft sand, trying to avoid the inch long kiawe spikes. The sun massages my scalp with its heat. He reaches for my hand as we walk along the water's edge.

We're a 3D postcard.

"Let's sit there," he says, pointing to a spot under the shade of some kiawe. We meander over and find a relatively thorn-free spot. I stare at the cloudless blue sky and rolling ocean. I feel safe.

And horny. *Going Back to Cali* plays in my mind's boombox. To me, this rap is normal sex. Good sex. Well, what I assume normal good sex feels like. Smooth like LL's lyrics. Hot like the groove.

He puts his arm around me and pulls me closer. I'm certain he knows what he's doing because everything happens like clockwork. He slides my glasses off, folds them, and lays them on a small patch of grass. I lean my head on him. His hand lingers on my bare shoulder. Then his fingers play with the spaghetti strap of my tank top. Like a wisp of cotton, his fingertips graze my collarbone. My neckline. My breath quickens. His hand slides down under my tank top. Searching. Finding. He pulls me onto him. I straddle him and his lips move up my neck to my mouth. I close my eyes. His tongue captures mine. Urgently he needs more of my skin. He unfastens my bra and runs his hands up and down my back, sinking his fingers into my flesh. His hungry hands plunge under the waistband of my shorts.

Dad.

He's kissing me harder and pulling down my shorts.

Dad.

I tear my mouth off his and quickly roll off, pulling my shorts back up. Hugging my knees, I rock in fetal position.

The dizziness is happening. I can't breathe.

"What's wrong?"

I can't answer. I make myself breathe slow and deep. I focus on a bunch of shells and pebbles nearby. I start counting them. Anything so I don't lose control.

"What's wrong, Rani?"

I'm still taking belly breaths. "I need to slow it down, Mark."

He nods and strokes my back. I can't tell him that his touch, even though it was making me feel crazy good, was punctuated by sickening flashes of Dad. The images were so strong. I'm shook up and frustrated. Tears cascade down my cheeks.

"Hey, it's ok."

We sit in silence. I inhale deeply and exhale slowly. I'm not sure how much time goes by but my breath eventually returns to normal. I feel a little better. Mark stands up and steps directly in front of me. He kneels down and cradles my face in his hands.

"Rani, I've never told anyone this," he whispers. His bright blue eyes sparkle in confirmation. He strokes my stubbly head and says, "I think I'm falling for you."

THE SINS OF THE FATHER

Sunlight floods the store porch. I bask in its glorious rays. And in the fact that I'm off for the rest of the day. The main street is empty. The only sound is the occasional chirp of birds perched in the colossal banyan across the street in front of the Big Wind Kite Factory.

Maunaloa seems deserted on quiet Sundays like this. I skip down the stairs of the front porch, whistling. I'm heading to Omar's house. On the smaller roads running perpendicular to the main street, trucks and cars are parked in front of the houses. But no one's hanging out in their yards. And there aren't any kids galavanting around the hood. Maunaloa looks like a beautiful, tropical ghost town. Then I get this funny feeling. Like naseeb is lurking in the red hibiscus shrubs waiting to pounce. I don't like it. So I ignore it. Instead I follow Bob Marley's recommendation—the one I heard on the radio a few minutes ago—to *Lively Up Yourself*. It works.

I've been plugging away on my new rap, "Love and War." I got the idea last Monday when I was at Hale O Lono. Monday was October

28th. What happened two years ago on that day devastated the entire island. No one on Moloka'i will ever forget it. It's the day that Aloha Island Air flight 1712 returning from Maui crashed into the side of the cliffs near Halawa valley. All twenty people on board—including Molokai High students and staff—were instantly killed. Since we only have one high school on the island, we have to travel to neighbor islands to compete for sports or other school events. There was a bunch of MHIS teams on Maui that weekend. I was there for a math team tournament. There were at least three or four flights heading back to Moloka'i at different times during the day. Many of us traded boarding passes at the Kahalui Airport. It could have been any of us on flight 1712. Sunday morning October 29, 1989, I was at Hale O Lono catching papio with my dad. That's where we heard it on the radio.

Each year on that day I'm pretty sure everyone on the island does something to commemorate the victims. Last year I went down to Hale O Lono by myself to pay tribute. I decided to do that again this year. Sitting on the rocky sand, the ocean was dark blue and calm in the harbor. I thought about my classmates. What would they be doing if things had turned out differently? I thought about their families. I thought about how much they've lost. How did they cope? How are they now? My mind wandered to other kinds of loss. Then to loss that women in my family have suffered. That's how "Love and War" was born.

Six days later it's done. It chronicles the struggles of multiple generations of women in my family. Including my mom. I want it to be perfect for the next 4eva Flowin' production. Omar agreed to give me an honest critique of it. I hurry ahead, excited to get to his house and spit my rhyme.

Practicing in front of Mark doesn't work. My genuine rehearsal attempts with him unavoidably go from rapping a few lines to giggling to making out. Not that I'm complaining.

Especially since I've kinda figured out how to freeze the yucky Dad thoughts and the fear. I was so tired of not being able to get my kiss on with Mark that I decided to try to fix it myself. I did some research at the public library and found some books, one about panic attacks. Super helpful. Now I can usually stop the panic before it gets out of control. That means more uninterrupted kiss time.

Oh yeah.

But dang. Now I can't get enough of Mark's lips. I want to make out with him all the time. I even got my first hickey. I covered it up with a bandana. Just like Samantha on *Who's the Boss*?

It gets better. A couple of days ago, Halloween night to be exact, Mark said he loved me. I'll never forget the scene. Caesar and Cleopatra at the wharf. Sitting in the open bed of Caesar's black Chevy 1500 4X4 lifted truck. Sharing hot bread. Warm butter and cinnamon softness under the starry night sky. Caesar, regal in his purple toga, wraps his arm around the majestic Cleo. He looks deep into her black-lined eyes and says she's the first girl he's ever loved. Besides his mom. Cleo drags him into his truck and they make out like Caesar's leaving for Rome the next day. All the while Cleo's thinking, *It's funny, Caesar, you're the first guy I've ever loved. Besides my dad.*

I turn right onto Mark's street and remind myself that I'm going to Omar's place for serious business, not to Mark's for monkey business.

From out of nowhere the sound of a woman's voice stops me

dead in my tracks. It's not the typical "Eh, Junior boy, where you stay?" or "Oh, da pahty was good fun." No. It's not the voice of a local woman. I try to pinpoint the location, inspecting all the houses and parked trucks and cars on the street. My eyes get to Omar's house. No one in sight yet. Then I turn my head to Mark's house next door. That's when I see her. I give her the once over. Probably thirty. Her long blonde hair is pulled back in a high ponytail. She's wearing a tight white tank top with "Los Angeles" printed on the front in silver cursive. And I know exactly why she's wearing it. The girl leads with her huge, round boobs. Seriously, she's got the biggest mammary glands I've ever seen. Her cleavage pours out and reminds me of a big 'ole butt on her chest. But the kutri doesn't have any junk in her trunk. I decide her triple D's must be fake. No skinny girl with a flat butt can have boobs that big.

I look down at my chest. It seems even flatter than usual in comparison to her fake ass monstrosities. So distracted by her silicone, I almost forget about where she's standing—Mark's doorstep.

NO! NO NO NO!

My enthusiasm crumbles.

Mark walks onto the porch. He gives her the gorgeous smile that's supposed to be for me. He leans down and throws his arms around her, pulling her close. Then he delivers a long, deep kiss.

That's supposed to be for me, too.

He pulls his lips away.

Finally.

She steps off the porch and says, "Bye, Mark." Flirty to the max. Then she blows him a kiss and saunters unsteadily toward the street.

I duck behind Omar's truck. Boob girl gets into a red Ford Fiesta, obviously a rental, and drives off. The car skids as it turns onto the main street.

Mark yawns, stretches, then goes back in his house. He swings the door behind him. It slams shut, startling me.

Crazy emotions swirl. Crazy jealous. Crazy sad. Crazy hurt. I clench my fists. My tears, like my mood, salty. I picture lifting Omar's truck above my head and smashing it into Mark's house, screaming every curse word I know. In English and Gujarati.

Then I imagine banging my head on a wall. A concrete wall.

I'm about to sprint back to my truck so I can get out of here. And descend into solo despair. By chance I notice an old, rusty navy blue Ford pickup. It reminds me of Stan Lee. What would he do in a situation like this? Simple. He'd march up to Mark's house and call his cheating butt out.

Thanks, Ol' Seoul.

I stomp through Mark's front gate and pound my fist on his door. He's grinning when he opens it.

"Expecting boob queen? Huh? Huh?" I manage to blurt before the blubbering begins. "You said you love me!" I sob while I hammer my fists on his chest. He takes it. And I keep going. "You slept with her, didn't you? I can't compare to her!"

Not quite the strong Stan Lee style unemotional confrontation I was hoping for. Better than nothing I guess. The tears keep streaming. I realize this feels exactly as terrible as when I saw my dad at Kanemitsu's with Wendy. My mind goes dark. Fast. My self-worth gets put in the rack. My brain tortures it. Both Dad and Mark said they loved me. But they both found another girl to love without telling me. What's wrong with me? How else can I explain this two-for-two record? I'm a worthless piece of chee. I hate myself. Who could possibly love me?

"Ra-Rani," he stammers. He drops his head into his palms and shifts awkwardly on his feet. Then he lifts his head and shakes it. "That was nothing. She doesn't mean anything to me. You—you're my girl." He reaches for my shoulder.

I push his hand away. "Don't touch me."

"Come in, Rani. Let's talk about this. Please," he says, stepping to the side and waving for me to enter.

"No way, you jerk!" Then I change my mind. I push him aside with all my strength. He stumbles back. I march into his house without taking off my slippers. Knocking my knuckles on my head I pace in circles in his living room. I try to figure out what to do. All I can picture is him and boob girl gettin' it on in here. The tears keep coming. I bury my face into my hands. When I lift my head I realize I'm sitting on his couch. I imagine them making out on the sofa. The way we have. My anger erupts again. I lean forward and push all the junk on his messy coffee table off. With one big sweep of my arms, magazines, beer cans, half-eaten musubi, cigarettes, a lighter, a straw with a burned edge, and a small glass pipe go flying onto the carpet. I jump up from the sofa and stomp out of his house.

Mark grabs my shoulder as I'm about to step onto the porch. "I'm sorry. So sorry. I love you, Rani! What can I do to make it up to you?" he asks. His somber eyes are fixed on me.

I give him a piece of my broken mind. "Nothing. And I was actually gonna go all the way with you. Not anymore! You don't love me. You only care about yourself. You're just like my dad." I back away from him. I can't help but wonder if my mom's felt this horrible.

"You had me so fooled. I can't believe I thought you were my boyfriend. I'm such a gullible dumbass." Then I get all up in his face and declare, "I'll make it easy for you—leave me alone."

My first straight-up rejection of anyone. I thought it would feel more empowering to stand up for myself. But right now I feel crappy. I turn and jet. But not before I hear Mark say, "I still want you, Rani!"

As I race off, I catch sight of Omar standing in his doorway.

LOVE SUPREME

Ken. That's Mark. And Barbie. That's the L.A. bimbo.

I found my old Barbie dolls in the storage room downstairs. And mom's sewing needles. Mom saves everything.

"I hope you feel this," I say out loud. I stab the needles into the dolls.

First into Barbie's unnaturally large boobs. *You stupid harlot.*

Then into Ken's fake smile. *Who's smiling now, you no good ghadhedo?*

Pathetic bawling ensues as voodoo doll therapy takes an unanticipated turn for the worse. I accept the naseeb Mattel has set forth—that it's Ken and Barbie. Now and forever. Not Ken and a blonde-buzz-cut-flat-chested-Indian teen.

Besides the dolls, I'd grabbed the telephone handset from the kitchen before I confined myself to my room. Just in case I wanted to call Mark and give him an earful. Which I decide is in order now, tears or no tears. Wailing, I pick up the handset.

But before I get a chance to dial, I hear a knock. Mom opens my bedroom door and asks, "Suu thhayu?" My eyes converge on her furrowed brow and it puts me off. I clam up.

"Nothing." I stare at the carpet.

"Play some piano. That'll make you feel better."

Really? That's all you have to say?

I peek at her without lifting my head. Her face has softened. I force my eyes back down. "Tried it. It didn't." Even though I hadn't. Recently I'd vowed never to play piano again. It'd been for Dad anyway. He's gone. So is my incentive to play.

I'm not sure how long she stands there. Watching me. Waiting. It seems like forever. All I can do is get more irritated.

Finally she says, "Well, if you want to talk, I'll be in the kitchen for another hour. Then I have to go back to the store."

The warmth in her tone jolts me out of annoyance.

You've been waiting for Mom to communicate with you like this!

Hearing about the store adds a familiar layer of guilt.

She's still working 24/7. If it's not at the store or restaurant, it's at home. Why was I cold? I'm an idiot.

I hear the door close. When I look up, she's gone. I'm alone in my four walls again. I wonder why it's so hard for me to be nice to Mom when she's being nice to me. It's like there's a switch inside me that gets flipped one way or the other depending on how she talks to me. And I can't control the switch.

The phone rings. I stare at the handset. I groan.

"Hello." My tone is cold and bored.

"Rani?"

"Yeah."

"It's Dad."

"I know."

"How are you, betta?"

"Fine." His spurious niceness makes my body writhe in disgust.

"Did you talk to Mom about Wendy and me moving in?"

No way. Fo' real?

What is it with these guys? Within the span of two hours, both Mark and my dad try to get me to do what's good for them. They're like puppet masters pulling on my strings. Maybe it's my fault. It's been me who's gone along with their commands. My mood plummets to a new low. I hang up the phone without answering him.

Nothing matters.

The phone rings again, but I ignore it. I open my notebook and start writing with urgency, trying to slow my downward spiral into total anhedonia.

The Rule of Men

I love you = I'm going to cheat on you because my needs come first.

My Rules

I'm a worthless piece of crap.

I hate myself.

Brain slap.

Stop wallowing and do something about it, Rani.

The phone rings yet again. This time I seize the handset, rip open my bedroom door, and fling the phone down the hallway. I slam my door shut and get back to writing. Now I'm determined to convert my melancholy and self-pity into a new rap.

190

I start laying down the words and something extraordinary happens. My brain synthesizes my ordeals in a new way. It forms amalgams of my relationships and my experiences. Mark and my dad merge. Boob girl becomes the girl that this man's world expects. The girl with whom I always compare myself. My thoughts flow and ripen into something tangible. Many hours—and tissues—later, I finish it.

LOVE SUPREME

<u>Verse 1</u>

It's myself I can't love.

Sure enough when he gets a hold of

my heart, it melts like wax.

And it feels like I'm on track

to find some inner peace

and cease the heartbreak, piece by piece.

An illusion of love confusing

my mind, causing my delusion.

If he thinks I'm worthy—I must be.

If he's my devotee,

I must be

earnin' the highest degree

in the school of love. But help me.

I still feel broken—amputee.

Keep lookin' to the outside to find

someone kind to convince my mind

that I am good enough.

I check the flow of the first verse. When I rap the last four lines, I ache in my core. Tears push themselves out of my eyes. See, I intended to write something that would make me—or any girl that heard it—feel better. Oddly, after I banged out the rhymes, I got more than an emotional remedy. I found unanticipated meaning in the words. Meaning that I hadn't intended. Almost like my inner self knew the real reasons things were happening in my life. That's why the words flowed easily. I grab another tissue and blot a couple of tears that drop onto my notebook. Some of the word smudge.

I still feel broken—amputee.

Dad.

Keep lookin' to the outside to find
someone kind to convince my mind
that I am good enough.

Mark.

A rush of anger strangles the sadness. I slam my notebook shut and push it away. The anger squeezes harder. I grab the notebook and fling it across my room. I watch it fly. It lands open, cover side up. It lays there, patiently waiting for me to get myself together. To get back to it. I take a couple of deep breaths and walk over. I sink onto the carpet. Then I slide my feet back. Lying prone, I flip the notebook over and find my slam poem staring at me. It lures me. I reread the poem. And now I'm finding unexpected meaning in these words as well.

A dark web of emotional and sexual merging.

Honestly I don't know why I wrote this line a month ago. It just flowed out of me. But today those eight words hurl the truth, kicking and screaming, into my face.

Closeness. Mind union. Love. My room. Private touch. Body union. Love.

That's how I learned to feel love. Because he wanted to do everything with me—to me, I felt loved. Sometimes, love meant secrets. The more secrets, the more he wanted me. Loved me.

Dad hurts Mom. *But I love you, Rani.*

Dad wants me. Alone in my room. *But I love you, Rani.*

I feel like I'm on a tiny boat at the edge of a giant whirlpool. It sucks me and all my tears down. My eyes are wide open and dry. I turn the pages back to "Love Supreme" and scan the rest of the rhyme as I capsize.

<u>Chorus</u>

A diamond in the rough,

but my heart be callin' my bluff,

cuz I am still empty.

<u>Verse 2</u>

Where does it come from,

my self-worth, and will it succumb

to society's beating and mistreating

that keeps me competing

with other girls instead of defeating

their mind-numbing greetings?

We so busy with the religion of beauty

and lookin' perfect—heavy duty.

Brainwashed into worryin' about the color of my lip gloss

instead of bein' a boss.

I was confused by all of this

promise of bliss that exists

in the scalpel kiss

of plastic surgery that I missed

my step and fell into the abyss

of low self-esteem, covered up in their silicone schemes.

And now I dream of love supreme.

Chorus

A diamond in the rough,

but my heart be callin' my bluff,

cuz I am still empty.

Verse 3

I gotta look inward

to escape this absurd

prison that keeps my heart

captive and makes it hard to start

lovin' myself. Left in the dark

where do I begin when

I never got it as a kid—

love by example—that was forbid.

So I looked to others

only to get smothered

by the superficial love drug,

needing a daily injection in my blood.

I gotta find my higher power,

in my own ivory tower

of unconditional love.

Prove to myself

bit by bit

that I'm worth it.

Chorus

A diamond in the rough,

but my heart be callin' my bluff,

cuz I am still empty.

I press my hand into the page with the third verse. Closing my eyes, I try to use a Jedi mind trick to make the positive intentions my new reality.

It doesn't work. I don't believe I'm worth it.

What I am is empty and scared.

Dad doesn't want me. He doesn't want me alone. To show my mind and body that he loves me. That I'm worth it.

I'm worthless because Dad doesn't want me.

Then I remember. Mark said he still does.

THE PEACE OF THE ROSES

Two days, six unreturned cajoling messages, one poem, and a dozen red roses later, I'm still not going to forgive Mark. As far as I'm concerned, it's over. I crumple up the card with the poem. I'm about to toss it into the trash but my hands defy my brain. I end up smoothing out the card then press it against my beating heart. My lips join the revolt. I smile. My eyes decide to get in on the insurrection. I reread the poem.

Rani,

these coming days

I'll strive to amaze

and leave you in a daze

with my love haze.

But first this bouquet to show you I've been

repenting and lamenting,

and now I'm presenting

this

apology

and hope you'll agree

to still have me.

—Mark

P.S. Dinner tonight? I'll pick you up at 7.

The hand-eye-mouth coordinated mutiny is victorious. My resolve weakens. Then it slips away like the setting sun I'm watching from the front porch of the store.

Ok. Just one more hang. For closure.

Twenty minutes later, Mark pulls up in his Chevy. It's all shiny. I can tell he washed and waxed it today. I try to muster anger. No use. All I feel are butterflies. He hops out and stands on the foot rail. He calls out, "Hey, queenie!"

Frown, Rani. Come on, frown!

Can't do it. Instead I manage a bizarre frown-smile hybrid. As I climb down the steps, I shake my head. I'm frustrated at my tendency to be dazzled by his charisma. He jumps off the foot rail and walks around to the passenger side. Holding the door open for me, he gives me a peck on the cheek.

"Kaluakoi, ok?"

"Yep," I say, masking the burgeoning elation with as much expressionlessness as possible. Why couldn't I have inherited Mom's poker face?

He drives and I'm silent. Neither of us mentions boob girl. He rambles on about work and ideas for 4eva Flowin'. His hand finds its way onto my knee and slides up a tad to claim its rightful place under my denim mini skirt. He's acting like nothing happened.

The resort parking lot is filled mostly with rentals plus a few local cars and trucks. I notice Pono's 4runner. Mark opens my door and extends his hand to help me down. We stroll to the restaurant and he puts his arm around me. Then he pulls me close and we walk attached at the hip. "Did I mention you look beautiful?"

"No, you didn't. And yes, I do," I say, suppressing a giggle and pouting instead.

He stops and steps in front of me. Suddenly it's like he's Rhett Butler and I'm Scarlett O'Hara. He puts his hands on my shoulders and draws me to him. He gazes down at me. My head angles back so I'm looking up at him. I can tell he just smoked and the smell of Salem Lights on his breath excites me. He lifts my chin with his left hand. I think he's about to tell me what Rhett told Scarlett in that scene where they were standing exactly like this. But instead he whispers, "I can't stand the thought of not doing this ever again." He holds my face in his hands, leans down, and kisses my lips softly.

I forgive you, Mark.

Geez, Rani, you're so easy.

The restaurant is packed with tourists. Mostly couples. We get seated at the best table. The one in the corner with the most breathtaking ocean view. Probably because Mark knows pretty much everyone that works at Kaluakoi. There's a bottle of Moet & Chandon on ice beside the table. My eyes are riveted to the placid ocean not far on the other side of these ceiling to floor windows. Right off the bat, Mark pops the cork of the champagne and pours me a glass. I try my first sip of bubbly. It tickles the back of my throat, but tastes crisp and refreshing. I glance at the bottle. It looks expensive. I know I should probably drink it slow. But I'm nervous so I down the entire glass.

Mark refills my glass and says, "I'm so sorry about the other day. It'll never happen again." Stroking my hand on the table he says, "I don't want to lose you. I love you."

"I love you too." My eyes fill with briny regret. "Don't hurt me again," I admonish through my tears. I take a gulp of champagne.

"I won't. I promise." He reaches over and with his thumb wipes away one of my tears. "Don't cry."

I blot my eyes with my dinner napkin, but the tears keep coming. I'm about to bury my face in the napkin and bawl when I spot Pono's reflection in the window. He's walking towards us.

Uh-oh.

I stop crying. I lay the napkin back across my lap. By now he's at our table, filling our water glasses.

"Hi Pono," Marks says, turning his head towards Pono. Mark's lips are pressed together and one side comes up.

"Hey Mark, hey Rani," Pono mumbles. His lips move up slightly, but there aren't any wrinkles around his eyes.

They stare at each other for a couple of seconds. Mark with his smug smile and Pono with his fake smile. My eyes move back and forth between the two of them. Like I'm watching a tennis match.

"Sorry I can't stay and talk. It's super busy," Pono practically growls.

"It's ok. No worries," Mark says.

What the heck is going on?

Pono picks up my glass and pours in the icy water. Some of it splashes onto the table, but I make like I don't notice. "Thanks, Pono," I say. I try to catch his eye.

"No problem," he mutters, not looking at me. Then he whips around and stomps off. I watch him disappear into the kitchen.

Pono's mad. I know why. The guilt starts a tug of war in my mind: Pono's warnings about Mark versus Mark's attention. But then the champagne hits me and I can't help but join Mark's team. Pono's side has no chance. I lean back in my chair and look at Mark. The tears from a little while ago seem like a distant memory. Like the champagne, his eyes intoxicate me. I'm aware that he's about to wine and dine me into capitulation. With my full consent. Well, with my underage, drunk consent.

Our food—and more champagne—arrives. We both got the surf and turf, potatoes, and asparagus. I'm famished and I scarf down the mahi and ribeye as I listen to Mark recount stories about his youthful escapades. The champagne turns into a love potion. I feel more and more enamored of Mark. He's still working on his steak when I push my plate slightly away. It's practically licked clean.

"Damn girl. You eat like a horse," Mark says. He chuckles and nods his head in approval.

"Uh-huh. And this mare wants dessert," I say with a sultry voice, lowering my glasses down my nose with one hand and eyeing him provocatively. When the waitress stops by our table, I order the chocolate cake with chocolate ice cream. It arrives quickly and it's humongous. I devour it before Mark's done with his dinner. We finish our champagne as we wait for the check. When it arrives, Mark pulls out his wallet and pays cash. I'm not sure how much everything costs, but there's a big pile of twenties on the small tray. Then he gets up and continues his gentlemanly behavior by pulling out my chair for me. I stand. He takes my hand. He whispers in my ear, "Time for my dessert."

The almost four glasses of Moet & Chandon I consumed make

me giggle. "Masala chocolate, I hope." Breathy and soft like Marilyn Monroe.

"Dark, spicy, and luscious." He licks his lips and stares at me all sexy.

The banter ends with me because I crack up. I'm laughing hysterically. He wraps his arm around me and hauls my wasted ass out of the restaurant.

Not fast enough.

Because as he's leading me out, my dad creeps up from behind us and throws one arm around each of us. Like we're all chums. He smells liquored up. Whiskey, I think. "Rani, I see you and Mark are..." Dad almost yells but then stops himself. He kisses my cheek. Wet and sloppy. Then it's like time stands still and everyone in the place is gawking at us, their breath sucked in as they wait to see what happens.

"Dad..."

Mark steps out of Dad's arm. Then he walks around and lifts Dad's other arm off me. "Pradip, don't."

Dad glances around the restaurant. I hold my breath hoping Dad will walk away and leave us alone.

"You were mine first, Rani," he says, his voice sharp but hushed. Then he turns and ambles away.

I watch him walk back to the bar. That's when I see Wendy sitting on a barstool. Dad whispers something into her ear. They both look at Mark and me for a second, then turn away.

I exhale slowly. "Close call," I say to Mark.

"Yeah. Let's get out of here before your dad changes his mind and I have to kick his ass."

My eyelids droop and my balance is off. I focus on walking straight in the parking lot. Mark laughs at me as I stumble. I'm relieved when we make it to his truck. He starts the engine and I search through his CDs. I pick Naughty by Nature and teehee as I skip to *O.P.P.* I crank it. Then I proceed to rap every word of it like the ill MC I think I am in my plastered state.

The lights are on at Omar's house when we pull up in front of Mark's.

"Let's get Omar and hang in your house," I garble.

"Naw, let's just you and me hang out. I want you all to myself."

Arm in arm we walk into his house. I fumble with the straps on my sandals and it seems like it takes me forever to get them off. I follow him into the living room. He turns on a sleek metal lamp, lighting the area just dimly. I notice that he cleaned up his crib. Everything seems neat and tidy. The coffee table is bare. All the boob girl clutter is gone. The white carpet is spotless. He sits down on the angular brown leather sofa and pats the space next to him. I stumble over and flop down. My eyes fix on the three evenly spaced modern paintings on his wall. They remind me of a life-size Rorschach test. I tilt my head to the side, trying to determine what image I see.

Today, definitely the Phallic Rock.

I cover my mouth with my hand and laugh.

He leans back. "How're you doing over there?" He eases me over so I'm nestled against him.

"Rilly good." I give him a dippy smile with my eyes half closed. Then I nuzzle my face into his burly chest. He smells like Drakkar Noir. I breathe him in. Long and slow.

"Come here." He pulls me onto him. He takes off my glasses very slowly. "Let me look at chu, girl." Then he runs his hands up and down my smooth, bare legs, now on either side of him. "Damn Sutra, you've got legs for miles."

He becomes a European conqueror, fully exploring his South Asian conquest. His lips skim my forehead. My cheek. My neck. His hands, like feather fans, lightly brush my arms. My spine. Red blouse and crimson bra become cabernet stains on the carpet. The front of my body, his canvas. He glosses over it with his velvet tongue.

I close my eyes and lean my head back. Love sounds unexpectedly come out of my mouth, arousing me more. Then he hikes my skirt up and firmly grips my waist. One of his hands drifts down.

"Oh my god, Rani." Hand lower. "You're the..." he utters, breathing heavy, "...the hottest woman."

Woman? I'm only sixteen.

"I love you, Rani baby."

Woman or baby?

Fingers slide under to dewy softness. I arch my back, gasping. "You're mine, Rani, only mine."

Really? What about boob girl? She's the woman. Did you tell her the same things?

The thought of Barbie sobers me up. Fast. Imagining Mark doing all this to Barbie kills my erotic vibe immediately. "Mark, stop. Please." I sit up and pull my skirt down. My thoughts jump, I can't stop the leapfrog in my mind. I know he said sorry. I want to believe his promise that he'll never hurt me again. But I've learned that words are easy to say.

With his words, Dad promised me the world. But all he ended up delivering was misery.

Now Mark is laying on the "I love you's," promises, and tantalizing caresses.

But the bitter taste of both their two-timing lingers.

Mark's head drifts back onto the sofa. He catches his breath. His eyes bore through the ceiling. "It's ok." He's working hard to keep his voice in check. Trying to sound patient.

It's his stonewalled face that makes me feel in the wrong. I turn towards him and put my hand on his. "So sorry, Mark." I try to show him sincerity with my eyes.

"Forget it, Rani." He doesn't look at me.

I feel super guilty. I don't know what to do. So I sit there. At some point I whisper, "I better get home."

He drives me home. We don't speak the entire time. For twenty-one miles, the *Rule of Men* is on constant replay in my mind.

SCHOOLED

On most days, the banyan in front of school is my safe zone where I hide, retreat, and avoid. Not today. Pono and Omar are standing under the tree. Their hardcore b-boy stances seem to forebode trouble. I cross the street from the parking lot to the school, slowing down as I approach them. I swear the outrage on their faces grows the closer I get. Instinctively I want to flee. I turn around and hustle back to my 4runner.

"Rani!" Omar hollers.

I stop. My back's still to them. I let my head drop.

Oh no. Can't escape this.

I take a deep breath. Then I pivot and schlep from the parking lot to the banyan. As soon as I'm within earshot, Omar shouts, "What the hell, Rani?"

I know I'm about to get the third degree. And I have an inkling it's about Mark. I hang my head and avoid their eyes. "Hi guys," I murmur.

"Where do I start?" Omar challenges. He's shaking his head like he's disappointed big time.

"What're you doing, Rani?" Pono demands. The dirty look he gives me makes my heart hurt.

My pissed off big brothers go ahead and scold the living crap out of me. And me the naughty little sister cowers. Tears fill my eyes.

"Let's see if I can sum it up," Pono says. By now his face is almost red so I can tell he's reached the boiling point. "I warn you about Mark. That he's a druggie. That it's weird for an old guy to hang out with a high schooler. But you ignore all that." He stops and turns his back to me and it dawns on me that my dad should be the one yelling at me about all this. Not my homies. Pono inhales sharply and faces me again. "He cheats on you. Then he buys you some flowers. Takes you to dinner. And you go home with him?" By now Pono's yelling and waving his arms.

And I'm sobbing.

Even his arms are mad.

But it's his eyes that rip into my soul. Even though he's acting mad, his eyes are filled with agony.

I grab Pono's hand and whimper, "I'm sorry. Sorry I didn't listen."

He yanks his hand away. He narrows his eyes. And flares his nostrils a bit. His lips are tightly pressed. So tight that they're quivering.

Omar continues the rebuke. "I know Mark. I've lived next to the guy ever since he moved to Moloka'i. Yeah, it's great that he started 4eva Flowin'. But he's a mack." He pauses, and exhales loudly. Then he softens his voice and says, "Rani, I've seen choke girls go in and out of his house."

More than one Barbie? Choke even?

Confusion festers. But I put the kibosh on their anti-Mark sentiments. I appeal Mark's case to the judge and jury. I pull myself together, stand up straight and put my hands on my hips. "No, it's not like that. He said sorry and I think he really meant it."

They exchange irked glances. Omar rolls his eyes.

I go on, only now I'm pleading. "He says he loves me. We didn't have sex. He didn't pressure me or anything." I contort the center of my face because I can't believe I'm explaining these details to them.

Pono lets out a frustrated sigh and takes a step back. Then he drags his fingers through his hair and says, "I can't take watching you crash and burn. You're killing me." His eyes are moist. He jams his hands in his pockets and stalks off.

My heart breaks as I watch him walk away.

So this is how it feels to hurt someone you care about.

And let me tell you that it ain't a good feeling.

I wonder if my dad felt like this.

I'm overwhelmed. All I can think to do is go over my record of straight-up Stan Lee style rejections.

1. Stan Lee to Rani

2. Rani to Mark (recently, overturned)

3. Pono to Rani

I glimpse at Omar. He lowers his head and plods away.
Et tu, Omar?

4. Omar to Rani.

TRUE COLORS

I'm about to explode. Turns out the third verse of "Love and War" doesn't work and 4eva' Flowin' is tonight. My plan was to fix it today because I was supposed to be off.

But no.

Lani, Colt, and Auntie Maile can't work today. Today's freight day at the wharf. And there's no way I'm gonna let Mom unload all those heavy boxes by herself. She'd break her back. Plus, we've got extra merchandise and food coming in today's shipment because we're prepping for Thanksgiving. That means the hauling and stocking will take all day. No downtime on the porch to write. Oh, and my poor mom will have to run the lunch service at the restaurant by herself because Shawn can't make it until the dinner service.

And we're in this predicament all because my dad bailed on us.

You suck, Dad. Did you stop and think that you'd be leaving your wife and kid to manage two labor-intensive businesses on their own. No. Of course not. A selfish bastard can't do that.

I have to find a way to calm down. Because right now I'm seething. If I can't settle down, I might mess up my performance tonight. I take a deep breath, determined to chill out.

We're heading to the wharf. Mom's at the wheel, and I'm in the passenger seat. Fortunately, by the time we reach town, I've defused myself. We turn left onto the long, straight road that juts into Kaunakakai harbor. Sunlight streams into the flat bed's cabin and Ravi Shankar's entrancing sitar fills our ears. I angle my head so that I can't see the road. It's like we're skimming the surface of the serene Pacific. For a second, the juxtaposition of the vast sky, open ocean, and sitar takes me somewhere else. Somewhere peaceful. I close my eyes and I'm in India, floating on a river boat in Kerala.

The truck makes a beeping sound as my mom backs up to the loading zone. Reality strikes and my eyes jerk open. The truck bounces as the forklift driver adjusts the palates of merchandise on the bed. I look around the dock. Wharf employees dressed in jeans, t-shirts, and hard hats zip about like worker ants. I shift sideways and watch some of them board the huge Matson vessel. People waiting for their cargo stand around the harbor office. Smoking. Chatting and laughing. That's when I notice Mom and I are the only females here.

After all the palates are loaded, we begin the drive to Maunaloa. Neither one of us has said a word since we climbed into the truck at home. I rest my elbow on the window sill and try to get lost in the scenery that goes by. Maybe it'll help me reach some kind of nirvana. Unfortunately, by the time we pass the turn off for Kala'e Road, my tranquil mind has become an agitated mess of loneliness and guilt. I'd been trying to think about the third verse. Ways to make its flow more def. But my thoughts don't want to do that. So now I'm sitting here obsessing about the far-reaching ramifications of Dad's abandonment. And about what Pono and Omar said the other day at school. And about how much I don't want to—no, can't—lose Mark. And if friendship and love is supposed to be this complicated. Suddenly, I feel drained. I sigh. It must have been louder than I intended because Mom turns her head and glances at me. I keep my eyes fixed out the window.

She looks back at the road. "Rani?"

I don't say anything at first, still wandering in my head. Adrift in the battling words of two boys and two men.

"Rani?" This time she taps my shoulder.

"Huh?" I don't look at her. Normally, I'd be stunned that she was initiating talk with me, that she was touching me. And I'd be trying to figure out why she was doing all that. But right now I don't have the energy to analyze her motivations. I close my eyes again and attempt to clear all the male opinions dominating my brain. I sigh. Again. Louder than I meant. Again.

"Rani, suu thhayu?"

"Nothing."

"Nah, khaasuu thhayu che. Tell me."

There's no way I'm about to explain everything about Mark, Pono, and Omar. I know she wouldn't get it. She might even get mad.

And though I've seen Dad's true colors, I can't help but think if things were like they'd been a year ago, I could've told him what was going on. He would've told me how to handle the situation. Problem solved. Case closed. Most likely, he would have directed me to stop being friends with all three of them. He'd say I only needed him.

Even though now I know that's whack, it would've been way easier than this mental turmoil.

"Tell me," Mom says again.

"I miss Dad," I blurt out. I regret the words as soon as they flit out of my mouth. I slide closer to the door and press my hands into the seat under my thighs. I peek at her, cringing inside. I'm expecting her to either cry or get pissed. Maybe even start screaming something about wanting to die.

She does none of those things. Instead, she pats my head and with a tranquil face, she says, "I know, betta."

Though I don't move a muscle, I'm freaking out inside.

Is Mom trying to show me her true colors?

LOVE AND WAR

Mo'omomi's packed. The number of hip hop enthusiasts that have surfaced at the dunes tonight is way more than last month. And there are a handful of girls.

I skip up the side stairs onto the stage and grab the mic from Mark. "Yo, yo, yo! How's everyone feelin' tonight?" I bellow. They thunder in approval. I strut to the center of the stage. Leaning slightly back. Swaying side to side. The crowd open fires on me with their spirit and vigor. It's hard not to vibe off their energy. It forces me to amp up my swag walk. And the crowd responds with hoots and hollers.

I'm about to drop one of the best raps I've ever written. Tonight's about the women in my family. My mom. Lalita ba. Agneya ba. And so many others. I inhale the crisp, salty air. It's like smelling salts. I nod at Skittles and he launches the haunting voice of Nusrat Fateh Ali Khan in *Mustt Mustt (Massive Attack Remix)*. Slowly he fades the vocals and lays out my beat. And it brims with robust Bally Sagoo bhangra samples. My Indian soul is aflame. I watch the crowd get enchanted by the first ever Indo-Pakistani influenced beats at Mo'omomi. Then like a satguru, I bust out my rhyming sutras.

You're finally free of his chains—invisible.

Emotional abuse, unseen—permissible.

Statue like, enslaved soul—survivin'.

Isolated wife, his alone—he's deprivin'.

He got no love for her—cuz his ego lackin'.

Wife a commodity—mirror crackin'.

Had a kid to appease the masses—curry culture.

Raise her as your boo—perverse nurture...

I enunciate each word of my rhyme clearly, deliberately. Almost by syllable. Because I want the delivery to be striking. As I'm spitting the first verse, all I can think about is my mom and her life. I wish she was here tonight.

The setting sun covers the crowd in a film of orange and yellow. The colorful, urban-fashioned hip hoppers remind me of a polychrome Lite-Brite. I get to the second verse and tell the story of how bad Agneya ba had it back in the day.

...and three generations back it's worse.

Unfaithful man—her curse.

Her solution—leave the situation.

His solution was her live cremation

Fire burning in his Indian eyes.

Demise covered up in his lies...

Then something amazing happens. I start to feel part of something big. Something universally feminine. Like all my women ancestors enter my consciousness. They root for me as I lay out the truth about their oppression. The next two verses come out with more gusto. Nearing the end of the fourth verse, I throw a lyrical grenade on the crowd.

...descended from this slaughter,

me and a thousand other daughters.

Navigating ancient rivers—muddy waters.

Taboo subject they hope we forget,

but it makes us hate ourselves—playin' Russian roulette.

How can we expect more

when we refuse to explore

our—own—war?

And the crowd reels from the impact. I close it out.

Kama sutra ain't all I'm good for.

Kids I bore, but there's so much more.

What you don't know

is that I'm settlin' the score.

It ain't all fair in love and war.

It's pau and the applause is ardent. I lift my head to the sky and offer a peace sign. My props to my mom and all my Gujju women ancestors. The moment is emotionally heavy. I feel drained. I wipe the sweat from my brow and let things settle for a couple of seconds before exiting the stage.

Instinctively, I look for Pono and Omar. Pono is nowhere in sight. Regrettably things still aren't back to normal with Pono and me. He's standoffish. He'll acknowledge me with a chin-up if we pass each other in the hall. But he won't stop to talk. He'll discuss class work. But nothing more. He isn't hanging out with me at lunch. He's acting like Lance did in one of my mom's romance novels. All distant with Julia because she broke his heart.

But I didn't break his heart. It's not like he's in love with me or anything. I know I frustrated him big time. Hurt his feelings. I wish he'd give me a chance to make peace with him.

I spock Omar in the throng. But he's surrounded by three girls. I think he's getting his flirt on! It looks like he's running off at the mouth and the girls are all giggly. Oh! He just put his hand on one of the girl's shoulders. Definitely don't want to cramp his style.

Especially since Omar and me are good. A couple of days after he and Pono gave me an extra large piece of their mind, Omar and I made peace. It happened at school. Omar was walking towards the cafeteria. We exchanged glances. Mine uneasy. His aloof. He did an about face and headed towards the library in a hurry. Avoiding lunch to avoid me. That felt like a sucka punch. Because the blindsiding force of it made this sucka realize that I had to step up my truce-making game.

Imagining a white flag in hand, I quickened my pace. "Omar!" When I was almost behind him I said, "Omar, wait up."

He kept walking with his hands deep in the pockets of his baggy jeans and his head down. The closer I got, the faster his blue and white Adidas high tops seemed to haul him away.

"Come on, Omar. Can I talk to you for a minute?"

He stopped without turning around. "What, Rani?" There was indifference in his tone. His head was up now and I was in awe of his higher than usual hi-top fade. I imagined snapping a photo. A truly artistic first rap album cover for him.

"I'm sorry for being such a dumbass."

He turned around and crossed his arms over images of Posdnuos, Trugoy, and Maseo on his oversized black t-shirt. He and De La Soul stared at me without talking.

"Omar, can we make peace? I miss you. And your clowning."

He inspected my face. I think he was trying to see if I was for real. The loud clock in my mind went tick, tick, tick. It seemed like five minutes passed without either of us saying anything. I couldn't stand the silence any longer so I conceded.

"I'll be careful with Mark," I said.

But inside I knew I couldn't really do it.

The truth is that despite all the undeniable reasons the boys had given me about why I should break up with Mark, I'm hooked. So hooked that I'm willing to overlook the glaring signs of his player status. Besides no one's perfect and he hasn't hurt me since the boob girl drama.

"Please, Omar. Can you forgive me? I'm sorry."

I was about to get down on my knees and beg when he said, "It's ok. You're still my homie." He smiled and that felt better than any amount of applause. "You know what this means, right?" he asked.

"What?"

"Game on for Rani ridicule."

"Bring it!"

"Oh, it's brung," he said, laughing. Then he switched into full on pidgin. "We go grind." We headed back to the cafeteria and he poked at my head. "You was plenny akamai before but now you stay one blonde."

"What? You think I stay lolo jus cuz I one blonde?"

Omar chuckled at my ridiculous attempt to speak pidgin. Even I cringed at its horribleness. I really wanted to fling my arm around his shoulder like we were bros. But I resisted and slapped his arm instead. Things were back to normal.

Mark's voice on the mic brings me back to the present. He's announcing the next MC. As much as I want to be his shadow, I know he's busy. Things are better with us too. He's not distraught about the Kaluakoi night anymore. And I'm over boob girl. I really want to get my hands on him after the show. Then I remember I won't get to hang with him tonight. Something about him being busy with errands because he's leaving tomorrow to visit his mom on Maui. An acrid taste fills my mouth like I swallowed a bitter pill.

So I have no one to chill with for the rest of the show. I find a place at the edge of the crowd. The next performance starts and I try to get lost in the MC's flow. But it's no use. I can't shake the apprehension that's descending on me like a vulture descending on a carcass. I decide to leave early. By the time I reach the path it's after dark. I stumble over a couple of small rocks on the shadowy trek to the parking lot.

Stan Lee emerges on the path. We're face-to-face. It's like a showdown.

He breaks the silence. "There's only one reason you made it onto the crew. You know that, right?" I can't really see his expression but his voice is menacing.

"Yeah. Because I can flow."

"Wrong. It's because Mark wants to hit that," he says. "He's playing you, Sutra. Making you think you're such a good MC, when in fact..." His voice trails off. In the dim starry light, I see him make a lewd thrusting motion with his pelvis.

My face burns. My lacrimal glands go on overdrive.

Don't cry!

Too late, the tears pour.

"Face it, Sutra. You aren't cut out for all this. You're just a little girl in a big man's world." He scoffs. "Run home to Daddy. Oh wait..." He pauses. I feel his icy stare. And then he goes for the jugular. "That's right. Your daddy left you. Yeah, Mark told me."

This isn't Stan Lee rejection. It's Stan Lee aggression. All out war.

It ain't all fair in love and war.

SOCIALLY CONSCIOUS SEXINESS

I thump my fist on my forehead, hoping to knock some sense into my head. I squeeze my temples with my palms. But no matter what brain manipulation methods I try, I can't get anything done on this essay about deforestation in the Amazon. It's Wednesday, the last day of school before Thanksgiving break. I resign myself to the fact that I won't accomplish any work today. I haven't even finished the agenda for our class council meeting later today. Mr. Silvo, our class advisor, will be totally disappointed.

Ugh.

Forget it. I pack up my papers and books and head out of the library. I grasp my stomach because it feels like I'm committing educational seppuku.

This on top of the homie harakiri that's already happened with

Pono. It's worse today. Because today is his eighteenth birthday. I've tried extra hard to reach out to him. Of course I wished him a happy birthday as soon as I saw him. I slipped a birthday card between his books in Nihongo. I wanted him to know that I was thinking about him on his big day. After all, you only become an official adult once.

Besides a fake smile, he didn't respond to my goodwill birthday gestures.

It's recess now so I head to the banyan. When I get to the end of the hall, I see Pono already there, sitting on the shady side. He's reading my card! And smiling! My knees feel a little wobbly as I stand here wondering what to do. That's when I think of Queen Latifah's rap *A King and Queen Creation*. Hearing the words and feeling the beat in my mind, I know what I have to do. Because Pono and I are homies that fit together like dope rhymes and a sick beat. Just like *A King and Queen Creation*.

Backed by the Queen's lyrical wind in my sails, I walk towards Pono. He looks up and shoves the card real quick between his books when he sees me coming. I put on my biggest smile. When I get close, I call out, "Hey, Pono!"

"Hey." He keeps a straight face.

"How are you doing?"

"Good. What's up with you?"

I sit down opposite of him. I stretch my legs and lean back on my hands. "Not much. Looking forward to the break." He doesn't say anything. So I ask, "What are you gonna do over break?" I'm hoping he'll open up a little more if we discuss our mutual disdain of Thanksgiving. It being a one-sided holiday and all. Well, that's how we see it.

Last year Pono and I spoke up in class about the way the holiday is typically portrayed. The rape and pillage of the nation's indigenous peoples is usually left out. And after class that day, Pono and I continued our discussion. He drew parallels to the destruction of the Native Hawaiians.

It dawns on me that my initial crush on Pono grew by leaps and bounds that day last year because—and I distinctly remember thinking this—ain't nothing more sexy than a socially conscious guy who knows his stuff. Remembering that now, my mouth tries to let a giggle escape. But I force my lips to stay shut. Instead I wait for Pono's answer.

He offers a half smile and says, "Not joyously celebrating the slaughter of indigenous people."

I nod. "Me neither."

Then we sit in silence. I stare at the grass. He tinkers with his pen. Neither of us looks at each other.

A minute or so passes like this. Finally he opens his mouth. Without making eye contact he says, "Actually I'm having a birthday party at Papohaku on Saturday. You should come."

YES! Oh happy, happy day!

The euphoria I feel with his invitation is extreme. I know this because *Motownphilly* starts blaring from my mind's boombox. This Boyz II Men song is my ultimate feel-good song. I have to press down on my hands with all my might and focus. Focus on not springing up and doing a Milli Vanilli-Snake-Cabbage Patch-RoboCop-Roger Rabbit-Running Man dance. Doing my best to not put Pono through this because we're not totally G yet, I grit my teeth and say, "Shoots."

LIKE FATHER, LIKE DAUGHTER

The bell rings. School's out for four days! And I'm going to Pono's birthday party! I want to prance to my car and do a little raise the roof dance along the way.

I cross the street to the parking lot. Omar comes running up and grabs my shoulder. "Did you hear about Stan Lee?" His eyes are wide.

"That he hates me? Yes."

He looks around to make sure no one's in range. "No, I mean about his mom?"

"No, what's going on?"

He leans in. "His mom was at Queen's Hospital. In the ICU. They flew her back to Moloka'i General yesterday. She's doing ok now, but it was touch and go for awhile. I just told Pono about it too."

"That's awful! What happened to her?"

"I heard that her junkie boyfriend got crazy high on batu and tried to choke her to death."

"Oh no!"

"Yeah. She's lucky to be alive."

"Did they put that perp in jail?"

"The word is that Stan beat the crap out of him first. Then the cops arrested the guy, all bloody and battered."

"Good for Stan."

Then Omar's face changes. It's as if he's staring through me. He smashes his fist into his open palm and says, "Yeah. I'd do the same thing if someone hurt my mom. Guarenz." He pauses, then looks more somber. Taking a deep breath, his lips in a slight pout, he softly says, "My mom is all I got."

Omar's scared of losing his mom. I get it. I mean the poor guy already lost his dad to prison. "You ok, Omar?"

"People do some fucked up shit when they're high. Blondie, now do you get why Pono and I don't want you to hang out alone with Mark?"

I nod. My good mood is gone. I hang my head as guilt and shame swirl around me. Mark's been visiting his mom on Maul since Sunday so I've had a chance to think. Not only about Pono and Omar's warnings, but also about Stan Lee's crude words. I was hoping that this distance from Mark would help me build up my courage to do the right thing when he gets back. Break up with him.

Nope. Not gonna happen.

And there's no way I'm telling Pono or Omar that I have two secrets about Mark. First, I'm not breaking up with him. Second, I'm planning on going all the way with him. I've tried to convince myself that it's ok not to tell them. In fact, it's not even straight-up lying.

But inside I know lying by omission is still lying.

I've sunk way, way down. Lying to my homies so they'll stay friends with me.

Am I turning into my dad?

BRIGHT FLOWER

It's strange to think that inside these walls people might be battling for their lives. Because from the outside, Moloka'i General Hospital looks like an oasis sitting on top of a Kaunakakai hill. Ocean view and all. Its serene atmosphere and lush manicured greenery is more reminiscent of a small resort than a hospital.

I park my truck in the parking lot and lift the pot with a bright purple orchid out of the old cardboard box on the floor.

There's an important backstory to the orchid. Yesterday was Thanksgiving and Mom prepared our favorite South Indian food. Masala dosa and sambar. With my right hand I tore off a piece of the crispy rice and lentil crepe-like wrap and dipped it in Mom's homemade coconut chutney. I was thinking about what Omar told me about Stan Lee's mom. By then I'd reached the dosa's curried potato filling and Mom noticed me deep in thought.

"You ok, betta?" Her voice and expression matched—both concerned and welcoming. And there hadn't been any drama.

So different than before. Maybe it's who she really is. I remembered the freight day drive to Maunaloa with her on Saturday morning. And maybe like that morning, she's showing me her true colors now. Who she could only get back to being once she escaped Dad. I felt warm inside because I realized that her kindness and sincerity on Saturday might have been why I connected so deeply with my performance of "Love and War" later that night.

Something clicked in me and I accepted her concern without my usual questioning. I decided to take a chance. It was a relief to tell her the whole story about Stan Lee's mom. As my mom listened, she brought her hand to her mouth and pressed it against her lips. Her eyebrows rose and her eyes expanded.

"Khaarob, khaarob, khaarob," she said, shaking her head. She pushed her half-finished plate away. In Gujarati she whispered, "Women suffer at the hands of men in so many ways. Sometimes you don't realize how bad things are until it's too late."

I wasn't sure what to say. But I hustled to find my words because I didn't want to miss any opportunity to have a real conversation with my mom. I thought about her and Dad. I said, "You've suffered because of Dad. You must have felt so alone all these years."

She lifted her eyes and they connected with mine. Without speaking, our eyes communicated something that should've been obvious all along.

We've got each other.

But it seems like we only figured it out that second. I didn't want the moment to end. It felt like we made peace. Maybe even that I could tell her anything.

Still I wasn't sure. And I wasn't about to rock our boat named

Fragile Reconciliation by telling her about how far things had gotten with Mark.

Another lie by omission.

Later that evening, I couldn't stop thinking about Stan Lee's mom. I had to do something. I told my mom that I was planning on visiting her in the hospital the next day. Mom suggested I bring an orchid. She said orchids represent strength. Since Stan Lee's mom had been fighting for her life, my mom thought it was fitting.

I bought the orchid plant this morning from Moana's. Pot in hand, I walk to the entrance of MGH. The hallway is empty and quiet. I find Room 14 and knock on the door. A woman's muffled voice tells me to come in. I push open the door. A beautiful woman is sitting up in the hospital bed. A blanket covers her legs. Her long shiny black hair is pulled to the side under a chin-neck bandage. Her exquisite face belies her age. She looks more like Stan Lee's sister than his mother.

Mrs. Lee smiles at me. I smile back. Then I notice Stan sitting on the other side of her bed. Out of respect for his mom, I suppress the frown that begins to form on my face. I hold my breath.

As soon as he sees me, he leaps up and pushes his folding metal chair back. It tips over and crashes on the floor. He snaps, "What're you doing here, Rani? Who said you could come visit?"

"I'm sorry. I didn't mean to bother you. I just wanted to drop this off for your mom." Turning to his mom I say, "This is for you, Mrs..."

"Call me Lee Myeong Hwa," she says, still smiling.

"Eomma..." Stan Lee grumbles, taking a step towards her.

I put the orchid plant on her bedside table. Like the Eye of Sauron, Stan Lee's evil eye follows me across the room.

"Thank you. You're Rani, right?" she asks.

"Yes."

"The orchids are pretty."

Like you, I think, but don't say. "I'm sorry for everything you've been through. I hope you feel better soon."

"Thank you." She turns her head to Stan Lee. He looks like he's about to blow a gasket. "I didn't know your friends were so kind," she says to him. "You're lucky to have such a good friend."

Stan Lee picks up his chair and sits back down, throwing one arm over the backrest as he turns to stare out the window.

I make eye contact with his mom and say, "I'll go now. Best wishes on a speedy recovery." I wave good bye.

"Thank you, Rani." She waves back with her fingers.

Before the door shuts completely, I hear her speaking in Korean to Stan Lee. I don't understand Korean, but it sounds like a reprimand. I smile to myself.

Ha ha, Stan Lee. Getting scolded like a tiny baby by your mommy.

I'm half way down the hospital corridor when Stan Lee's voice stops me.

"Rani, hold on," he calls out.

I stop and wince. Then I turn around, expecting to get my head chewed off.

I hoist up my glasses, lean my weight on my back leg and cross my arms. I change my mind and put my hands on my hips. I change my mind again and tuck my arms behind my back. Then I stretch my arms up in the air and clasp them behind my head. I keep fidgeting in place, frustrated at my inability to keep the b-girl stance I'd intended. I drop my arms and stand there. Straight and boring.

"Rani," he says, like he's a boss. My boss.

"Yeah?" I put my hands in my pockets and trace a line on the linoleum floor with the tip of my camo Converse high tops.

"Thanks for the orchid. My mom digs it."

I'm not sure if his lips even moved when he said that. I nod.

Not that looks are everything, but Stan Lee's really handsome when he's not cutting me down. I give him a run down in my mind and suddenly feel jipped because all I've seen before is his ugly attitude. Right now, he's like a different person. He's tall compared to other Asian guys on Moloka'i. Maybe five feet eleven. His hair is literally perfect. A little longer on top and combed to the side. Every hair in place. And if he's my boss then his strong physique presents itself like a year-end bonus under his large tank top, baggy jeans, and dark brown converse high tops. His cologne's subdued yet intriguing. A refreshing break from the smell drench most guys seem to use. Without a doubt, he's the most fashionable man I've ever seen on Moloka'i.

"One more thing," he says. "Stay away from Mark."

No way.

Automatically I'm in a b-girl stance. I'm irritated by his command. I want to say, "Don't tell me what to do. Mark's mine." But I can't get myself to be direct. So I say, "Whoa, Stan Lee, what are you talking about?"

He doesn't answer. He turns around and walks back to his mom's room. I'm mad at myself for not saying what I wanted to say. I try again, but all I manage to yell out is, "Hey Stan Lee, it ain't all fair in love and war!"

He keeps walking, raising his right arm and giving me the finger without looking back.

I thought I'd feel like all that and a bag of chips after visiting Stan Lee's mom. But Stan Lee's little visit has got me feeling more like a bit of that and a sack of poop.

I drag my pathetic self across the parking lot. I happen to glance up at the small satellite building on the other side of MGH, The Moloka'i Women's Health Center. What I see makes me duck my head. I open the driver's side door of my 4runner and jump in. I slide down in the seat. Coming out the front door of the MWHC are my dad and Wendy. They're holding hands. I raise my head and sneak a peek. Dad's got his arm around her shoulder. I slink back down in the seat and scratch my head. What's Dad doing here?

He never went with Mom to any of her doctor's appointments. This one time last summer she had massive back pain and I had to take her to the ER because he "needed" to go out. Turns out she had a kidney stone. The ER doc gave her a bottle of strong pain medicine to help her until the stone passed. I remember she and I drove to the store and restaurant right after they released her from the ER. We worked until closing. If Mom had cancer or something, would Dad still have bailed?

Duh.

But there he is now. By Wendy's side.

Now I feel like none of that and a truck load of dung.

IT AIN'T PAKALOLO

Today is Pono's birthday party. I brew up some extra strong masala chai and pace the kitchen. I sip and contemplate the perfect music selections for his gift—an 80's hip hop tape.

I end up with a caffeine buzz and a solid list of tracks I know he'll love. Mom hands me a small plate of penda. She stayed home later than usual this Saturday morning to perform an extended service ritual for Thakorji. She's been more dedicated to Him recently. For me that's like winning the lottery. The lottery of prasad, that is. Because more service time for her means more sumptuous Indian treats for Thakorji. And me. I bite into the penda. "Umm." I chew the milky-sweet-cardamomy-nutmegy goodness slowly. I give Mom a quick look. Her face is serene as she washes a pot. "Thanks, Mom."

"Ha, betta," she says as she rinses.

Mom and I are way better. Right now's a perfect example. Yes, technically she's made all this prasad for Thakorji. Yet she's only made my favorites. I mean she could have made ladoo or kheer. She didn't. She made keri no rus, penda, gulab jambu, and rose-essence kulfi. My four all-time favorites. And I figure that's real love. A kind that's unselfish. A kind that Dad didn't understand. Gratitude spills out of my mouth. "I love you, Mom."

"I love you, too," she says, balancing the pot on the dish rack. She's trying to talk to me. And I'm trying to appreciate her acts of love. Our relationship is like a kid learning to ride a bike. We've got communication training wheels for now. But we're practicing. Little by little we'll ditch the training wheels and be fully in sync.

I shovel the last penda into my mouth. "Need some help?"

"No, it's ok. I know you still have to work on the tape. Jah betta. Tape banava."

We exchange smiles and I head to my room.

Two hours later I step back from my desk and behold the finished product. Lying there against the teak wood, the tape seems to emit beams of sacred light. It's an 80's hip hop cassette tape miracle.

Side A

Grandmaster Flash & The Furious Five: The Message

Queen Latifah: Ladies First

Afrika Bambaataa: Renegades of Funk

Rob Base & DJ EZ Rock: It Takes Two

Kurtis Blow: The Breaks

MC Lyte: Paper Thin

De La Soul: Buddy

Run DMC: Kings of Rock

JJ Fad: Supersonic

<u>Side B</u>

Roxanne Shante: Roxanne's Revenge

Eric B & Rakim: Paid in Full

Boogie Down Productions: Poetry

Public Enemy: Don't Believe the Hype

L'Trimm: Cars with the Boom

Run DMC: My Adidas

Beastie Boys: No Sleep Til Brooklyn

Salt-N-Pepa: Push It

LL Cool J: I'm Bad

After a quick shower, I throw on my bikini, shorts, tank top, and glasses. I check my hair in the mirror, smoothing it a bit. It's grown. Two-tone now, with black roots and blonde tips. I grab my beach bag, the tape, and scamper down the steps to the truck. I pull onto the main road and head west. The ocean on the left is flat and shimmery turquoise. The sky ahead is cloudless and rich blue. Queen Latifah and Monie Love rap about *Ladies First*. I grin, anticipating good things to come for this lady.

I decide to make a pit stop in town to get another small gift for Pono. Downtown is busy on this Saturday morning. Most of the parking stalls on either side of the street are filled. Some of my classmates are cruising the sidewalks. It's especially packed in front of Friendly Market and Misaki's. People are busy loading grocery bags into their trucks. Luckily I find a spot in front of Moloka'i Fish & Dive. I park and head in.

After an exhaustive search through all the shirt racks, I strike gold. A dark green tank top with a killer design on the back—the words "Moloka'i Style" and an image of a surfer shredding on an overhead wave. Tank top in hand I walk over to the register. To my surprise Stan Lee's there, paying for some bait and tackle. I stand behind him quietly hoping he'll pay and leave. Without noticing me.

No such luck.

He turns around and sees me. He raises one eyebrow and smirks. "Whatever," I mumble under my breath and step up to the counter.

Stan Lee walks out the door. I finish paying. My mind's on Pono's party. So when I head outside, I almost bump into Stan Lee. He's right next to the front door, leaning his left shoulder against the wall. His arms are crossed high and tight on his chest.

"Rani."

"What?"

"I gotta tell you something. I was gonna call you later, but since you're here..." There's a weathered bench under the store's large windows and he sits down. I'm not sure what to expect but something tells me to give him a chance. I sit next to him. He doesn't say anything at first. We people-watch.

After a while I speak up. "How's your mom?"

"She's good. She got discharged this morning. The doctor said she should be back to one hundred percent in a couple of weeks," he replies, his voice monotone.

"That's great."

"Yep." Stan Lee leans his elbows on his knees and rubs the back of his head with his hands. Then he blurts, "You need to be careful, Rani."

"About what?"

"About Mark."

"What're you talking about?" I hide my irritation. I'm tired of everyone's Mark-bashing. Ever since the Kaluakoi dinner, Mark's been giving me much respect. Full on Aretha Franklin.

Stan Lee sits up and pivots slightly towards me. On his face I see an emotion I haven't seen before—worry.

"Mark's using again."

"I know he drinks."

"No. He's using drugs again."

I shift uncomfortably on the bench.

"Earlier this month he started acting funny at work. Then he didn't show up a bunch of days. I had to cover for him with the bosses. I got busy the last couple of weeks with taking care of my mom and Mark went to Maui last week. So I let it go," Stan Lee says. "I know he got back last night. I went over to catch up and see if everything was ok." He stops and lowers his head.

I've wanted Stan Lee to talk to me in a meaningful way for so long. But now that he's doing it, I don't like what he's saying.

Just get to it already.

"What happened?" I ask, my annoyance breaking through.

"I knocked on his door. He didn't answer. It was unlocked so I went in." Stan Lee looks up at me. I see the whites of his eyes all the way around his brown irises. The rest of the story gushes out. "He was lying on the couch totally strung out. On the coffee table there was a small bag of clear, chunky crystals, batu by the looks of it, a glass pipe, and a lighter. I couldn't wake him up for a long time."

"Shit." I cover my mouth with my hands, remembering the pipe I'd seen at his place.

"When I got him up he went straight for the pipe and the crystal.

Shocked the hell outta me. All I could do was stand there. He smoked right in front of me." Stan Lee opens and closes his Fish & Dive bag. "Finally got my head out of my ass and tried to stop him, but he attacked me."

Neither of us speaks for a few minutes. I try to wrap my head around the situation. I sweep my fingers across my palms. They're sweaty. My head's spinning.

I know what's happening.

I take belly breaths and try to stop the bad Mark thoughts. I focus my thoughts on Pono's birthday party. I visualize Papohaku beach and the ocean.

"You ok, Rani?" He sounds muffled and distant.

I can't say anything at first. I just nod my head. Then, going against what I expected, my body slows down and the panic dissipates.

Stan Lee asks again. "You ok, Rani?"

"I'm ok."

We sit quietly for a few more minutes watching cars and trucks drive by. Eventually, Stan Lee says, "Be careful, ok? My mom's alive, but it was a close call. Mark got violent with me and I'm his good friend. You're..." He stops himself. "Just be careful."

"Ok."

Stan Lee stands up and stretches. "I gotta get going. My uncle's waiting for me at the wharf. Going trolling today."

I look up and smile. "Good luck. Hope you catch some big ones."

"See ya, Rani," he says with a straight face. He turns and walks towards his truck.

"Hey, Stan Lee," I call out. "Thanks."

Without turning around or stopping, he throws me a shaka.

Mark and I are supposed to hang out tonight. I vow to myself to confront him then. This time: no excuses.

No. Wait a minute. This is a big deal. Huge. It's freakin' batu. Not pakalolo. Stan Lee's mom almost died because of it. That's it. I'm going to do it now. I get up and charge to a payphone, determined to call and confront Mark. I pick up the handset and bring it to my ear, quarter in hand. Then I hang it up. I'm torn. I want to do it now, but it might get heated. And I don't want to be late for Pono's party.

I end up filing Stan Lee's warning into my mental "to do" folder for tonight. Jumping into my truck, I drive to the west end.

THE DARK SIDE

I don't pass a single car for the first fifteen miles. I turn right onto Kaluakoi Road for the remaining five-mile drive to Papohaku Beach Park. About three miles down, I spot a car. Whoever's driving must be going really slow because in no time we're almost bumper to bumper.

Oh no.

It's our Cressida and Dad's driving. There's a woman in the passenger seat. From the back, her straight short black hair tells me it's not Mom. My mind goes blank. I follow them on autopilot. They park at Kaluakoi Resort and step out of the car. Naturally the woman is Wendy. I watch them stroll towards the Resort. Dad's got his arm around her waist.

Clutching the steering wheel, I hesitate. I see Dad rub her back and that small gesture of affection helps me make up my mind. Pissed, I march after them.

They head into the restaurant. I stop outside its wide entrance. I weigh my options as I walk back and forth near the adjacent gift shop. I try to convince myself to leave and go to Pono's party. But I can't resist the impulse to spy on them. I push logic aside and proceed in. I scan the dining area.

Gotcha.

They're sitting at the corner table. The same one Mark and I sat at. They're holding hands. Wendy's throwing her head back in laughter. Dad's chuckling. They're having a freakin' ball.

You never did this with Mom.

I stomp over to their table. I hear Dad say, "Our baby's going to get my good looks and your brains." More laughter.

Baby? She's pregnant?

It hits me. That's why they were walking out of The Moloka'i Women's Health Center yesterday.

I'm frozen at the edge of their table. Dad eyes me for a second, then turns his attention back to Wendy. I keep standing there, mute. Dad looks at me again. "Yes, Rani? What do you want?"

Here's my chance to tell him off. To tell him what I really think about everything he's done and how it's been for Mom and me.

But I choke.

Dad shifts back to his discussion with Wendy. They continue talking. Like I'm not even there. My brain does a Dad download.

Hadn't I cut the cord?

He wasn't supposed to be able to hurt me again.

What's going on?

A baby?

Are they going to get married?

A half-sibling and a step-mom?

How will Mom feel?

He used us.

He left us.

He used me.

He left me.

I don't know how long I stand there. Unexpectedly, Wendy turns her head to me and says, "Rani, we could all be one happy family. Pradip, me, the baby, you and your mom. It's up to you." Her expression is as serious as liver failure.

I feel like she ripped off a large scab, then poured a beaker of sulphuric acid on it.

I turn and jog, weaving between the tables. I can hardly see past my tears. I can't seem to get enough air, even though I'm breathing fast and hard. When I'm out of the restaurant, I start running.

I make it to the parking lot. I find the nearest pay phone. I call Mark. He answers, but he doesn't sound like himself. Between sobs and labored breaths, I unload everything that happened. He tells me to stay put. That he'll be right over.

I crouch on the grass next to a black Ford Fiesta and bury my head in my knees. I can't stop crying. I can't think straight. Minutes pass. My tears slow down. An engine roars nearby.

Next thing I know, Mark's arms are around me. "Rani," he says. "Let's get out of here."

We get in his truck. I lean my head against the window and close my eyes. We don't drive far. He parks at the Paniolo Hale lot.

I follow him down the narrow dirt path to Make Horse Beach. He's carrying a small cooler and a backpack. The path ends and opens up to a seemingly untouched cove. The wide deserted beach with its white sand is a sharp contrast to the dark blue and foamy white waves.

We walk to the far right side of Make Horse. I'm numb. Like I'm not really here. Like I'm a robot. He pulls out a blanket from his backpack. I help him spread it under the shade of a couple of kiawe. I settle down at the edge. He sits behind me, enveloping me in his arms.

Even in his strong embrace, I feel detached. I become absorbed in the waves crashing onto the shore.

He kisses the back of my neck. "How're you doing?"

"I don't know."

"Sorry about your dad."

"Yeah. Thanks. And thanks for coming to get me."

"Anything for you, Rani."

Those words.

I don't move, but my tears flow.

Mark notices and says, "Hey, it's ok, it's ok." He squeezes me tighter. After a few minutes, he asks, "Want something to drink?"

I wipe my face with the back of my hand. "Sure, why not." He hands me a Bud Light. I crack open the can and guzzle it down.

"Can I have another one?" I down half the second can and then take sips. Feeling a little better I stretch my legs on the blanket. He lays down with the back of his head on my thigh.

His eyes track down mine and seem to offer consolation. And so do his words. "You wanna hear some haole jokes?"

"Ok," I reply. He tells me a bunch. At first I chuckle. I chug my third beer and the jokes get even funnier. Soon he's telling me stories about his days on the mainland. All I can think is how hilarious he is. By now I'm on my sixth beer and alternating between rolling on my side in laughter and trying to listen attentively.

Suddenly I have to pee really bad. It takes me awhile, but I finally find a hiding place behind some rocks. I cop a squat. After I'm done, I stumble back. Mark's facing away from me as I approach. I see him shove a pipe and a small plastic bag into his backpack. He doesn't realize I've returned until I kneel down on the blanket behind him and sling my arms around his shoulders and chest. He touches my arm, then pulls out a bottle of Cuervo from his backpack. I plop down onto the blanket, facing him.

"How about it?" He holds up the bottle. His smile is huge. He seems more awake. Like he drank ten cups of coffee.

"Sure." I study his face as he unscrews the cap. "Cheers!" he exclaims and takes a big swig. Then he gives me this strange look. A look that worries me a little. His eyes are squint. He's staring at me like he's a hawk and I'm a juicy mouse. He props the bottle against the cooler and grabs my face in both his hands. He kisses me hard. It feels like I'm gagging on his tongue. He pulls away. Then he passes the bottle of Cuervo to me.

I take a swig of the amber liquid. Immediately I take another. My head's spinning. Time blurs. At least I've forgotten about my dad. And I finally get to what I should've asked Mark a long time ago. I take one more gulp. "Mark," I slur, "do you use drugs?" This simple question took me six beers and three swigs of Cuervo to gain the courage—or lose the inhibition—to ask.

"Alcohol," he says. He takes another swig and hands the bottle back to me.

I take a drink. Somehow I manage to say, "No, I mean other drugs. My boys warned me about you." I feel myself wagging a finger at him in what seems like slow motion.

Mark doesn't answer. Instead he rummages through his backpack and pulls out a small plastic bag with clear crystals, a five-inch glass pipe, a lighter, and a small straw.

That's the pipe I saw on his coffee table. And the straw with the burned tip!

He holds out the stuff for me to see. My glazed expression and silence give him the green light.

Using the slant tip of the straw, he packs a pinch of the crystal through a small hole into the chamber of the glass pipe's bulb. Then he rolls the spark wheel of the lighter and holds the flame really close to the bulb. The flame almost touches the glass. He moves the flame in circles under the bulb. The crystal starts to melt and turn to smoke. The smoke fills the chamber and he inhales slowly from the mouthpiece, keeping the flame near the bulb. Then he shuts the lighter off and inhales a bit more.

Drunk and dazed, I don't move. I can't move. I'm like a piece of petrified wood. Time seems to be moving at a snail's pace. A strange feeling takes over. It's as if I'm sitting up on the kiawe tree observing him below. Like he's in a gritty documentary on batu use.

He packs more crystal and smokes it.

I watch, paralyzed. My vision fades in and out.

He packs the bulb yet again and says, "Here," holding out the pipe and lighter to me.

"No, I'm good." I try to force my eyes fully open.

He lights it and takes the hit himself. That's when the darkness spreads across his face. He mutates into someone—no, something— else. His expression is wolfish and scares the crap out of me. I imagine jumping up and running back to the parking lot. But all my wasted ass can do is scoot away on the blanket. I push myself with my feet and try to get myself to the other side. My coordination is off, and I end up collapsing on my back. He eyes me for a second then reaches out.

"Get over here, Rani," he snarls, dragging me by my feet closer to him.

Next thing I know he's straddling me. His mouth swallows mine. I can't tell where his tongue ends and mine begins. It kind of hurts but feels good too. His hands are all over me. He yanks my tank top over my head, almost ripping it. My glasses go with it. I feel my bikini top around my neck. He's touching, rubbing, squeezing.

"You're mine, Rani," he growls. "And I want all of you."

His left hand reaches down and tears off my shorts and bikini bottom in one swift motion.

"Wait, wait. Hold on." I grope to find my shorts.

He pushes my hands away.

"My head hurts. I-I wanna rest."

He pulls down his board shorts.

"Stop," I whisper. It doesn't come out like the scream I want. I try to shove him off me.

With one hand he grabs my hands and holds them over my head.

"No, stop." I can't get my legs to kick him off me.

He has me pinned down completely. He reaches below with his free hand to his groin.

"Stop..."

"Shut up!" He moves his hand up to cover my mouth.

Then, sharp pain. I try to scream again but his hand seems to sense it and presses down harder.

Fade to black.

TLC

"Rani, wake up. Rani."

Faraway, familiar voice.

Lifted.

"Rani, please wake up."

Eyelids flutter open for a few seconds. Enough to catch a glimpse of kiawe floating in an ocean of deep blue sky.

I bolt up.

Where am I?

I feel sticky and crusty. As if I ran the "block" for PE, then didn't take a shower all day. And the sweat on my body got all dried up. Now it encases me like the fried batter on tempura. I sweep my hand over my face, starting at my chin and working up to my forehead. My hand remains idle on my forehead for a second, then moves down the back of my scalp. Tiny grains of sand rain onto my body.

"Rani, betta, drink," Mom says, handing me a pyalo.

"Mom," I say, taking a sip of cool lemon water. Then Mom holds out my glasses. I slip them on and everything comes into focus. I look straight ahead and see my bookshelf and closet doors. To the left, my dresser and mirror. And next to me, my desk, boombox, and stack of CDs.

My room.

I try to sit up.

She places a damp washcloth on my forehead. "Rest now, betta."

She adjusts the pillow under my head. I feel queasy. My head's throbbing. So is my crotch.

My crotch?!

I sit up again. The washcloth drops from my forehead onto the front of my tank top. With both hands, I grab the edge of my blanket. I notice bits of dirt and sand trapped under my fingernails. I lift the edge of the blanket and glance under. The towel that's wrapped around my waist loosens as I move and the ends fall open. My eyes widen because I'm not wearing any bottoms! Lightning strikes and the events of the day fast forward in my mind. Pono's party. Dad and Wendy. Mark. Make Horse. Beer. Cuervo. Crystal. Pain.

"How are you feeling, betta?"

I lie back down. I focus on the white of the ceiling. But all I see is red. After the pain, my mind is blank. How did I get home?

"You didn't show up for Pono's birthday party," she says patting my hand. Tears fill her eyes. "He said something didn't feel right so he went looking for you. Someone told him they saw you get into Mark's truck."

"Pono found me?" I turn my head to face her.

"Yes." She slips one hand into mine and strokes my forehead with the other. "Rani, betta, what happened?" she asks.

I study her face. Her eyes and brow radiate understanding. Her mouth is relaxed and her full lips are slightly open.

I remember this look.

It's the same one she had after I shaved my head. Only then I was confused and I ended up resisting her TLC. And even though we've gotten closer, I haven't told her anything about Mark. But now it feels right.

Before I can get to the whole story, I have to get through a decade of tears. My face contorts and I cry. Like a baby. Like the doctor just pulled newborn me out of my mom and I took my first breath, then let the wailing rip. Thick, clear, viscous snot drips from my nose. But there's no nurse here to use the suction bulb to suck it out for me. Good thing Mom hands me tissues. Sitting up, I blow a ton of it out.

"It's ok, betta, tell me what happened."

I try to get a hold of myself, but the tears keep coming.

Mom must know I'm not ready to talk yet. She changes the subject. She switches to Gujarati. "Have I ever told you about your great grandmother, Agneya ba?"

I nod. "Lalita ba did."

A lovely young Gujarati woman in Dharmaj. 1937.

I close my eyes and remember that sweltering afternoon in my grandparents' Nairobi apartment. Lalita ba and I are sitting cross-legged on the cool, grey concrete floor of the tiny kitchen. I'm watching her trim the giloda for my least favorite shaak. She's ignoring my disapproving stare. I have no idea why but it's then that she decides to tell me about her mother. In Gujarati, she says, "Rani, you have to listen to this. Listen closely. Don't ever forget."

Lalita ba begins with facts. Agneya ba was born and raised in

Dharmaj. Her parents arranged her marriage to Suresh, the son of a wealthy local politician from Bhadran. Everyone thought it was a perfect Chha Gaam union. But Suresh dada had several affairs and affair children. When Agneya ba found out, she wanted to leave him. He didn't like that idea.

That's where the second verse of my rap "Love and War" took root! Its flow germinates in my head.

His solution was her live cremation.

My rhymes and Lalita ba's account fertilize each other. They intensify each other's growth. Lalita ba's voice grows clearer. I picture her dropping a partially trimmed giloda into the large stainless steel bowl and waving her knife around like a magic wand. She's an enchanted raconteur. And I'm all ears.

By the time Agneya ba returned home from her friend's place that evening, it was dark. She hadn't noticed the windows boarded up from the outside. Or that the large copper water vessel near the spice shelf had been removed. Had she known she would soon die, she would have worn her white sari.

Images of Agneya ba's murder come together in my mind like a climactic film scene.

As the flames leaped about her, Agneya ba frantically searched for an exit from the small kitchen of their Dharmaj home. She pounded her fists against the thick, wooden door, now securely locked from the outside. She screamed, "Bachao! Bachao!" No one came. All four walls were burning. Desperation and fear turned into resignation as the oppressive heat from the blaze enveloped the room.

Agneya ba grabbed the shears from her sewing tin and quickly snipped off her thick, long, black hair. She shaved off the remaining hair with her husband's razor. A small blessing that he kept his toiletries neatly arranged on a floating shelf in the kitchen, under the only mirror in the house.

I'm rubbing my short hair. I visualize Lalita ba balancing the knife on the edge of the bowl. She presses her palms together in prayer. Then she bows her head slightly and concludes the tale with a persuasive version of the way she saw things.

It became increasingly difficult to distinguish the raging fire from Agneya ba's bright red sari. Only her chestnut colored Gujarati face could be seen, all the more radiant with her bald head. Aware of her imminent immolation, she thought about her daughter. All at once her eyes revealed a glimmer of defiance. This was the last time Suresh dada would control her fate.

I open my eyes. I'm nodding. I touch my face. It's dry. I'm not sure when my tears stopped. Then I see my mom. She's crying. I'm pretty sure she's thinking about the time Lalita ba told her the same story. I hand her some tissues. She smiles at me through her tears. We sit and cerebrate together.

When her tears slow, she wipes her eyes and blows her nose. Still in Gujarati she says, "The men in our family shatter people they say they love." She pauses and strokes my forehead again. What she says next breaks down the last layer of my invisible wall, the one I'd been surrounding myself with to keep her from knowing everything. "Rani, betta, Mark hurt you, right? Tell me everything. Pele thee."

She takes my hand in hers and holds it tight. I work my fingers in between hers. We turn into the Wonder Twins, our powers activated by our interlaced fingers. Our eyes unite. I feel safe. Even though we've spent the last ten years at odds, we've finally come together.

And it's around our mutual understanding of an unspoken reality in our lives: that generations of women in our family have been broken by men behind closed doors. Maybe the youngest generations, Mom and I, aren't exceptions. It just happened in a different way.

But today, Mom and I are ready to face the truth. The truth will allow us to start the process of healing ourselves. Of strengthening ourselves. Of ending the cycle of suffering at the hands of men.

Still holding her hand, I confide, "Mark hurt me. But it started with Dad." She nods. Then I tell her everything. All my deep, dark secrets.

BROKEN PROMISE BEAT DOWN

At first I don't recognize him. He grips the porch railing and climbs one step at a time. His t-shirt looks like a red and white tie dye. Blood. I check out his hands. They're smeared with dirt and dried blood. His left eye is swollen shut. It resembles a bullseye with a ring of black and blue. The middle of his face is puffy. Blood drips in vertical lines from his nostrils. A deep cut on his right upper lip oozes. He stops on the fifth step and leans against the railing, struggling to catch his breath. His right sleeve is bunched up. The dreamcatcher tattoo.

Mark.

I jump up. My notebook and pencil fall on the porch floorboards. I rush over to him and help him up the stairs.

"What happened?"

He lowers himself onto the bench taking care to keep his left leg straight. That's when I notice a deep gash on the unbent leg. It extends from the bottom edge of his board shorts to the top of his knee.

"Karma," he whispers. He turns his head slightly to the left so his right eye can maintain visual contact.

It's January 3rd. I haven't seen Mark since November 30th, the day at Make Horse. I heard from Omar that the cops got Mark the next day for "acting crazy" in town. That same day, they shipped him over to Kekela, the psych ward at Queen's Hospital on Oahu. I don't know what his "acting crazy" was, but I guess it was bad enough to end up in in the hospital. When he got out, Omar said Mark went to Maui to stay with his mom.

My mom wants me to press charges against Mark. In the past I would've said, "Fo shua." Heck, I would tell someone else to do that. But I haven't been wanting to take it to the popo. I don't know why. I'm tired of thinking about it. It's probably because—and I'd never admit this to anyone—part of me wants to protect Mark. I mean it wasn't him that day. It was him on batu. But the other part of me knows that's pretty messed up.

Mom said she understood. And Mom's all Gandhi. So I know she wouldn't organize a Mark-beat down.

Pono and Omar know what he did to me. Did one of them do this to him? I'm pretty sure Stan Lee knows since he knows everything about Mark. And despite him not being a huge admirer of me, would he have beat Mark up?

Or was it because of the batu? A smackdown from Reynold?

"Who did this to you?"

He doesn't answer. He can barely hold up his head.

"Lemme take you to the ER. You might have some broken bones. Maybe you need stitches or antibiotics or something."

"No."

My mind races with ways to help him.

Then Make Horse bursts back into my mind.

I'm confused.

"I'm so sorry, Rani," he mumbles.

I almost accept his apology. But then I remember Pono and Omar's reactions. They were ultra pissed. They still are. They can't understand why I'm not enraged. They're little guardian angels on my shoulders yelling, "Call the cops!" and "He should be in jail!"

But I don't feel angry at Mark. I'm just mad at myself. Hating myself.

How could you be so stupid? You didn't listen to Pono, Omar, or Stan Lee?

You deserved it.

You led him on.

Just like Dad.

This spirals into daily bouts of sadness and death wishes. Just like Mom. I guess it's true what they say—the apple doesn't fall far from the tree.

"Sorry, Rani."

"Sorry?"

"Sorry for what I did to you," he says. "I didn't mean to hurt you." He pauses and cautiously lets his upper body drift back to the porch railing.

"Happy late birthday. I wanted to tell you in person last month. But I just got back on-island this morning. I got you the *2Pacalypse Now* CD."

"Thanks."

Thinking about my birthday makes me sad. I turned seventeen with none of the fanfare I'd hoped for because it was only one week after Make Horse. So when December 7th rolled around, I wasn't in the mood for celebrating.

Mom tried to cheer me up by preparing my favorite meal. Mater paneer and naan. She even asked Auntie Maile, who was on Oahu for a couple of days, to bring back a dream cake from Zippy's.

Pono and Omar tried to get me to hang out. But I chose to hide on the deck of my house and focus on tragedy. Mine at first. But then I condemned myself to thinking about a real tragedy. Specifically World War II. Everyone knows that December 7 is also the day Pearl Harbor got bombed in 1941. About four and a half years later, Hiroshima and Nagasaki were annihilated by A-bombs. It seemed like the perfect birthday brain slap to reread *Gen of Hiroshima*, volume 1 and 2. Yep. That was quite an effective brain slap strategy. Thoughts of little Gen and his family post-nuclear bomb devastation shook me out of self-pity. I noshed on dream cake and on the reality of my life, easy by comparison to Gen's.

Mark interrupts my birthday recollection. "I started smoking ice here and there in August. But it snowballed," he says. "It made me do bad things."

That sounds like Dad.

The pills also made him do things he didn't plan on.

"I'm going to rehab on the mainland. I'm leaving Monday. Clean and sober for good this time. I promise I'll never use again," he says.

At first I'm hopeful. Then I remember the promise he made after the boob girl fiasco—he promised not to hurt me. Broken promise #1. Broken in a way I never imagined. I guess there are many ways to hurt someone.

I don't say anything. I pretend duct tape covers my mouth and think about what Omar said. *A real man would never hurt a woman like that.* No matter what.

And that's when the anger comes. And it erupts like Kilauea, blowing the duct tape off.

"Why, Mark? I trusted you. I loved you!" I shout.

"I know I fucked up! I want to make this right. Tell me what to do."

"It's too late!" I pace back and forth, one arm crossed and the other up so that my forehead is balanced on my fingertips.

Bit by bit he pushes himself up from the bench. He hobbles over and tries to touch my shoulder.

"Don't touch me!" I back away. The bench stops me. I collapse on it. I bury my head in my hands. "Why would you say you love me but then hurt me? Why would you promise not to hurt me but do it anyway?" I thump my balled-up fists against the sides of my head. "I hate myself."

I thump harder.

"No, Rani. Stop. And don't say that. Come on, I'm sorry." He's hovering over me. Out of the corner of my eye I can see him reach down. But then he stops himself and takes a step back. He says, "I..." He pauses. "I love you for real. I've never loved anyone like I love you."

I stop thumping. I look up.

"What?"

I watch him limp back to the other bench and ease himself back to sitting. Then he says, "After I get back from rehab, you gotta give me another chance." There's earnestness in his voice. "Rani, I don't want to be like my dad. Or your dad. I have to change. I want to be a better man."

His words hit me like a tranquilizer. I chill out instantly. I believe him. And I like what he's saying. I even justify his words in my mind. My dad never admitted to being wrong about anything. Never took responsibility for his actions. But Mark's stepping up. Maybe there's still a chance for Mark and me.

"Really?"

"Yes. Anything for you, Rani."

No, Mark. Anything for you.

THE COUNSEL OF MY BOYZ

"Mark came to the store yesterday all buss up," I tell Pono and Omar.

They exchange glances. We're chillaxing on the deck of my house. Awaiting the Gujarati feast Mom's preparing. Dhal, bhaat, oondhiya, bateta nu shaak, and rotli. Mom suggested this gathering to celebrate two seventeenth birthdays—Omar's and mine.

"Better late than never," she'd said in her thick Gujju accent.

The boys have never eaten Indian food, let alone Gujarati food. I'm confident they won't be disappointed.

They take sips of the refreshing kachi keri no baflo that Mom's whipped up for us. I notice Pono's hand as he grips the pyalo. I glimpse at Omar's hands. Four hands with scabs and bruises on the knuckles and fingers. Especially on the right hands.

I can't believe I didn't spot the evidence as soon as they walked through the door.

"Ok, you guys, what's up?" I watch their every move. They turn their heads in different directions, their eyes zipping from each other to the ocean to the deck.

"You guys did it, didn't you?"

"He knew he had it coming," Omar says, staring at his knuckles. "He didn't fight back much."

"Mark's lucky we didn't kill him," Pono adds.

"Tell me what happened."

"Mark asked Stan Lee for a ride back to his house from the airport yesterday," Omar starts explaining.

"Too bad for him three of us showed up," Pono says, his lips pressed together. "We took him to Make Horse. The same spot I found you." Pono shifts his eyes to me.

Did Stan Lee help beat up Mark for my sake?

But then I get it. No.

For his mom.

I'm grateful that they'd want to protect me enough to beat the crap out of Mark for revenge. And also because of Pono's thoughtfulness. The warnings. Finding me at Make Horse.

"We let Mark know what we thought of what he did to you."

An eye for an eye.

Makes the whole world blind, Gandhi would say.

"I don't know what to say," I adjust my glasses and stare at my feet. I want to express so much more than thankfulness. It's funny: I can write pages and pages of serious rhymes, but I can't find the words right now when I need them.

"You don't have to say anything, Rani," Omar says.

Pono nods. "Yeah, Mark got what he deserved."

No one says anything for awhile.

Pono breaks the silence. "What else happened when Mark came to the store?"

I fill them in. Mark's apology. His plan on going to rehab. His idea on me giving him another chance when he gets back.

"Another chance?" Pono huffs impatiently.

"Marks wants one. I'm not sure yet," I mumble.

Pono shakes his head then looks at me like someone's just blown chunks on him. Like I've said the most disgusting this ever said in the history of the world. "Oh boy, Rani," he begins.

"Whoa. Hold up. Why are we more mad at Mark than you are?" Omar interjects.

"I am mad," I say without conviction.

Omar looks at me in dismay then says, "No way in hell, Rani. Don't let that a-hole near you again."

"Don't you see? He still wants to do what he wants to do. Don't listen to him," Pono pleads.

I nod. "You're right."

I know they're right. My rational brain has given me the same advice. But my emotions are a force to be reckoned with and my rational brain has already been trampled. Only my boys don't know this.

"He said he doesn't want to be like his dad or my dad. That he wants to be a better man. That he really loves me and—" I say, stopping myself because Pono's eyes catch mine.

Oh shit.

He glares at me.

I look away, silent.

LOVE DRUG REHAB

A tsunami warning? That's the first thing that comes to mind when our annoyingly loud telephone rings, ripping me out of slumber. I lift my head up and check out the bedside clock. 12:30 a.m. January 13. The sound continues.

Oh.

It's the phone.

Ugh.

No one calls us past 10:00 p.m. I roll over and heave the comforter over my head. The ringing is dampened. Then it stops. I'm about to doze off. It rings again. Vexed, I kick the comforter off and jump out of bed. I stagger into the dark hallway. I use the wall as a guide and make my way to the kitchen. I grope the counter for the phone. It's still ringing. I find it and grab the handset. I cradle it between my ear and shoulder.

"Hello?" I'm not fully coherent.

"Rani, is that you?"

"Yeah."

"It's Mark. What're you doing?"

"Oh hey, Mark. Sleeping." I'm groggy.

"Oh sorry. How's my queen?"

I wake up. Fast. I don't feel like a queen. Queens don't get raped. My body stiffens.

Mark went to the mainland last week to start rehab. Somewhere in L.A. I haven't talked to him since he left.

"Umm. Ok, I guess."

He had told me before he left that they're not allowed to call anyone when they're inpatient. How comes he's calling me now?

"I miss you, Rani," he whispers.

His words are like a magic wand. My emotions push my rational thoughts out the window.

Now my body turns to jelly. I have to rest my back against the kitchen wall so I don't slip. "I miss you, too." I press the phone harder against my ear. There's loud music in the background. Sounds like country. I really hope they let him listen to hip hop in rehab. If they knew Mark the way I do, they'd know that beats and flow would be more therapeutic for him than honky tonk music.

"How's rehab?" I ask.

"Oh, I checked out early. Didn't like it." He's slurring his words.

Checked out early? What?

"Where are you?"

"At a bar."

What. The. Frick. "A bar? What else are you using?"

Silence.

"Mark, what else are you using?" I'm about to go apeshit.

"A few hits won't kill me. One last hurrah, Rani baby."

Then I hear rustling and scrunching. Like someone's grabbing the phone from him.

"Ronny, Ran-ee, whatever your name is. Mark's with me now. You better back off."

A woman. She sounds plastered.

I hear a scuffle. Mark's back on the phone. "Sorry, that was just some random girl in the bar."

My anger oozes like pahoehoe. "I can't believe I was going to let you back into my life."

"Calm down, Rani. I'm sorry."

"Don't tell me to calm down! You're just like my dad!" I scream. "You'll never change!"

"Baby, come on. Give me one more chance."

Really? Is he reading from some bad Hollywood screenplay?

"No!"

"But I love you, Rani," he whimpers.

But I love you, Rani. Just like Dad.

"You're the only good thing in my life," he continues. "I'll be back on Moloka'i in a week. Clean and sober, I promise. I need you. Help me stay on the straight and narrow."

I listen.

"Please don't give up on me."

"I don't know," I whisper.

"But I love you, Rani," he whispers back.

My anger slides away.

But I love you, Rani.

Hurt and love.

Love and hurt.

Lurt.

Hove.

I start thinking about ways to help him when he gets back.

One last chance.

I'm about to say that when the kitchen light comes on. I turn around. Mom's standing near the light switch. She walks over and grabs the phone from my hand. I guess she woke up when she heard me shouting. Did she hear what I said? Does she know who I'm talking to?

"Mark, this is Rani's mother. Don't ever call her again. Don't ever come near her again. Leave her alone or I'll call the police." She hangs up the phone.

She did. She does.

I'm shocked. And scared that Mark will be mad at me. I grab the phone. But I drop the handset in my frenzy. I retrieve it. My fingers reach the dial pad, but I realize I don't have his number in Cali. My hand grips the phone tighter.

I can't call him.

I drop the handset onto the receiver. I want to yell at Mom. But I'm mute. She grasps my shoulders and says, "No more Mark."

Aghast, I slog to my room. Mom did what I couldn't have done myself—she ended it with Mark for me. Once and for all. She straight-up put me in my own rehab—from Mark. Just like she did with Dad.

She's protecting me.

I fall onto my bed and close my eyes. Gripping my chest I'm transported to that scene in *Indiana Jones and the Temple of Doom*.

The flames light the otherwise dark pit. I feel the scorching heat. As the Thuggee henchmen chain me into the cage, I whisper salutations to Shiva. Over and over.

Mola Ram, with his horned ceremonial headdress, moves toward me. His hand's extended. He calls out to Kali, raising his hand to the large image of the goddess overhead. He lowers his hand slowly, then shoves it into my chest. He pulls out my beating heart. He laughs sinisterly, holding my heart up to Kali.

I sob.

GAUNTLET

Me and my non-pregnant, STD-free reproductive system wait for Mom outside the bathroom of The Moloka'i Women's Health Center. My follow-up appointment with Dr. Perry went well. My nether region is okkie dokkie. I smile to myself. Things are looking up.

But then my good fortune plummets. Way down low. To my consternation, Wendy Nagaoki's walking towards me.

"Rani, what're you doing here?" she asks.

Wendy's the last person I want to see. She's rubbing her baby bump and smiling. I try to think of a good excuse for why I'm here. Luckily she doesn't wait for me to answer.

"A kick," she says, pleased.

The maternal-ness of her high-waisted elastic band jeans and polka dot blouse makes me want to hurl.

She grabs my hand and presses it onto her basketball.

"Right here. Feel that?"

I feel it alright. Like a kick in the head.

"Twins. Girls."

Of course.

I roll my eyes and purse my lips. The idea of their perfect little family of four literally shoves my eyeballs up and my lips together. I can't take it anymore. I plot an exit strategy.

Knock her out?

No, that might hurt the babies. It's not their fault she's a tramp.

Tell her to take a hike?

Possibly.

Be polite?

Yeah right.

I'm not sure how long I stand there pondering. Long enough that Wendy says something else.

"Your Dad really wants you to be there for your little sisters." Her serene gaze and Mona Lisa smile make me think she actually believes we could all be The Brady Bunch. I'm speechless.

"Your Dad's at the drugstore. He'll be back soon if you want to see him."

I'd rather swallow my own vomit.

"Maybe another time. I gotta go." That's when I see Mom coming out of the bathroom. "Mom, over here," I call out. I wave my arms like I'm a landing signal officer at the airport. I'm desperate for support from my real family. Mom waves back and walks over. Then I realize Mom and Wendy haven't actually been face-to-face since everything happened.

Uh-oh.

I'm not sure what it'll be like when they face off. Before I have a chance to say or do anything, Wendy throws down the gauntlet.

"Oh hi, Meera." she says. "It would've been nice for us all to live together. Especially now that Nila and Nala will be part of the family." The sweet smile is gone. Instead she's glaring at Mom. I imagine Wendy pulling out a laser gun and releasing a burning stream of mockery straight at Mom. Wendy sighs and relaxes her face. Then she turns the stream into a blast. "Pradip's so loving. He's going to be an incredible father," she says. She smirks and strokes her protruding belly.

I glance at Mom. The pearls of sweat forming on my forehead are like evidence of Wendy's imminent victory.

Astoundingly, Mom picks up the gauntlet. With an expression of pity, Mom says, "Oh, Wendy. I wouldn't live with you and Pradip even if that meant I had to be homeless." Her thick Gujarati accent adds to the dramatic effect. Then Mom smiles. "I actually wanted to say thank you. Thank you for taking Pradip off my hands." Her smile widens. "You can keep him. And his bullcrap."

Wendy's look is priceless.

A FRESH START

Mom's verbal beat down of Wendy stimulated my flow. And now I'm transforming her toughness into a bravado rap of epic proportion. Epic because I'm also drawing inspiration from powerful women in history.

I'm spitting some rhyme ideas about Razia Sultan. I'm hoping to find a potent way to incorporate her disdain of being categorized as a sultana into the intro of my rap. The girl wasn't about to be pigeonholed into being merely the wife of a sultan. Which is what sultana means. No way. She expected to be called sultan because she ruled Delhi with the prowess that is generally attributed to a man. I'm willing to bet she governed better than any man.

The living room is my stage. Mom's velun is my mic. The sofa and coffee table are the crowd. I'm working my motionless fans hard with my sick flow.

Don't call me Sultana.
Blazin' it down, settin' off the alarm-a.

I'm a charma' with plenty of armor.

More like Cleopatra spittin' your mantra.

"Oh, there's my velun," Mom calls out.

My flow gets dammed.

In her thick Gujju accent she says, "Carry on, Rani. I want to hear it. The bakri can wait." She walks over and sinks into the sofa.

I'm mortified. Though Mom now knows all about MC Sutra and 4eva Flowin', she's never heard my rhymes. I mean I've wished that she'd see me in action. But I never thought she'd really be interested.

My face is burning. I can't get my mouth open. I stare at her. With her brown polyester pants and beige faux silk shirt, she blends into the taupe and burnt sienna striped sofa. She crosses her legs and clasps her hands over her top knee.

I'm all bared teeth. I want to yell "eek!" and run to my room. But I end up standing there like I'm flaunting my custom fit 24K gold grillz. Upper and lower.

"Rani, rap for me," she says.

With her Gujju accent, it sounds like she said, "Rep for me."

I relax my face. And snicker.

"What's so funny?" she asks. It sounds like, "What's so punny?"

"Oh, nothing is punny. Let me get on with repping for you," I say in a mock Gujju accent. I can't keep a straight face. I stifle my laugh. It comes out like a reverse snort. Mom smiles.

I know I'm dragging my feet. But letting myself openly tease her accent a little bit is a good sign. It means we're comfortable enough around each other to be real. Six months ago this would never have happened.

Enough avoiding. "I can't rap in front of you, Mom. I don't know why, but I'm too nervous. Sorry."

"But you rap in front of so many people," she argues.

"I know. But you're my mom. It's different."

Mom crosses her arms. Her brow rests in its V. Her eyes shift up and left. And remain in that position while she thinks. She looks like she's trying to figure out some incredibly difficult math problem. Which actually wouldn't take her this long because she's kind of a math genius. Then she gets this mellow expression and shifts her eyes to me. "Well, can I read your raps?"

I slog the two steps to the sofa and rest my behind next to her. As much as I'm embarrassed to rap in front of her, deep down I'm overjoyed that she's asking to read my work. "Ok." I hand her my notebook.

She grasps it in the same reverent way she does her holy *Bhagavad Gita*. She turns to the first page and starts reading. I melt into the thick sofa cushions. I watch her. Her face changes as she immerses herself in my world. The curve of her mouth. The angle of her eyebrows. The diameter of her eyes.

I must have fallen asleep because the next thing I know Mom's stroking the top of my head. I strain to focus my eyes on her. "Huh?" I fumble with my glasses.

She points to a page in my notebook. "This one. 'Widow.' It's my favorite," she says. She's looking at my head. Then she runs her fingers through my hair. It's grown some more. Practically a pixie cut. I dyed it back to black yesterday after work because I kinda like me au naturale.

She pulls her hand away from my head. "Rani, these lines make me sad." I follow her finger running over four lines.

A dark web of emotional and sexual merging,

and I am emerging

as his mirror.

He tries to make things clearer.

Then another line.

A better life that was my intention.

A tear lands next to her finger on the page. She quickly dries it. She rubs her eyes and whispers, "It's always been about what he wants." She shakes her head, "I'm sorry, Rani."

"Sorry?"

She raises her head and looks straight at me. In Gujarati she says, "Sorry for letting him be in charge of everything. I thought he was being a good dad to you. He spent all his free time with you. He taught you so many American things. I thought I had to let go of being your mom because he could give you more than I could."

She grabs my hands and squeezes. "I was mad at him for not treating me like a wife and for treating you like a princess. Many times, I had these feelings that things weren't right. That he was hurting you. But I ignored it. I let it happen. I let him hurt you. I should've kicked him out long ago. I'm so sorry."

"It's ok, Mom."

She wraps her arms around me. She keeps hugging me and saying she's sorry over and over.

Guess it turns out we both thought he was being a good dad. And it's partly true. He did many good things with good intentions. But those things blinded both of us to the bad things he did to us. And since it was like I didn't exist to my mom, it's not surprising that I felt closest to someone who hurt me but also made me feel good.

Then Mark pops into my mind. Funny. Because with him it was the same as with Dad. Another rendition of love and hurt. A repeat of me letting go of the bad things he did to me because he did good things also.

"It's ok," I say again. I lean back and smile at her. My smile widens as hope descends. "Hey, Mom, there's something I have to do." Taking the notebook, I leap up from the sofa. I grab a pencil from the kitchen counter and walk onto the deck. The Moloka'i channel is smooth and flat. I admire its cerulean sheen. Then I set up a mini lyrical lab on the deck table. I settle into a chair. I realign my glasses and glance one more time at the ocean. I flip open the notebook to my slam poem. I take a few minutes to read it again. I'm drawn to two lines.

and I am emerging

as his mirror.

And I think about how mirrors are a reflective surface. Mirroring someone is imitating them. In a weird way all I could do up until now was reflect whatever Dad and Mark wanted. I couldn't work on figuring out my wants. My needs. My identity. They forced me into a corner where I was convinced I needed them. So I let them do whatever they wanted. I existed for Dad. Then for Mark. I was their mirror.

Then I scan the rest of the poem to some other lines that compel contemplation today.

I'm worthless.

Nothing.

Dead.

When Dad abandoned me and when Mark was gone, I cracked. I became a cracked mirror in a void. I had nothing to reflect. So I was nothing.

But that's all about to change.

An hour and a half comes and goes. As do several whales in the channel. I put down my pencil and exhale slowly. Done. A new ending to the slam poem that started it all.

Until Mom sees me. First time in all my seventeen years

she reaches out—emotionally.

Quells my fears, wipes my tears.

Says, betta, widows in India are forced to shave their heads.

Society views them akin to being dead.

Forced tonsure,

prostitution and oppression they endure.

Made to fast,

seen as social outcasts, the lowest caste.

A state of social death forever.

But, betta, you have a choice.

You can get through this pain,

you can grow your hair again—

thick, strong.

With it, my sense of self grows—I belong.

My perception of choice.

The strength of my voice.

Knowledge of my good fortune

to save myself

and show my future daughter

how men control women—

through mental slaughter.

Infuse her with the views

to escape all kinds of abuse

so maybe she can choose

positive self care and

long hair.

I'm happy with the new ending. It lets me get a fresh start. Free from my dad. Free from Mark. And slowly, I will become my own person.

I'm so done blaming my parents, Mark, and Wendy. My daddy's gone. And I'm so done looking for another one.

LOVE OUTLAWED

It hits me when I'm alone. The sadness. The anger. The fear. The shame. Three months after Mark raped me, these feelings still hammer me.

You drank like a fish. You let it happen. You deserve it.

Brain slap. I squeeze my knees tighter with my arms. I press my face into my lap. I'm hoping the pressure I'm exerting on my body will stop the running commentary in my head. That's when I hear my name.

"Hey, Rani."

I lift my head off my lap and grab my glasses from the shelf behind me. I slide them on. He comes into focus. It's Pono. He's standing on the other side of the counter looking like a gorgeous mirage in the desert that's been my day. "Oh hey, Pono." I get up from the step stool. There haven't been any customers for awhile. Enough time for a little emotional purgatory.

"How're you doing?" Pono asks.

"Ok, I guess. What brings you to Maunaloa? Wait! Let me guess. You want to try our new self-serve nachos. That's it, right?"

"How'd you guess?" He crosses his arms and gets this confused look on his face. Then he recovers and throws me his classic foxy Pono smile.

"Wanna go hang out on the porch?" He uses his thumb to point in the direction he wants to go. Like he's a hitchhiker.

"Umm..." But right then, two customers enter the store. One of them is clearly a tourist. The silky, multicolored aloha shirt he's wearing and the lobster red color of his face and arms are a dead giveaway. He grabs a shopping basket and walks to the refrigerated section. The other customer, La'akea, walks up to the counter and asks for a pack of Marlboro Lights.

"It's ok. I'll wait." Pono moves aside.

I ring up La'akea's cigarettes and take a quick look at her. She seems worse than the last time I saw her. Much worse. Her arms are covered with burns at varying stages of healing. The sores on her face seem to have coalesced into two big sores on either side of her nose. Her tattered t-shirt hangs like an oversized poncho on her pencil thin frame. Several of her front teeth are gone.

I wish I could do something to help her. But all I do is take her money and hand her the cigarettes. And a free book of matches. She doesn't say anything as she leaves. I watch her limp out of the store.

The tourist steps up to the counter. He unloads his groceries. I glance at Pono. He pretends to be browsing the canned goods aisle. He picks up a can and brings it close to his face. He pretends to examine it. The thumb and index finger of his free hand cup his chin and his lips are in a pout. I almost laugh out loud because it's a can of green beans. He catches my eye and holds the can over his head, mouthing yum while rubbing his belly. I end up making a weird hacking noise because I can hardly hold in the laughter that starts way down in my belly.

"Sorry," I say to the tourist man. After he pays, he grabs the paper bag, smiles, winks, and says, "Mahalo and aloha." Automatically my mouth goes all Billy Idol as I watch him walk out of the store. I eye Pono. I can tell he heard it too. I know the tourist guy was probably trying to be nice. Maybe he even thought he was being respectful of the Hawaiian culture by using some of its words.

Pono traipses back to the counter. I shake my head and grimace. "Unbelievable," I say.

"Uh-huh."

I lay my forearms on the counter and interlock my fingers. He does likewise with his forearms from the other side. Our faces are less than a foot apart and our eyes connect. I remember the little flutter in my heart I used to feel when we were this close. He gives me this lopsided smile. As if he's happy and worried at the same time. He inches his hands toward mine. I watch them surround my hands. Then close in. I stare at his hands on my hands. I'm trying to keep my cool but my eyebrows shoot up.

"I'm worried about you. You always say you're ok when I ask. I kinda don't believe that."

"It's sweet that you're worried." I force a smile. "But I'm ok. Really."

"I dunno, Rani." He shakes his head and presses his lips together. It looks like he's deep in thought. Then he suggests, "We could go hang out sometime this weekend. After everything you've been through you must need to vent."

"That's ok, Pono. Don't worry. I'm ok. Besides I have to work."

Pono's lopsided smile becomes a slight sulk.

Pono's been acting strange. Like when Omar badgers me at school, Pono miraculously appears and kicks the clowning up a notch. Then there's lunch. Whether I'm eating alone in the cafeteria or under the banyan, Pono shows up. Lunch tray in hand, he settles down next to me. Eager to discuss this or that.

Needless to say my thoughts have been going this way and that.

Does he like me?

No, he's just being a good homie after everything that's happened.

Stop reading into things! You're not even over all the Mark fallout. Plus you're not Pono's type.

But what's up with the stepped-up attention. Bordering on flirting. Maybe he likes me, likes me.

Wishful thinking.

Anyway, it doesn't matter. I've banned myself from guys. I can't trust myself when a guy gives me attention. I might end up his mirror. Or something else. As my mom put it last night when we were talking about Dad and Mark, "Just because a man calls you his rani, doesn't mean he'll treat you like one. You might end up his kam vaari."

Seems so obvious now. My two-for-two record as Dad's princess and Mark's queen proves that. Both times I dove into the relationship. Head first. Doing whatever they wanted simply because they sweet talked me.

I run my hand over the back of my head. It's growing out super thick. Almost an Indro. I can't wait until it's fully grown.

Pono exhales and crosses his arms.

I know Pono has been looking out for me. Above and beyond. He's been an amazing friend. But I'm not taking any chances. Until I'm able to figure things out, I'm keeping my walls up and fortified. For now, my head and heart are safely tucked away from any male influence.

Sorry, love, but you're outlawed.

"Thanks again for offering, Pono. You my best homie."

Right when the words "best homie" come out of my mouth, I swear I see him cringe.

"No worries. And, back at cha," he says with downcast eyes. "Homie."

B-GIRL STANCE

Omar rolls into the Maunaloa Community Center like he's MJ. "What's up, Rani girl?" his Airness asks as he plants himself in the empty chair next to me. I get a load of his threads. Red and white on black Michael Jordan Chicago Bulls jersey. Baggy jeans. A pair of fire red and white on black Nike Air Jordan V's.

"Lookin' good, Omar."

"Dressing like Mike gives me confidence," he whispers. "Not that this playa needs any more confidence," he professes a little louder.

I giggle. "So you ready for the meeting?"

"Yup. Dressed to kill. Check. Powerful testimony. Check. How about you?"

"Fo' sure."

Tonight's big. The Ranch is still trying to get Maui County approval to build a massive pipeline to pump water to the dry west side. They want to keep expanding the undeveloped land here. There are even rumors that they want to build a gated community of luxury homes near Papohaku. And though the EPA approved Molokai's Federal Sole Source Aquifer designation, the Ranch hasn't given up on getting their hands on the island's fresh water. The feds are on our side, but no local who opposes the pipeline wants to take any chances. And so the community center is packed. Pono's going to be a little late, but he'll be here. He wouldn't miss this for anything.

The Chair from the Maui County water committee calls the meeting to order. He reviews the issue to be discussed and the procedures for the meeting. I go over my testimony one more time. I smile to myself because my points are tight. The adrenaline is pumping in my brain. So is *Mama Said Knock You Out*. I can always count on LL Cool J's motivating rap to play in my mind's boombox exactly when I need it. I look around and everyone seems ready to go. All this heightens my desire to take a stand against the developers.

Then Omar says in a hushed voice, "Hey, don't look now, but your dad and Wendy are here."

Of course I look. Yup. Dad and Wendy stroll in. They find a place to stand against the wall near the front. My body tenses and my fists ball up. I'm scared I'll panic. I've waited so long to be here. To speak my peace. I don't want to miss my chance because of Dad. A minute or so passes. I realize my mood or feelings haven't changed. No trouble breathing. No tears. My body and fists release. I exhale slowly in relief. I'm still amped up to testify.

I refocus on what the Chair is saying. I try to forget about Dad and his floozie. After a half hour of testimony, mostly in opposition, the Chair calls my name.

You know your stuff. You're ready to deliver.

I walk up to the mic imaging I'm on the 4eva Flowin' stage. And I'm ready to drop a verbal bomb.

And that's exactly what I do. Only today it's in prose.

Honorable Chair and Committee Members,
My name is Rani Patel and I'm here to testify in opposition to the proposed pipeline...

When I'm done, I deliberately turn around to the left first. I want to see my dad. We make eye contact. I give him a quick b-girl stance. Then I walk back keeping my narrowed eyes on him. I maintain a frown and a slight pout. My head stays tilted back a little. My arms are high on my chest, crossed, with my hands under each of my pits. His eyes grow wider as I walk down the aisle. Now it's like a staring contest. My eyes remain unblinking. He's got a blank look at first. But he can't keep up with my b-girl determination. He blinks and his head drops. I think I see defeat on his face.

As I approach my seat, I chill. And grin. I plop down and Omar elbows me. "Yo Rani that was off the chain!" The next person starts their testimony. Omar and I listen. Then he elbows me again. "Hey, I saw you give yo' b-girl stance to your dad. Right on, sistah. How're you feeling?"

"It felt good." We smile at each other then tune back to the testimony being spoken.

Just did me.

I'm kinda astounded. The me I just did was sure of herself. She finished what she set out to do. What she wanted to do. What she believed in. Despite the stress of seeing someone who doesn't have her back anymore. She was self-assured when it counted.

Wait a second.

Why am I surprised? I've had it in me all along. Except I didn't make the connection.

Tonight MC Sutra handled my biz. And she's not some different personality or some figment of my imagination. She is me. I am her.

BUT I LOVE YOU

The line for hot bread is longer than I've seen it in awhile. No one's talking. The silence makes me notice the throbbing in my feet for the first time tonight. The restaurant was noisy and crazy busy. It wouldn't have been so bad if there was someone there besides me and Mom. What I really should've   done after closing, especially for the sake of my overtaxed feet, is gone straight home. Like Mom. And soak my feet or something. But I'm willing to take a little more pain because of what I'll get. I'm thinking butter and cinnamon tonight.

My eyes drift up to the vibrant full moon. It's practically flaming in the night sky. The beauty of it summons the animal in me. I get this urge to howl. I imagine throwing my head back and doing it when I feel a hand on my shoulder. I turn around.

It's Mark.

Oh-no.

Oh-yes.

I haven't talked to Mark in a couple months. We've been

incommunicado since Mom broke up with him for me. I think I've worked through most of my feelings about the rape. I think I've gotten over Mark, though I've maintained my self-imposed ban on guys. Not that it matters. It's not like there are any guys lined up at my door. No guys pulling a Bob Marley *Waiting in Vain*.

But just like that, my guy hiatus is over. Because one look at Mark and this she-wolf is all *Hungry Like the Wolf*. Duran Duran to the max. He's as virile as ever. Like he's regained his normal muscle weight. I don't see any sores or fresh burns. His teeth are pearly white. I can't find any evidence of batu use on him.

He gives me a chin-up and says, "Hi there, Sutra." The words roll off his tongue like LL Cool J's permission to the girl in *Jingling Baby*.

I try to sound as casual as possible. "Mark. Oh hi."

"Been awhile, huh?" He slides his hands into his baggy jeans. Then he smiles. The tingling feelings inside me awaken from their months of slumber.

"Yeah." My face feels hot. I peel my eyes off him and force them to stay focused on my black-on-black high tops. The white soles and Adidas insignia seem to glow in the dark. I tug at my acid wash high-waisted denim shorts. I shift my stance.

"How've you been?" I think I hear tenderness in his voice. Or maybe that's what I want to hear.

"Fine." I don't look up. "How are you?"

"I'm good. Just got out of rehab on Maui. Clean for over a month."

I lift my head and smile. "Cool. I'm happy for you." I'm not sure what else to say. So I stand there and fiddle with the bottom edge of my tank top. My glasses slip down. I don't notice them perched precariously on the tip of my nose. Not until Mark reaches out and brings them into line. Our eyes link. Within seconds, the jumbled up parts of my brain about Mark—the parts that I've tried to bury— rise up from the depths of my hippocampus and frontal lobes. Like vampires in the depths of night, the neurons that still connect Mark to love, hurt, and feeling good about myself arise from their coffins. I'm flooded with memories of his charisma. And mesmerized by his drop-dead hotness.

It's like all my hard work at staying sober from Mark-the-love-drug just went out the window.

So this is relapsing.

For a second I think about how easy it is to fool yourself into thinking you're over something. And if you stay away from it, you may convince yourself that you're completely over it. But when it's staring you in the face, like a frosty beer to a recently sober alcoholic...

All Mark sees are my wide eyes and frozen mouth. Now he's the wolf and I'm a deer caught in the headlights.

"Let's get out of here, Rani." He grabs my hand and draws me towards him. He presses his forehead into mine. I catch the familiar whiff of cigarettes and beer.

Clean? Doubtful. Don't trust him. Don't go with him.

Oh yum. That smell still turns me on.

Things are proceeding so fast that my rationality and emotions don't have a chance to find common ground.

My emotions triumph over my rationality.

"Ok," I say. I forget my hot bread zeal. Instead, I fall into a Mark fervor. We hop into his truck. Driving west out of town, he pumps his stereo. Chubb Rock's *Treat 'Em Right* is on blast. I'm hoping Mark'll take a hint.

There aren't any other cars on the road when he turns right on Kala'e Highway. My eyes drift down and left. I keep tabs on his right hand. I see it meandering towards my thigh. I'm pretty sure he can feel the heat radiating off my body. By now I'm almost feverish with desire. I can't resist capturing his wandering hand. I position it in its proper location on my upper thigh. Where it always used to be when we drove.

Guess it's true. Old habits die hard.

He slides his hand under the frayed leg opening of my shorts. I exhale slow and heavy. Just as his fingers reach my thigh crease, we pull into the Kalaupapa lookout parking lot. He jerks his hand away because he has to use both hands to crank the steering wheel. He barely makes the turn to avoid crashing into the metal fence along the edge of the lot. He slows the truck down. Then he catches his breath and parks. I don't see any other cars or people around.

I haven't taken a sip of alcohol, but I'm feeling high off the unexpected thrill of what's happening. Plus I'm not thinking straight. In fact, I'm not thinking at all. I'm just going with it. Just following his lead. My old Mark brain pathways are operating full throttle and I'm on automatic pilot. I want to do whatever with Mark. Let him do whatever to me.

He opens my door and before I can climb out, he thrusts one hand under my knees and one behind my back. He lifts me out. He slams the door shut with his leg. He carries me across the well-lit parking lot to the dark edge of the forest. Then he steps onto the narrow pine needle covered trail. There aren't any lights on the path. I can't see a thing. Somehow he avoids the protruding tree roots that I know jut out all over the place.

When we reach the bench next to the lookout, he lowers me down gently. We sit side-by-side. I'm ready to go at it. I lean in to kiss him. But he stops me. And I'm confused because I thought that's why he brought me here.

Nope.

He wants to talk first.

"Rani, baby, I'm so sorry for everything."

"It's ok," I say. I get up and straddle him. I throw my arms around his neck.

This is what he wants. I want to make him feel good. Then I'll feel good.

Running my fingers through his hair, I try to kiss him again. He turns his head to the side so my lips land on his ear. "Easy there, little lady," he says. "I wanna tell you something first."

"Ok." I try to slow my breath. "I'm listening."

"I never meant to hurt you."

"Uh-huh."

"I'm so sorry. Can you forgive me?"

"Yes." I attempt to kiss him again.

He dodges me. "Do you love me?" he whispers into my ear.

"Yes." I kiss his cheek.

He kisses my forehead. Then my nose.

Finally!

"There's something else," he says. He kisses my lips. My chin. My neck.

"What?" I manage to say, my voice breathy.

He kisses my neck again.

"There's a girl on Maui," he whispers.

As soon as he says that, it's as if someone threw ice cold water in my face. Like someone put a "t" in front of the "h" in horny. "What?" I back up and off his lap. I take a few steps away from him. He jumps up and puts his arms around me. I start to ask him about it again but before I get the words out, his tongue's in my mouth. I tear my mouth away. "Wait a minute, what?"

He runs his hands up and down my back and says, "She's pregnant. It was a one-night thing. But I gotta take care of my mistake. I'm moving in with her." By now his hand is on my okole. "Rani, I don't love her. I love you. I want to work it out with you." And with that he pulls me to the ground. Now I'm lying on top of him. He kisses me hard. At this point, I'm all mixed up.

Still it feels familiar.

Love = Hurt.

His hand slips under my tank top.

Dad's love = Repeated hurt.

He deftly unhooks my bra.

Mark's love = Repeated hurt.

His hand veers down. "Rani baby, sorry I keep messing up. I have to help her. But I want you."

And the chaos makes my mind take its usual leap into the chasm of worthlessness. Even though I thought I'd sealed it up for good over the last couple of months.

They hurt me because they're damaged. They hurt me because I let them.

He shoves his hands under the waistband of my shorts.

They hurt me because I deserve it. They hurt me because I'm worthless.

"You should come live with us on Maui," he whispers. Then his mouth becomes a leech on my neck. His words, and what his mouth is doing to me, extract my Dad-memories from the deepest recesses of my brain. Those old sick recollections are pulled out and thrown into the current turmoil with Mark.

What's happening now is the same chaos I'm used to. It's what I've grown up with.

I'm at a crossroad. Because it would be so easy to take the path of least resistance and do what Mark wants me to do.

Then Mark yanks my shorts and panties. Before I know it, they're down at my knees.

Dad is happening to me again.

That's when my tangled thoughts start to become ordered.

It wasn't me with the problem. It was Dad. It's not me this time either. It's Mark.

He's sucking on my neck with such tenacity that it aches.

Stop trying to figure things out. Stop trying to make excuses for their unacceptable behavior. They abused me. Straight up, it was—is—wrong.

I mobilize all my strength, tear myself away from Mark. I pull up my shorts and panties. I start running.

And I don't look back.

RIGHTEOUSNESS

Pono once told me that Native Hawaiians believe that rain is a blessing. Does heavier rain mean more blessing? I'll have to ask him next time I see him. But I think it does. Because this torrential downpour keeps the customers away. And I get uninterrupted time under the porch roof to finish my epic bravado rap, "Revolution." I even remember two lines I'd made up on the spot way back during the 4eva' Flowin' audition.

Bam!

And those two lines are now the sick hook to this rap. Three sweet verses and the hook, done. I close my notebook. I'm satisfied. I listen to the rain pelting the metal roof of our store.

I look over at the restaurant. No cars in front means no customers there either. And that means Mom's getting some down time too. I'm glad. Things are so different for her now. In a good way. That's when *Love and War* pops into my mind.

You're finally free of his chains…

It's amazing how much more this line means today than when I first wrote the rap. There are only a few weeks until graduation and my mom's definitely free from his chains.

So am I—from many chains.

I've seen Dad around town with super preggo Wendy. I haven't talked to him. He tried to contact me a few times but stopped after Mom reminded him that if he tried again, she'd call the cops.

I haven't seen or talked to Mark in over two months. He moved to Maui to live with his baby mama just like he said he would.

Good riddance.

When I think about my dad saga—that repeated itself as my Mark saga—I mostly feel disgust. I shudder and shove the identical narratives from my mind.

I concentrate on the steady rain. I like steady. I know what to expect. I know how to handle it.

This is what steady means to me:

1. I study.
2. I work.
3. I talk to Mom.
4. I stay away from booze.
5. I've made friends with a couple of girls. Paula and Chantel. They're in the environmental club with me at school and they seem nice. And drama free.
6. I keep it real with Omar and Pono.

Pono hasn't let up on the one-on-one hanging out with me at school. I've kept my guard up though. My mind's still been flip-flopping between *he likes me* and *he likes me not*. I can't fathom how someone who went out with the splendid Emily Angara would ever go for someone like me. He's probably already got his eye on another girl like Emily if she won't take him back. I'm just trying to enjoy hanging out with him without overthinking it. Besides, it's cool talking to him about college stuff, graduation, and our rhymes.

But then maybe two or three weeks ago, I started to feel more relaxed around Pono. And when his hand accidentally brushed mine—or he fixed my glasses on my face—I felt a few butterflies. And some chicken skin! Haven't had those feelings since I left Mark at the lookout.

Last week I found the mixtape I'd made for his birthday back in November. The one I never got a chance to give him. I listened to it. By the time Salt-N-Pepa finished rapping *Push It*, my brain pushed my Pono crush back to the surface. My walls came down and I let myself bask in the glory of crushin' on Pono. I'm not gonna tell him, but I think I'm ready to trust myself with feeling the crush, even if he isn't feeling anything like that for me. I still have to give him the tape.

Yep, things are all G.

I yawn and stretch my arms. It doesn't seem like the rain's going to let up anytime soon. I watch it beat down on the ground. Its steady rhythm puts me in a trance. I yawn again. Drowsiness drags my eyelids down. I'm about to nod off when I hear the rumble of a truck. I open my eyes and lift my head. It's Pono's 4runner pulling into the store's parking lot.

He bounds up the steps with his head down. He lands so hard that it jars the old wooden floorboards. Dripping with water, he grins at me.

"Hey, Rani," he says, slicking his hair back to push the water off.

Time lags. Chaka Khan's *Ain't Nobody* plays in my mind's boombox. Pono's tilting his head back and I imagine that his eyes are closed. I delight in the beads of moisture on his smooth, dark skin and the way his white t-shirt clings to his well-built chest. Rain blessing number two.

"Rani. Hey," he says again.

"Oh hey, Pono." I blink my eyes and try to erase the silly expression off my face. "What're you doing here?"

He sits down on the bench opposite me and leans back with his arms crossed. "Looking for you," he says with his foxy smile.

I smile back. Normally, this time. "Hey, do you want a towel? You're soaked."

He nods.

In a flash I grab a towel from inside. "Here you go."

"Thanks. Better."

"What's up?"

"On my way to work. Thought I'd stop by to say hi."

"Cool. But you got all wet."

"It's ok. I've got extra clothes in the truck." He wipes his legs with the towel. "It's slow cuz of the rain, huh?"

"Yeah, I'm glad. Gave me time to finish my latest rap masterpiece."

"And? What's it about?"

"Oh, it's another bravado rap. For the next 4eva Flowin' jam."

"Awesome! Can't wait to hear it. I'm still working on mine."

"What's yours about?"

"Shit," he mumbles under his breath. He looks away, laughing nervously. "Promise you won't laugh."

"I promise." I cross my heart and put my hands together in prayer.

He's still looking away. "It's about a girl."

I sit up taller and cover my mouth with my hands in surprise. I'm sort of disappointed. Tilting forward I say, "Oh. Hmmm. A hypothetical girl of your dreams, or...a real girl?"

He stalls. His face gets a little red. He takes off his slippers and wipes the water from his feet. "A real girl." He keeps his eyes on the floorboards.

"What?" I cup my hand behind my ear and angle my head towards him. "I didn't hear you," I say.

He shakes his down-turned head, then mutters, "A real girl."

"Ohh. Hmmm. I wonder who she is..."

He shrugs. "You'll never guess."

"Does she go to our school?"

"Yes."

"Is she a senior?"

"Yes."

I stand up and pace across the porch. I cross my arms over my chest and run through all the senior girls at our school that I think he might like. "Give me another hint."

"She's super smart," he says with a slight smile.

"Paula?" I guess.

"No."

"What else?"

"She's funny."

"Richelle?"

"Nope. She's sweet."

"Rayna?"

"A'ole. She's beautiful."

"Crystal?"

"No!" he exclaims. He cracks up.

I don't really like this game and want it to end. "Ok, so Pono and blank, sitting in a tree, k-i-s-s-i-n-g…"

"Real mature, Rani."

"Yep. Didn't I tell you? Mature's my middle name," I say, sitting back down on the bench. Now the steady rain just irritates me.

"Ha ha ha."

"Come on. I'm tired of guessing."

"She's got killer taste in music."

"Chantel?"

"No."

"Ok. Come on, I give up."

"She raps."

My eyes widen and I hold my breath.

"She's Indian…"

I stare at him. I can't move.

"It's you, Rani," he whispers.

"Me?"

Rani, you idiot. Is that all you can say?

"Yeah. I've liked you for a long time. That's why I broke up with Emily. All I could think about was you."

The butterflies rustle and slowly start flying around. "Why didn't you tell me sooner?"

"I wanted to, but you were with Mark."

"Oh. Yeah." I pause. "Pono, I never told you this but I've had a crush on you since the beginning of junior year. Right when you started going out with Emily so I had to hide it. Then I tried to forget about my crush on you because of Mark." I cross my legs and rest my elbow on my knee. I drop my chin on my hand. "Recently I've let myself remember."

"Really?" he asks, with that sexy smile of his I love.

"Hey, can you spit a verse or two of your new rap. Pretty please?"

"It's a surprise. You'll have to wait until I perform it."

"Oh, man. Come on. A couple of lines then?"

"Ok. The first two lines only." He takes a breath and spits.

When she arrived on the scene,
I knew there was something about this Indian queen...

I grin so big. "I can't wait to hear the rest." The butterflies gain momentum and I imagine Pono's Melle Mel and I'm Chaka Khan. We're on stage and he's rapping.

"So now what do we do?" Pono asks.

His questions get me off stage and back to the porch. I want to say, "Duh, Pono. I run into your arms. We passionately kiss and live happily ever after." But what I say is, "I don't know."

We both got into our first choice colleges. Me, NYU. Pono, Columbia. When I found out, I was stoked that we'd be in the same city. Not only in the same city, but in a hip hop mecca.

We sit in comfortable silence.

After awhile he says, "Well, we're definitely friends."

"Yep. No doubt. Best of friends." I bite my thumb. "Now it's your turn not to laugh at me. It's about to get all cheesy up in hea'. Full on cheddar."

He laughs.

"Remember how you said you'd do anything for me?" I ask.

Pono nods. "I still would."

"That's the thing, Pono. I know you would. You already have. My dad and Mark only said the words but did what they wanted. What was good for them. Not you, Pono. You always do the right thing. Even if it's not the best thing for you."

Pono smiles.

I continue with my trés fromage parle. "I really want to be with you. My heart says, 'Jump on it, girl!' My head says, 'Hold up. Check yo' self first.'" I drop my head and eyes. "I'm hoping my heart and head connect soon."

He moves to my side of the porch. Putting his arm around me, he says, "That sounds good, Rani. Take your time. That's one of the things I like about you. You think a lot."

"Some people would call that crazy," I say, laughing.

"I call it queen-like."

I lean my head on his shoulder. We sit listening and watching the rain as it drenches everything. I remember the question I had about the rain. But instead of asking him about it, I decide that everything about today is a blessing.

And I decide to trust myself and go with it. Taking the leap of faith, I say, "Hey Pono, I think my heart and head just connected about one thing."

"Oh yeah, what's that?" he asks.

"That I really want to kiss you."

He grins and gives me a chin-up. Then he changes his expression to a serious one and says, "I don't know, Rani." He crosses his arms tight and shakes his head. "What kind of guy do you think I am?"

I give him a look. "Really?"

"Ok, ok. But just one kiss. Don't try anything else," he says with mock sternness, wagging his finger at me.

I slide closer to him. I think he was expecting a little peck.

Suddenly, it's like we're in Casablanca. And he's Rick and I'm Ilsa. I confess that I've never stopped loving him. Then we kiss like we did in Paris.

RANI REVOLUTION

"Yo, 4eva Flowin', you ready?" Pono calls out.

Applause, cheers, and whistles come from everywhere. Pono, Omar, Stan Lee, and I are keeping the monthly 4eva Flowin' hip hop jams going. Without Mark.

"The first MC to throw it down brings a fresh perspective that only a rani—a queen—can. Give it up for MC Sutra!" Pono yells.

I've climbed these steps to the stage a few times before. But tonight's different. I climb, knowing more who I am. I climb, knowing that I have worth. I climb, knowing who my friends are. I climb, knowing Mom's got my back. All this makes me a hot stepper.

I take the mic from Pono. Louder whistles and clapping.

"It's MC Sutra here. The girl in effect who's about to put you in check with this important subject. Cuz boys, if you brought up correct, then ladies get the foremost respect."

DJ Skittles lays out the tight beat and I spit.

Don't call me Sultana.

Blazin' it down settin' off the alarm-a.

I'm a charma' with plenty of armor.

more like Cleopatra spittin' your mantra.

Brain so big I attain my own rain.

Don't need your ball and chain

cuz I'm gonna sustain my reign.

What I'm sayin' got you obeyin'.

Crushin' your cranium—mantis prayin'.

You be crass, checkin' on this ass

while I be smashing your rhyme window like glass

Call my solution a female revolution,

retribution in the form of rhyme electrocution

Tonight, the rhymes flow easily from my lips. As I lay out another two verses, I'm grateful. Grateful that rap isn't my savior anymore. Nope. I've saving myself. And now, my rap is part of me. By the time I get to the last verse, I'm high. On life.

To my ladies, it's up to you—

stay strong through this life like you are bamboo.

His control ain't love, do not misconstrue,

you be Marie Curie,

free to disagree and get a degree,

not under his lock and key,

your true potential set free.

Stand up to the persecution

and make your contribution.

Call my solution a female revolution,

retribution in the form of rhyme electrocution.

My name is Rani Patel—aka MC Sutra—and I'm in full effect.

AUTHOR'S NOTE

I am a physician who practices psychiatry. Like Rani, I'm also a Gujarati Indian who's lived on the island of Moloka'i. And I've loved hip hop and especially one of its elements—rap—all my life! To make Rani's fictional story gripping in a unique way, I wove in pieces of the three cultures I grew up in—Gujarati, Hawaiian, and hip hop.

I am wondering if some of you readers are angry or frustrated with Rani Patel. Why couldn't she become empowered sooner? Why does she depend on guys so much? Why did she keep going back to Mark? Didn't she have any sense? And then there's Meera Patel. Why wasn't Meera angrier at Pradip for sexually abusing Rani for so long? Why didn't Meera do anything to protect Rani?

As a psychiatrist, I've spent over fifteen years helping children, teens, adults, couples, and families—from all walks of life—steer through the murky waters of emotional struggles. Sadly, many of my patients have been sexually abused. By listening, understanding, bearing witness to recollections of abuse, and providing guidance to facilitate healing, I've gained insight into how people who are sexually abused think, feel, and act, as well as how overarching family dysfunction can enable it to continue.

In creating Rani, I wanted to give readers a realistic view of how one form of sexual abuse, incest, can affect the lives and interpersonal relationships of girls who suffer through it. Rani's thoughts, feelings, and actions are characteristic of many of my patients who have survived incest.

Incest has tragic consequences on the lives of children and adolescents. Yet in treating these youth or adult survivors, I know many can recover. But what happens in between? Rani's story is one version of this.

There's a reason Rani does not display crystal clear girl power throughout her journey. Incest typically takes away a girl's power. She may appear to have it all together on the surface. But underneath, she is sad, anxious, confused, not confident, dependent on male attention, and not able to socially connect with females. Just like Rani.

Why is it difficult for sexually abused girls to become empowered? The most basic answer is that sexual trauma affects brain development. Plain and simple. It can damage the hippocampus. It can affect brain circuits that connect the body's response to the brain—the autonomic nervous system, the hypothalamic-pituitary-adrenocortical axis, and the neuroimmune process. This physical damage results in emotional symptoms that the abused youth unknowingly thinks, feels, and acts upon. These symptoms can include, but are not limited to: overthinking, intrusive memories of the trauma, flashbacks, physiological reactions to trauma triggers, negative automatic thoughts, self-blame, nightmares, inability to experience positive emotions, and self-destructive behavior.

Rani exhibited all of these symptoms at different times throughout her story.

Sexually abused youth may get "lost" in these symptoms. They may accept the symptoms as who they are instead of as their brain's reaction to the abuse. So they may "speak" through their symptoms without being able to talk about how the abuse affects them.

Remember when Mark first French-kissed Rani? His kiss unlocked memories of her dad's abuse and she immediately got confused because in her experience intimacy was always linked to incest. Of course, she didn't have the insight to connect these dots so her body reacted with a panic attack. And when Rani tries to tell Mark about her father's abuse, she can't find all the words. She ends up thinking about how her mind would "escape (dissociate) when it happened."

Youth who suffer through incest aren't aware that they're missing out on the normal development of trust, autonomy, self-care, self-worth, assertiveness, or stable platonic and intimate relationships. Instead their personalities are shaped and damaged by serving as a sexual object and/or playing a sexualized role even without improper physical sexual contact. This leaves the youth with clashing feelings of being needed, loved, and special but also used and trapped. Ironically, they, like all youth, have an innate need to preserve their primary attachment to their parents. They may desperately hold onto their abusive parent because it is only in the context of the abusive relationship that they have learned to function. They have not formed their own identity separate from their abuser.

Sexually abused youth suffer emotional turmoil in silence. And, particularly with incest, discussion is discouraged by family and society. Stifled, these youth will not focus on how harmful the abuse is. Rather they will fixate on what feels good in the relationship with the abuser. They will pursue the good feeling relentlessly because it is the only thing they can control. Or so they believe. Abusers take advantage of this and manipulate the youth into keeping secrets about the wrongdoing. And so the cycle of sexual abuse is perpetuated. As they grow up, the abused youth may be vulnerable to being in relationships that replicate their abusive relationships. They may end up with older, abusive, and controlling partners.

So how do sexually abused youth heal?

Healing starts with insight. And insight begins when abused

youth escape the muteness of trauma, when they begin to find words both to separate themselves from their symptoms and to verbalize their experiences, thoughts, and feelings. This allows empowerment because they realize they are not what their thoughts and feelings tell them. They recognize that they are experiencing a biologic trauma response.

In reality it is difficult for many youth who've suffered sexual abuse to gain insight. To help my sexually abused patients achieve insight, I recommend they engage in some sort of written or artistic expression as part of their treatment. This can help them establish order to the chaotic memories in their mind and construct a trauma narrative which they can then connect to their symptoms.

Rani used poetry and rap to express herself. But the fact that Rani was able to gain insight as quickly as she did is unusual. If anything in the story is unrealistic, it is that.

The ensuing healing process can take months to years to complete. I might explain it to my sexually abused patients like this: even though you may be seventeen years old chronologically, you are still only about eleven or twelve emotionally because the sexual abuse forced you to remain stuck at an earlier emotional developmental stage. And this isn't fixed overnight. It takes time to catch up on the emotional development. I also tell these patients that for every year they suffered the sexual abuse, it may take that many years to fully recover. This is not to make them lose hope, but rather to encourage them to go easy on themselves and to be open to taking time to complete each phase of healing to the best of their abilities.

—Sonia Patel

For more information on the phases of healing from sexual abuse, or for more information on sexual abuse in general, please refer to the following books and websites.

BOOKS

1. Adams, Kenneth M., Ph.D., *Silently Seduced: When Parents Make Their Children Partners*, Revised & Updated. Health Communications, Inc. 2011.
2. Herman, Judith, M.D. *Trauma & Recovery: The Aftermath of Violence—From Domestic Abuse to Political Terror*. Basic Books, 1992, 1997.
3. Siegel, Daniel J., M.D., *The Developing Mind: Toward a Neurobiology of Interpersonal Experience*. The Guilford Press. 1999.

WEBSITES

1. Kluft, Richard P., M.D., Ph.D. *Psychiatric Times*. January 11, 2011. www.psychiatrictimes.com/sexual-offenses/ramifications-incest
2. American Academy of Child & Adolescent Psychiatry, Facts for Families, #9, Child Sexual Abuse, March 2011. www.aacap.org
3. Rape, Abuse, & Incest National Network. www.rainn.org
4. Survivors of Incest Anonymous. www.siawso.org/page-5143

GLOSSARY

808: the sound of bass from stereos. Also, the area code for the state of Hawaii.

A'a: (Hawaiian) lava flow that's rough, loose, broken, and sharp.

Agneepath: (Hindi) title of a 1990 Bollywood action-drama film. Translates to *path of fire*.

Agni: (Gujarati) fire.

Ali'i: (Hawaiian) chief, chiefess, ruler or monarch.

Aloha: (Hawaiian) love, affection, compassion or sympathy.

Aloha mai no, aloha aku: (Hawaiian) When love is given, love should be returned.

Akamai: (Hawaiian) smart.

A'ole: (Hawaiian) no.

Ba: (Gujarati) grandmother.

Banava: (Gujarati) to make or create.

Bachao: (Gujarati) rescue.

Batu: (Slang in Hawaii) crystal methamphetamine.

Betta: (Gujarati) dear or my dear.

Bhadran: (Gujarati) a chha gaam village in the state of Gujarat.

Bhagavad Gita: (Sanskrit) Hindu scripture that is part of the epic Mahabharata.

Bhatt: (Gujarati) rice.

Bhus: (Gujarati) enough.

Bolo head: (Hawaiian pidgin) bald.

Buss up: (Hawaiian pidgin) bust up, broken or damaged.

Chee: (Gujarati) feces.

Chha gaam: (Gujarati) refers to six villages in Gujarat: Dharmaj, Sojitra, Karamsad, Vaso, Bhadran, and Nadiad (Savli is also considered by some as part of chha gaam).

Chicken skin to the max: (Hawaiian pidgin) goose-bumps.

Choke: (Hawaiian pidgin) a large quantity.

Chuup: (Gujarati) be quiet.

Da kine: (Hawaiian pidgin) any person, place, thing, situation, action, or description.

Dada: (Gujarati) grandfather.

Dharmaj: (Gujarati) a chha gaam village in the state of Gujarat.

Dirty lick'ns: (Hawaiian pidgin) getting spanked or beat up.

Ganesh: (Hindu) Hindu diety with elephant head who is known as the remover of obstacles.

Get 'em: (Hawaiian pidgin) you got this.

Ghadhedo: (Gujarati) donkey.

Giloda: (Gujarati) tindora or ivy gourd. The immature fruits of this tropical vine are cooked as a dry curry in Gujarati cuisine. The taste is akin to bitter melon.

Gooso: (Gujarati) anger.

Gopi: (Derived from a Sanskrit word) a cow-herding girl famous within Hindu religion for her unconditional devotion to Krishna.

Grind: (Hawaiian pidgin) eat. It usually means to eat voraciously.

Guarenz: (Hawaiian pidgin) guaranteed.

Gujju: (Slang in Gujarati) Gujarati.

Ha: (Gujarati) yes.

Haole: (Hawaiian) foreigner. nowadays, usually refers to a white person.

Hanabata: (Hawaiian pidgin) childhood days. Also refers to mucus.

Hawaiian homestead: an area of land, aka Hawaiian home land, in trust for Native Hawaiians by the state of Hawaii under the Hawaiian Homes Commission Act of 1921.

Hele aku: (Hawaiian) to go away.

holoholo: (Hawaiian) to go for a walk, ride, or sail.

Huaka'i po: (Hawaiian) night procession, especially the night procession of ghosts that's also called 'oi'o.

Jah betta: (Gujarati) go, my dear.

Juguu: (Gujarati) peanuts.

Jus makin' any kine: (Hawaiian pidgin) unrestrained behavior.

K'den: (Hawaiian pidgin) ok then.

Kam vaari: (Gujarati) woman who works. Usually refers to a woman who helps clean house. A servant.

Kanak attack: (Hawaiian pidgin) intense feeling of fatigue after eating a big meal.

Kava: (Tongan) roots of this plant are used to produce a drink consumed by various Polynesian cultures. The drink sedates and is used mainly to relax.

Khaarob: (Gujarati) bad.

Kilauea: (Hawaiian) an active shield volcano on the island of Hawaii (the Big Island).

Kutri: (Gujarati) female dog.

La'akea: (Hawaiian) sacred light or sacred things of the day, as sunshine, knowledge, happiness. It can be a name.

Lau lau: (Hawaiian) wrapping or wrapped packages. Also means packages of ti or banana leaf containing pork, beef, salted fish, or taro tops baked in the ground oven or steamed. Lau lau is usually served at a luau.

Liliko'i: (Hawaiian) passion fruit.

Lo-life gang: gang formed in Brooklyn in the 80's. They wear only Ralph Lauren clothes. The name comes from the second syllable in Polo.

Lolo: (Hawaiian) crazy or feeble-minded.

Maaf kaaro: (Gujarati) forgive me.

Mahalo: (Hawaiian) thank you

Mahiole: (Hawaiian) feather helmet.

Maile: (Hawaiian) a native twining shrub, Alyxia olivaeformis. Maile is often used to make lei.

Makai: (Hawaiian) ocean. Generally used when giving directions to specify that something is ocean-side, or opposed to mauka, or mountain-side.

Making A: (Hawaiian pidgin) making an ass of oneself.

Mana: (Hawaiian) supernatural or divine power.

Mangalsutra: (Hindu) a traditional Hindu wedding necklace. The groom ties the necklace around the bride's neck during the ceremony. The bride continues to wear it as a sign of her marital status.

Mhare mari jawuu che. (Gujarati) I want to die.

Nah, khaasuu thhayu che. (Gujarati) No, something has happened.

Naraka: (Sanskrit) the underworld.

Naseeb: (Gujarati) luck, chance, doom, or fate.

Naupaka: (Hawaiian) a flowering shrub found in the mountains or near beaches in Hawaii.

No ack: (Hawaiian pidgin) stop showing off or quit acting up.

No make: (Hawaiian pidgin) cut that out.

Nokrani: (Gujarati) woman employee or woman servant.

'Oi'o: (Hawaiian) procession of ghosts of a departed chief and his company. Commonly called "huaka'i po."

Okole: (Hawaiian) buttocks.

Pahoehoe: (Hawaiian) lava flow that's smooth, ropy, and rolling.

Pakalolo: (Hawaiian) marijuana.

Papio: (Hawaiian) young ulua fish.

Patang: (Gujarati) kite.

Pau: (Hawaiian) finished, ended, over, all done, or final.

Pele thee: (Gujarati) from the beginning.

Phat: Slang, something cool or excellent, such as a likable rhythm.

Pikake: (Hawaiian) Arabian jasmine introduced from India.

Pouthu: (Gujarati) mop.

Pradip nu salu aakhuu mathu kaaru che hagi. (Gujarati) Pradip's entire head is black still.

Prasad: (Hindi) a food that is a religious offering in Hinduism.

Pua'a: (Hawaiian) pig.

Pyalo: (Gujarati) cup.

Salo: (Gujarati) swear word for idiot.

Sati: (Hindi) Indian funeral custom where the widow immolates herself on her husband's funeral pyre.

Satguru: (Sanskrit) true guru.

Satsung: (Sanskrit) a traditional practice in Hinduism where practitioners sit together with a guru or a group of spiritual students and discuss religious topics or chant.

Seppuku: (Japanese) refers to ritual suicide by disembowelment with a sword. Traditionally practiced by samurai as an honorable alternative to disgrace. Also called harakiri.

Sewa: (Gujarati) service.

Shaka: (Hawaiian pidgin) the shaka sign is a hand gesture in local Hawaiian and surf culture. It has various meanings when given, such as howzit, thanks, or ok. It is displayed by extending the thumb and smallest finger while holding the three middle fingers curled.

Shaak: (Gujarati) vegetable. Also refers to curried vegetables.

Shoots: (Hawaiian pidgin) to express agreement.

S'kebei: (Hawaiian pidgin) dirty old man.

Spock: (Hawaiian pidgin) look, see, or check out.

Steez: Slang, style with ease.

Sutra: (Sanskrit) a thread that holds things together. Originally referred to a collection of aphorisms written down on palm leaves and sewn together with thread.

Suu Thhayu? (Gujarati) What happened?

Tapa: (Tahitian) barkcloth made in the pacific islands. It often has a specific print. In Hawaiian, it's called kapa.

Thakorji: (Gujarati) in Hinduism, Thakorji means Lord of the House and is the honorific name given to a form of the diety Krishna. Also called Shrinathji. Instead of worship, sewa (service) is offered.

Thali: (Hindu) a large, round stainless steel plate.

Thu mari chokri chu, mari princess. (Gujarati) You are my girl, my princess.

Uttarayan: (Gujarati) the International Kite Festival in Gujarat.

Vaitru: (Gujarati) work.

Vaso: (Gujarati) a chha gaam village in the state of Gujarat.

Vasun: (Gujarati) dishes, pots, or kitchenware.

Velan: (Gujarati) Indian wooden tapered rolling pin for making flat, thin breads.

Vidwa ne kussee kimut na hoi. Thuu vidhwa nathee. (Gujarati) Widows have no worth. You are not a widow.

Where you stay: (Hawaiian pidgin) Where are you?

ACKNOWLEDGMENTS

Props and thank you
to my Cinco Puntos crew
for effecting Rani's debut.
First to the Byrd family for putting this book on their publishing queue.
Lee, my incredible editor guru.
Bobby's skillz on the DL, tried and true.
John's tireless pitching to.
Jessica Powers for believing in Rani and the guidance she did imbue.
Mary Fountaine's behind the scenes follow through.
Ezequiel Peña's fresh cover art that let Rani breakthrough.
Isabel Quintero & Robin Kurz for their helpful inquiry and literary review.
And shout out to a few
friends and family I turned to.
They helped me see this book through.
Annis Lee Adams read the first new jack draft, still told me to continue.
Kristen Lindsey-Dudley reminded me about my MD view.
John Manaligod my kuya who encouraged Pono and Rani's pas de deux.
Edgar Esmeralda helped to keep it real with his DJ preview.
Rina Chung gifted me with her big picture point of view.
Joanna Gordon for her young adult purview.
Hiren and Carrie Patel for their business how to.
Hansa Patel for sitting through my Gujju interviews.
To James, Maya, & Joaquin Manaligod, my faithful retinue: I love you.